WINTER SWALLOWS

Maurizio de Giovanni

WINTER SWALLOWS
RING DOWN THE CURTAIN
FOR COMMISSARIO RICCIARDI

*Translated from the Italian
by Antony Shugaar*

Europa
editions

Europa Editions
27 Union Square West, Suite 302
New York, NY 10003
www.europaeditions.com
info@europaeditions.com

Translation by Antony Shugaar
Original title: *Rondini d'inverno. Sipario per il Commissario Ricciardi*
Translation copyright © 2023 by Europa Editions

Library of Congress Cataloging in Publication Data is available
ISBN 978-1-60945-727-3

de Giovanni, Maurizio
Winter Swallows

Art direction by Emanuele Ragnisco
instagram.com/emanueleragnisco

Cover design and illustration by Ginevra Rapisardi

Prepress by Grafica Punto Print – Rome

Printed in the USA

To Concetta and Maria Rosaria.
To their smile, behind the clouds

WINTER SWALLOWS

THE END

I'm sorry, Brigadie'.
I'm so very sorry.
But it's worth the trouble to try to explain it to you, because maybe it's not my fault, when we come right down to it. Or really, not entirely my fault. Even though it was my finger that pulled the trigger.

The blame, if you ask me, ought to be put on dreams. Dreams are such stinkers, Brigadie'. They're devious and treacherous, dreams are. They'll convince you that reality, deep down, isn't entirely real, that you can change it, that you can improve on it. Dreams create something in your head that tricks you and defrauds you, because afterwards, without them, you can't bring yourself to go on living.

Dreams, you know, Brigadie', aren't always the same. It depends on the time of year. When the difference between the world that spins around you and the one that you have in your head grows larger, when the abyss that separates them grows deeper and gives rise to subtle, insidious melancholy, impossible to get out of your head, that's when you become sad, and then sadder. That's when you find yourself behaving like a fool.

When you reach the depths of despair.

And of all the times of year, this is the worst. Because Christmas, with its sweetness and joy, with its candles and bagpipers and season's greetings, is over now, and it won't be coming back, and you look around and suddenly see the smoking ruins of everything you'd hoped for and the fog envelops and conceals what truly awaits us. These are the days of shattered dreams.

New Year's is an awful thing, Brigadie'. Just awful.

Objectively speaking, it's just another ordinary day in the middle of this winter, and this time it's a Saturday, too, not even the end of the weekend, so that afterwards you still have Sunday to collect your thoughts.

But for whatever reason we've all agreed that it's New Year's, the one day of the year when you have to reckon up a balance, add up the pluses and minuses, draw a nice straight line to separate the old, unsuccessful dreams from the new ones. New Year's. What a con game.

As if you could really be reborn. As if everything that we are, everything that we've built, was no longer worth anything and now we must—or at least now we ought to—venture off on who knows what hazardous undertaking, just because we've pulled a sheet off the calendar representing a day, a month, a year. As if that really changed anything.

You know, Brigadie', dreams are what we live on. Our own dreams and the dreams of others.

If you saw what I see every night, three times a night, in the eyes of those who look at us, you'd understand that it's dreams that keep life going. And that if dreams are a way of running away from reality, and madness is living in another reality, then we're all crazy, Brigadie'. Every last one of us. Stark raving mad.

In the midst of the music, through the smoke and the gleam of the glasses, I can see people's eyes. I can see their eyes as they lean closer to understand the lines that we recite and sing, as they're captivated and swept away by the characters, tinged with joy or rage, as they turn damp-eyed with emotion, as they pause, raptly, at the sight of the chorus girls' bare legs.

People's eyes, as they fill up with dreams.

What do you think, Brigadie'? That's what people are looking for when they come to the theater. They don't just want to spend an evening, take their wife or girlfriend out to get a breath of air or fill their bellies with cheap wine. They want to dream. They want a reality that's different from their everyday lives, for a couple of hours, including intermission. If you stop to think about it, it's cheap at the price, isn't it? Just a few lire for two hours of dreams.

But the problem is that we have dreams too. All the illusions that we scatter over the audience from the stage, three times a night, infect the actors and actresses too, the musicians and chorus girls. Impossible to be immune. Any more than it is for doctors who treat typhus or cholera. There's always a risk of contagion.

And when that happens, then one of us, one of the cast with a smile stamped on their face under the greasepaint, shedding fake tears, with a dramatic quaver in their voice, wearing a threadbare stage tailcoat or a top hat or fishnet stockings—one of us starts to dream. And when that happens, there's bound to be trouble. Big, big trouble.

Because our dreams are born of dreams.

In order to do this job well, you have to believe in it, even if you're a two-bit musician, even if you're nothing but a dancer in the chorus line or a green, apprentice actor, and that goes double if you're the starring actor or the leading lady. By sheer dint of repetition, you wind up believing the sweet words of love you whisper, or sigh, or sing, or bellow, Brigadie'. And you start to confuse real life with the life you churn out on the dusty floorboards of the theater's stage.

And that's why New Year's is the worst day of them all. Because you think to yourself: I can't take another year of this. I need to reshuffle this deck of cards. Until even the craziest solution starts to seem possible to you.

You have to put the blame on dreams. Dreams just fool you, they make you do the craziest things. In a sleepless night, as you ache from missing a familiar hand and smell, that special taste, that special smile, you wonder to yourself: Why not? After all, if *you stop to think, if I just do this or that, it might turn out fine, everything might take a turn for the better. You just remove an obstacle or two; it's no big deal.*

But it is a big deal, Brigadie'. It's a very big deal. There are so many things that have to fit together, so many details that don't come up in dreams. Life isn't like the stage, where all it takes is a song to conceal reality. Life is different.

Now I know that. Now I understand.

So that's why I'm telling you that it's not my fault, not all my fault. I put the blame on this time of the year, these damned holidays when people hug you and tell you: Happy end of the old year, happy beginning of the new year. But there is no end, and there is no beginning, everything continues exactly the same as it was before. These damned holidays when we pop corks on the stage and in the audience, when we exchange our dearest regards as if it were going to be years and years, literally forever, before things finally go back to ordinary life, the usual gestures, the usual hidden sidelong glances, those glances that bespeak yearnings and frustrations, hopes and despair. Best wishes and joy of the season, we all tell each other, and it's never clear that one person's joy must necessarily be another's despair, that one person's life can become another's death.

Best wishes and joy of the season. What utter nonsense.

I put the blame on dreams, Brigadie'. On the fake lives we lead in the secrecy of endless nights. The imaginary lives that transform ordinary everyday moments into an unbearable burden, and so you find yourself doing things you would never have imagined. Then you have no alternative but to hide what happened, hoping that no one else will figure it out and that your dream can come true. The dream, then, is really to blame. The dream is the real culprit, Brigadie'.

Then, all of a sudden, you read in someone else's eyes the one thing you've always dreaded: the spark of understanding.

God, I'm so very sorry.

That's the worst moment of them all, you know that? When you realize from some small act, some stray gesture, that there's someone else in the world who has figured it out. And the dream, which sat there until just a moment ago, glittering, solid, real, and eminently attainable, starts to crumble, to dissolve into empty air. From that instant, the only thing you can think to do is protect it. Somehow erase that spark of understanding. Because, you tell yourself, if I eliminate it, I can still get away with this. I can still get away with it.

And that's why I pulled the trigger, Brigadie'. I had to defend myself. I had to defend that dream.

I was fighting for the life I'd built night after night, for the dream I'd constructed moment by moment and that I thought I'd achieved by now. And not just on stage. Not just in a song. Not just in make-believe.

Happy end and happy beginning. Maybe it's true, Brigadie'. If you want there to be a beginning, then there necessarily has to be an end.

That's why I'm telling you all this, and I need you to believe me. I had to do it, and you understand that, don't you? Because I'd glimpsed the spark of understanding in those eyes. In those damned green eyes.

I'm sorry, Brigadie'.

I'm sorry I shot Commissario Ricciardi.

One of the things that the young man has learned, in these days that have taken him from summer's heat to winter winds and chill, and then back around to the warmth of sunshine, is to be aware of the weather.

They'd never discussed it as such during their lessons. And yet the fact remains, he muses as he walks up the slight incline that leads to the old man's home, that in the time he's been taking the old man's lessons, his own perception of things has changed, and not just professionally speaking. It has been a change as subtle as it's been inexorable. He sings differently now, everybody tells him so. It's not clear exactly what's new and different about the way he plays and modulates his voice, but everyone has noticed the change: both the audience of his fans, who never miss a single one of his concerts, and those who work with him. But no one knows where it is he goes one or two afternoons a week, when he heads out on those odd strolls from which he doesn't return until much later in the evening.

The young man smiles. The most precious gift, the most significant achievement has been the acquisition of awareness. Before meeting the old man, he thought that he'd been a virtuoso musician, but still basically cold. He felt a certain lack, a foggy absence. Now, however, every time he picks up his instrument, every time he completes an introduction, every time he opens his mouth to sing, he understands that he's telling a story. Now he knows that, aside from keys and chords, he needs to tune *himself* to match the sentiments wrapped up in that song.

Now he realizes, without any doubt or hesitation, that he needs to play a part, just like a great actor. He, who plays and sings, becomes for a few minutes the author of the piece. Like a medium, he needs to allow the phantoms imagined by a poet and a musician to take possession of his hands and his voice, so that he can narrate an age-old story. Each time starting over from scratch, every time as if it were the first. Without thinking of anything else; not the lights or the applause or the eyes wide open in the half-light before him—none of it can exist for him. Only the story. The story, and nothing else.

And so his hands have that new and limber ease that he never could have imagined he'd acquire, not even after years of lessons and practice. He's become a virtuoso, a first-rate virtuoso, even as his reputation for knowledge and skill has grown. He senses that there's so much more left to learn. That old man knows a great many things that he has yet to teach him; and the young man is hungry to learn.

As always, the diminutive housekeeper answers the door, her eyes downcast, an instant before he can ring the doorbell. He always wonders how she does it, where she manages to spy on him, how she sees him coming; there are no peepholes, and in the building's window he never spots anyone looking out. Then she leads him, her house clogs clopping ahead of him, all the way to the old man's bedroom, and then vanishes.

The young man opens the door and senses the atmosphere. He has learned that there's a subtle, almost imperceptible variation in the air that dictates the climate of their time together; every single time is different, unpredictable. There have been afternoons when no mention has been made of music at all, and the topics discussed have been varied and scattered; except when it's over, the young man realizes that they've talked about a song, or even more than one. Those have been the most useful lessons. Other times, after a brusque and fleeting greeting, the old man has played his magical, venerable instrument; and the young man has sat there, motionless, observing those arthritis-twisted fingers fly up and down the neck, captivated by a heavenly sound and transported who knows where by age-old passions.

In time, the young man has stopped asking or demanding. Now he just waits, grateful to have been given admittance; grateful for what he receives; grateful to be able to sit there, in the treasure chamber, amidst the stacks of books, perched on an uncomfortable stool a foot or so away from the worn leather armchair. Over time, he's grown familiar with every fragment of that chaos, governed by an illogical order. Over time he has learned. And he's still learning.

The old man is standing, with his back turned, next to the open window. The air is soft and warm even up here; the after-noon is lashing down on the sea. The city's voices arrive muf-fled. And there's a different screeching, like a congregation of piercing whistles.

The swallows, says the old man. They've returned.

The young man halts his step in midair, as if the old man had shouted a warning that he was about to step on a land-mine. His voice. What is it, about his voice? A tone that he'd never heard before in such an ordinary, workaday phrase. As if he'd just unveiled the day and the hour of the world's end.

The young man observes the old man's back. He's often wondered what he must have been like when he was young. What kind of life did he have, that man of such immense tal-ent, about whom legends are told and of whose performances there may still survive some long-forgotten recordings—maybe, maybe not, no one knows for certain. When he decided to come learn from him, the young man had to work hard to track him down. The old man seemed to have dis-solved into thin air, vanished from this world and from the domains of music, outside of the variegated canvas of an environment where everyone knows everyone else.

He must have been striking, quite charismatic: that much the young man had decided right a way. Sure, he's not much to look at now, he's let himself go, with the stringy, thinning hair, too long, the prominent, hooked nose and the haggard, sunken eyes, but he stands erect, he's quite tall. And talent is the best cosmetic.

Why had that phrase caused a shiver to run down the young man's back? What was there in those words that seemed so ineluctable, so definitive? *Buonasera*, Maestro.

Sure, springtime has arrived, you can tell from the . . .

No. Not springtime. The swallows. Those are swallows. Don't you hear them?

The old man had spoken with a harsh edge, cutting and annoyed. He hadn't specified some detail, he'd expressed a completely different concept. The swallows are one thing, springtime quite another. The young man nods his head, hastily. Of course, certainly, Maestro. The swallows, of course.

They build their nests in the rain gutter that runs right in front of this windowsill. They aren't afraid of me, you know? I look out and they still keep on coming and going, coming and going. Then, without warning, they vanish. I always expect that, one time or another, with all of these cars, with the exhaust and the noise, with the heat and the cold that arrive so unexpectedly, they'll finally fail to return. But they always return.

The young man nods foolishly, behind the old man's back. The beginning of their conversations is almost always incomprehensible, only to become clear in time. Usually.

The old man's voice is low, practically croaking; very different from when he sings. The swallows, you know. The swallows don't understand anything. They don't look at the world. They leave and they return. They think only of themselves, the swallows. Over the years, I've developed an idea, about the swallows. I think they dream. But they have only one dream.

The young man wonders if he's supposed to reply. The old man acts as if he's expecting some response, but the words that the young man utters out of courtesy for the most part drop into the void, unanswered; so for the past few months he's started saying what he thinks at the exact moment that he thinks it, and as if by enchantment, that's proved to be the best approach, he's obtained the occasional glint of understanding in those cataract-veiled eyes, even the occasional wrinkled smile.

A dream for each swallow, Maestro? he asks. Or do they all have the same dream?

There follows a fairly lengthy silence; he can't tell whether the old man is pondering the question or whether he's ignored it entirely. At last, the old man says: The same for each, I think; otherwise, they wouldn't all do the same thing, would they?

He turns and stares at him, fixedly. Expressionless. Motionless, his hair tousled lightly by the springtime breeze tumbling in through the window. The young man lowers his gaze, shuffles his feet uncertainly. Then the old man speaks.

Once I made the acquaintance of a swallow. I've never told anyone about it, in all these many, many years. But today they've returned, and you're here, and I need to leave this story with someone, before dying. I've been thinking about it all night.

Maestro, what are you saying? You mustn't think about death at all. You're fit as a fiddle. And you have so many things still to tell me, so much still to teach me . . .

No. I don't need to teach you anything at all. And I haven't taught you a thing, except which old steamer trunk to delve into and extract whatever you need to perform each song you sing. But this time, I'm going to tell you the story of the swallow I got to know, when the world struck me as full of colors, full of all the colors imaginable: and then it lost one of those colors. A single solitary color, all the others still remained; but knowing that you'd never again see this one specific color makes you die inside, little by little, one grain of sand after another, like in an hourglass. And in my hourglass, there's practically no sand left now.

What are you saying, Maestro? I'm not ready, I can't just . . .

No one's ever ready, *guaglio'*. Never. If you're ready, then you're perfect: and that will mean you can sing no more. That's the reason, don't you see that? You sing if you're imperfect. If there's a crack, a fissure that lets light through. What we sing is imperfection, pain, and passion. Otherwise, it's all pointless.

The young man sighs. That conversation is like a knife to his heart, it terrifies him. When did he begin to love that crazy old man so dearly? When did that happen?

Tell me, Maestro. Tell me all about the swallow.

The old man steps over to the case, he bends over with some effort, he snaps the fasteners open the same as always. He pulls out the instrument, he caresses it. His hand trembles.

Then he goes over and takes a seat in the armchair. The young man holds his breath, just as he does every time.

He recognized the chord, the start of the introduction. It's not one of the more famous songs, the ones you hear wherever you go. The young man takes in every movement of the claw-like fingers, every excursion of the aged hand up and down the neck of the instrument. But at a certain point he notices something else: the old man's eyes are fixed on the window, on the bright blue air of the bright blue city as it darkens in the springtime evening, amidst the swallows that come and go from the rain gutter, rebuilding the nests they abandoned last autumn.

The old man's eyes are steady and expressionless. And yet, the tears roll slow and viscous down his bristly cheeks.

Maestro, the young man murmurs. Maestro, please. If it's too much . . . if it's too much . . . don't do it, play a different song. I beg of you.

The old man's eyes remain fixed, unwavering, but he smiles. No, he says. You have to hear this. I'll stop after each verse and

I'll tell you the story. Because someone needs to know about that swallow.

He resumes the musical introduction, then starts to sing:

Tutte ll'amice mieje sanno ca tuorne,
ca si' partuta e no ca mm'hê lassato.
So' già tre ghiuorne.
Nisciuno 'nfin' a mo' s'è 'mmagginato
ca tu, crisciuta 'ncopp' 'o core mio,
mm'hê ditto addio.

E torna rundinella,
torna a 'stu nido mo' ch'è primmavera.
I' lasso 'a porta aperta quanno è 'a sera
speranno 'e te truva'
vicino a me.

(All my friends are sure that you're coming back,
that you're just off on a trip somewhere, not that you've left me.
It's already been three days.
No one so far has ventured to imagine that you,
who've grown to be a part of my heart,
have told me farewell.

So come home, little swallow,
come back to this nest, now that it's springtime.
I leave the door open when evening falls,
hoping to find you again,
by my side.)

And here he stops singing. Continuing to play slowly with those magical fingers of his, he begins telling the story.

The story of the only swallow that didn't come back.

I

Smoke. Voices, the sounds of crockery and glass. Waiters who move among the tables, carrying large trays, precariously balanced. Music, young actors and feisty actresses. On the stage, there's a dance number being performed, but it seems to attract little if any attention from the audience, who are chattering, laughing, arguing about politics and soccer.

Every so often a dancer manages to extract smiles and comments from the crowd, though nothing offensive, nothing crude. The Teatro Splendor is a classy place, a theater with ambitions, and if anyone overdoes it, under the effects of the moderately priced wine or hard liquor, they are promptly but courteously shown to the door by the cordial head waiter garbed in a Stresemann, or stroller jacket, and then deposited on the street outside, still drunk and abandoned to their fate, to stagger along in the late December winds, cooling their overheated spirits, if only, that is, these late December winds were actually cold.

But tonight, when Christmas is just a memory and people's fates dangle teetering between the grim past year, now on its way out the door, and the hopes of a better new year, this evening, while the first show is over and the second performance is nearing its end, it's hard to concentrate. The cheer is artificial, the money is short, and so it's best to spend your time at the gambling tables, in search of an excitement or an encounter that certainly won't be found out on the street, where you'd be surrounded by glum faces and the persistent calls of the shopkeepers whose establishments are still packed with unsold merchandise.

The attractions play out, one after the another, wearily. The revue isn't bad, not bad at all, otherwise the Teatro Splendor would never have booked it, certainly not in the month of December. The place is full, but three shows a night and the painful awareness that the only real interest is for the headliners certainly do nothing to heighten the artistic excitement. The occasional sporadic burst of applause accompanies the conclusion of a small comic skit with two actors tricked out as penniless commoners.

It's at this point that a renewed wave of attention spreads across the audience, like a sudden gust of sea breeze. The newspapers are folded and set aside, the last gulp of wine is swallowed in haste, and those who had wandered off to greet someone hurry back to their seats. Silence falls.

A man steps forward to the center of the stage and kindly informs the audience that the show has reached its high point: *la canzone sceneggiata*, the theatrically dramatized song. A little number filled with undistilled passion and abounding in rich sentiment, which has given this revue its evocative name: *Ah, l'amour!* It will be performed, as always, with masterful skill and conviction by none other than Michelangelo Gelmi, vocalist and actor, renowned for his work in the theater and even on the silver screen, along with the beautiful Fedora Marra, his sweetheart and partner in art and in life. The song will be performed by Maestro Elia Meloni, on the guitar, accompanied on the mandolin by the young Maestro Aurelio Pittella, a rising star in the musical firmament. Playing the part of the unfaithful friend and lothario, the up-and-coming thespian Pio Romano. It's quite the opposite of the state of affairs offstage, where Gelmi and Marra lead a life of unblemished fidelity (a buzz of muffled voices from the audience, and here and there a burst of laughter, abruptly suffocated by the emcee's angry glare), the song that the gentle audience is about to enjoy is *Rundinella*, by Galdieri and Spagnolo, written in the year of Our Lord 1918, and indeed it tells the story of a heartbreaking betrayal. Singing it will be Michelangelo Gelmi, while Fedora Marra and Pio Romano will play the unfaithful couple.

The emcee thanks the audience and hurries offstage, only moments left before the audience grows menacingly restless. Now the musicians walk onstage, an older guitarist and a tall, lanky, slightly awkward young man carrying a mandolin. They both sit down on a pair of stools at the side of the stage, exchange a glance, and then the guitarist strikes up the introduction. The mandolinist comes in after him. The sound of the mandolin cuts through the theater's smoke-filled, heavy air like a keening lament.

Now a couple makes its entrance, holding hands. The man is young and tall, well dressed and impeccably groomed. His neatly combed, brilliantined hair gleams in the stage lighting, his neat mustache frames a dazzling white smile as he gazes lovingly at the woman whose hand he's holding. He's certainly a handsome gentleman and here and there in the audience, ladies give a quick touch-up to their hair.

Most of the eyes in the house, however, focus on *her*. A stunningly gorgeous brunette, her slender figure is expertly highlighted by a dress that theoretically points to a working-class background but in point of fact emphasizes her generous bosom and long legs. After a moment's silence, the mandolin's voice is submerged by an extended round of applause punctuated by shouts of admiration. Fe-do-ra! Fe-do-ra! Like an impassioned whisper, like a call for help. Like a tacit act of submission on the part of her faithful subjects.

The actress remains focused, already unswervingly embedded in her part, and she knows full well that a smile of appreciation to her adoring public would only shatter the enchantment. The audience is there to see her. To see her, her astonishing beauty, her acclaimed bravura; and because of what the rumors say about her relationship with her husband, the man who discovered her, her Pygmalion. The man whom she is supposedly betraying, at least according to whispered insinuations, with a mysterious lover about whom nothing more is known.

The two of them take up their marks on the side of the stage opposite the musicians, right at the exact moment that the introduction is ending. Behind them, a painted backdrop portrays a geographic contradiction in terms: Milan's Duomo looming over canals plied by Venetian gondolas.

Michelangelo Gelmi makes his entrance. He's on the far side of fifty; his hair is thinning, and has been dyed a deep, raven black. There's what looks like an inch of greasepaint on his face, to conceal the purplish capillaries of the habitual drinker that he is. His commoner's garb does little to disguise a certain chubbiness, but his gait is confident and his gaze is fierce: when he treads the boards of a stage, he's right at home.

The applause arrives in a wave, fervid and decisive. It has none of the pervasive veneration reserved for the man's wife, but it's still clearly filled with warm affection. The audience loves the old lion, long in the tooth though he may be. They're grateful for all the thrilling stories he's told them.

Michelangelo breaks into song. The words are familiar to everyone in the house, the music is lovely and well performed. The people in the hall settle in to listen, with one eye on the singer, the other on his wife as she artfully pretends to canoodle with her illicit lover.

Gelmi sings about his friends and how they pester him with questions as to his woman's whereabouts, and admits that he lacks the courage to confess to them that she's abandoned him. That you—he sings, thumping his fist against his chest—nourished and raised on my heart, have told me farewell.

Come back, he begs her. Come back to me. I'll leave the door unlocked, even at night, and I won't even ask where you've been, if only I wake up to find you beside me. With his song, the man rivets the eyes of the audience upon him, without once turning to look at the two treacherous lovers. One spectator, caught up in the frenzy of make-believe, tries to draw his attention to the couple. But Gelmi goes on singing, heartbroken: now he expresses his fears for his little swallow, flown off into strange and unfamiliar cities, his concern for the risks that she's running. The members of the audience turn their eyes to the Duomo and the gondolas, sharing his concerns. At that very same instant, the two lovers point to the monuments painted on the backdrop, like a pair of tourists on a trip.

Again, he begs her to return to him, through that door left unlocked. The music highlights the verses of the song, Gelmi staggers under the weight of that unspeakable burden, or perhaps from an excess intake of wine, or both things together. He runs a hand over his face, to chase away the specters of loneliness. The audience rumbles in heartfelt empathy.

In the meantime, Fedora starts shooting glances in the general direction of Gelmi and the two musicians, as if in the throes of uncertainty; as if, magically, her husband's words, so freighted with anguish and sorrow, had broken through, reaching her in spite of the distance, insinuating a seed in her heart. "Am I doing the right thing?" the woman's eyes seem to ask. Can it have been the right choice to flee to new and distant cities, under unfamiliar spires or surrounded by gondolas, in pursuit of a fleeting infatuation, while abandoning her true love?

The mandolin embroiders the interlude between the refrain and the last stanza, while the guitar executes a grim, rhythmic counterpoint. The young mandolinist stares at the actress, as his left hand flies lightly over the instrument's neck; the guitarist looks up at Gelmi's face at the exact instant that the singer is about to start in on the final, heartrending stanza.

And Gelmi starts in.

Come back, he sings, addressing her directly, looking into her eyes, placing his hand on his heart, his voice cracking with his suffering. Come back, I no longer know what to say to the friends who ask about you. Then, seized by a sudden need to speak the truth, he tells her that only one friend hasn't asked about her. His best friend. For that matter, how *could* he have asked? No one has seen him for a while now. He must have left town, he adds under his breath, as if considering this detail for the very first time.

Among the people in the audience—even though they know the song by heart and have come to see the show many times before, possibly even earlier this same evening—a slithering surge of shock and disgust is palpable. A couple of soldiers, sitting at a table in the back, burst into bitter and mocking laughter; one of them extends index and pinky fingers in the Italian symbol of cuckoldry—the deceived husband—summoning a shocked objection from an elderly gentleman. Everyone turns their eyes to the couple on stage, who have stepped away from the backdrop where Milan and Venice inexplicably merge, moving toward Gelmi as if simulating a return home.

The mandolin and guitar raise the volume of their frantic dialogue and underscore the situation's dramatic intensity. The well-dressed young actor puts on a show of self-confidence, kissing the woman on the cheek and staring at the vocalist in order to place the stamp of finality on his unmistakable victory. Gelmi extracts a pistol from his pocket, and the firearm emits a sinister metallic gleam in the strong glare of the spotlights. A sigh runs through the audience like a gust of wind, and a matron utters a suffocated shriek of fright. The young actor twists his face into an expression of exaggerated terror, his right arm extended forward, his hand fanned open in a vain attempt to halt his rival's bellicose intentions. Then he retreats, stepping backward to leave Fedora alone and unprotected, in a clear display of his cowardice. Gelmi, in a frenzy of rage, staggers unsteadily forward and shoots the young man.

The sharp crack of the blank round startles the spectators, while mandolin and guitar, in a rising crescendo, weave their wonderful embroidery. The actor that the emcee introduced as a young, up-and-coming thespian steps back again, raising both hands to his chest, his eyes bulging as he emphatically extends his arm in the woman's direction, only to collapse to the floor, accompanied by a chorus of hate-filled whistles from the audience.

Now Gelmi turns the weapon toward his wife. A thin plume of smoke still issues from the barrel of the handgun. His hand shaking slightly, one foot set slightly ahead of the other, his pancake-laden face still betrays the red blush of violent passion. Perhaps in some extreme attempt to placate him, the woman blows him an improbable kiss. A kiss of farewell. Or else a belated request for forgiveness.

Gelmi fires the gun.

The actress is catapulted backward, a rag doll already, feet lifted off the boards, arms thrown wide. Her interpretative performance of death is quite different from her fellow thespian's, far more realistic, far more unsettling: especially because on the white bodice of her costume a large dark stain is spreading.

The mandolinist interrupts his final solo with a piercing, scratching sound, which resembles nothing so much as a despairing sigh, and leaps to his feet. The guitarist looks around. He seems to awaken from a momentary catnap, then slowly desists from his strumming. Gelmi stares at the pistol in his hand, as if it were an unfamiliar animal.

From the floor of the stage, where he lies ostensibly dead, the promising young actor opens his eyes and observes the section of set he can glimpse, unsure whether or not he should move. Fedora Marra, leaning back against the painted panel, midway between Milan and Venice, has a surprised expression on her beautiful face; a gush of dark blood streams out of her mouth, dripping down her chin and onto her neck. It's too late for her to savor the last, thunderous burst of applause that is offered to her in overjoyed tribute by the exultant audience.

A moment goes by, and then a woman, sitting at the table closest to the stage, lets out a scream of horror.

II

If anyone on the late afternoon of December 28th had bothered to make a judicious comparison of the gait of the man walking along Via Toledo with the same man's gait on the previous day or, for that matter, on any other day of the year currently nearing its end, they would have noted absolutely nothing out of the ordinary, nothing to distinguish this day from any other.

The same identical tilt of the head, bent to observe the pavement directly ahead of him. The same identical regularly cadenced step, betraying neither haste nor indecisiveness. His hands plunged as usual into the pockets of his unbuttoned overcoat, both quarters flapping about his legs in the gusts of variable wind, inexplicably warm for the season. The usual flyaway lock of hair dangling back and forth across his hatless forehead. He alone, among the strollers and striders that crowded the sidewalk, walked with his head uncovered, slightly annoyed at the absence of a proper seasonal chill. The cold was noted particularly for its absence at that year's end.

In short, nothing unusual at all, save perhaps for the time of day, strange for a man accustomed to spending his time in the office, and who usually only allowed himself a walk through the open air long after the end of his regular shift. Yet here he was, Luigi Alfredo Ricciardi himself, a detective with the rank of commissario, on the staff of the city's royal police headquarters, striding briskly in the general direction of Via Santa Teresa, and the apartment in which he resided. He hadn't resigned his position, no, far from it: it's just that, lately, and only occasionally, if there were no outstanding matters of any particular seriousness, he had tried to leave the office no later than the end of his shift.

There was no one actually monitoring his progress, at least not that afternoon; had there been, they might have been astonished to note that the commissario failed to stop at number 107, where he resided. No, today he didn't turn and walk through the broad street door, didn't stroll past the enormous concierge, giving her his usual preoccupied nod of greeting, as she sat impassively in the little booth fronting her tiny cubbyhole of a ground-floor apartment.

Without either slowing down or turning to either side, Ricciardi veered across to the far side of the street and continued on his way.

Here the street began its gentle uphill climb, at the end of which extended the forest surrounding the venerable palace—the Reggia—of Capodimonte. The atmosphere was unusual. Christmas was past, and it was still a few days to New Year's; one could sense a breathless suspense in the air, rendered even more unmistakable by the unusual temperature, the product of a persistent scirocco wind from the south, the momentary victor of the perennial battle with the winds of the north. Still, the commissario seemed so absorbed in his thoughts that he noticed nothing of all that.

Indeed, such was the case. Ricciardi, behind the façade of an impenetrable demeanor that he'd tirelessly cultivated for a lifetime, was currently struggling with a new and unfamiliar emotion, which he was having some difficulty mastering.

He heaved a deep sigh as he crossed the bridge that overlooked the Sanità quarter, teeming with activity like an overturned anthill. He knew what awaited him in the impending crossing, but the deed he was girding himself to perform gave him the courage needed to face up to any and all pain.

The Sanità bridge. The favorite destination of the city's sui-
cides. A broken chorus of chaotic thoughts assailed his mind
even before the edge of his peripheral vision began to fill with
the awful sight of a half dozen evanescent bodies, riddled
with bone fractures, shattered spinal cords, and the internal
swelling of hemorrhaging organs, all the result of violent
impact with the ground, some seventy feet below. A wingless
flight through the empty air, in the hopes of forgetting, erasing.
A flight of pure suffering, in order to put an end to suffering.

One woman whispered to him of her lost love. An old man
blurted out words about his dead wife. A young man cursed his
debts; a man in his prime spoke of his son, killed in combat.
Ricciardi hastened his pace, wondering for the millionth time if
he'd ever be able to forgive himself for what he was doing.

Ghosts, he thought. Ghosts. And among all these ghosts,
the worst of them all, the most treacherous and violent ghost
of them all. The ghost of his own hypothetical, possibly unat-
tainable happiness.

What was bringing him to the forest surrounding the
palace, on this senselessly hot late-December afternoon? What
had knocked down the wall built up, painstakingly, brick by
brick, in nearly thirty years of all-too-conscious folly?

An image, a ghostly image, he thought, answering his own
unspoken question. Yet another image, not so very different
from the crowd of phantom specters that were crowding
around him, demanding his attention, pleading for his sympa-
thy, his understanding of the pain and sorrow of their uproot-
ing from life. An image.

The image of a young woman whom he had watched—with
his own eyes, through the scrim of the glass panes of a drawing
room, as if it were a scene from a silent film at the movie theater—as she rejected in no uncertain terms the proposal of
marriage proffered respectfully by a suave and captivating
German officer in full-dress uniform; a young woman who had

then immediately strode to the kitchen to turn a calm, determined smile toward the window on the opposite side of the
street. The window behind which Ricciardi himself stood
watching, helplessly, as events unfolded—his heart furiously
trading punches with his dazed mind—about which he could
do nothing, neither to hinder nor mend them.

Once he had finally left the bridge behind him, and as the
shrieks of the dead gradually faded from his mind, he thought
of the new surge of energy driving him: the impetus that now,
in both a literal and metaphorical sense, was carrying him in
the opposite direction of both police headquarters and his own
home.

In those fleeting instants that followed hard on the heels of
his realization of what had just happened in the apartment
building across the way—after glimpsing the stunned expression on the German officer's face, the appalled reaction of
Enrica's mother, and the young woman's father's head tipping
ever so slightly forward and down—he had felt a growing,
heavy burden of responsibility for the events he had just
watched unfold. The gaze and the smile that the young woman
turned in his direction were communicating an unequivocal
message: Here I am, do you see me? I'm right here. I've just
turned down a future, a family, children. I've rejected the proposal of a handsome, wealthy, charming man. I did it here, in
my home, in the presence of my family, so that they would all
understand exactly what I wanted to declare.

I wanted to declare, openly, that I love you—you, who have
been watching me in silence from that window. You, whom I
feel so close to me, even though you maintain your distance.
You, whom I tried to get to know better through poor sweet
Rosa without success. You, who I know loves me, I can sense
it, even though for some unknown, unfathomable reason, you
continue to remain far, far away.

And now that I've done it, that smile told him, it's up to you to make up your mind how you want to act. Because I want you, you or nobody else. I won't settle, I won't accept second best, I won't choose someone else just to fill a void, I won't go in search of company just to escape loneliness.

I want *you*.

That's what he'd heard her say loud and clear, with nothing more than a smile from across the street. And a man like him simply didn't know how to evade his responsibilities.

The real point was that all this had made him happy. And happiness, mere, ordinary, wonderful happiness was the one feeling that Ricciardi had no idea how to handle.

Enrica had rejected the German's proposal on the evening of her own birthday, October 24. Ricciardi had waited until the afternoon of November 7, waiting at the corner of the museum, close to a sufficiently busy intersection to justify a chance encounter. As he had hoped, it was raining. It was coming down hard, in buckets; columns of water driven by the chilly, cutting wind. The young woman had passed by, the way she did every Monday, on her way home from her father's hat and glove shop where she helped out, when she could. Ricciardi, who was still, after all, an investigator at heart, knew to the finest detail the habits of that highly methodical young woman. Enrica was holding her overcoat lapels snug to her throat with one gloved hand, and with the other she was bracing her umbrella against the wind, struggling to maintain that flimsy shield.

She started in surprise when Ricciardi emerged from the nook where he had been waiting and planted both feet squarely before her. *Buonasera*, he said courteously. *Buonasera*, Enrica replied, every bit as courteously. May I accompany you? the commissario asked her. Why certainly, she replied in a calm, steady voice.

They walked along together for a stretch in the rain, in silence. The rain poured off of Ricciardi's hair and overcoat;

Enrica covered him with her umbrella, moving closer, and he made no move to withdraw. As they began to approach their respective homes, neither she nor he showed any signs of wanting to stop. They continued across the bridge, until they reached the narrow lane that ran alongside the church and led to the farmhouses of the Masserie dei Cristallini.

It was a silent, solitary place, poorly lit and clearly neglected: if anything, the driving rain and chilly wind made it even less hospitable. But for the two of them, alone at last, with so much to say to each other and such great fear they might not be able to convey their respective messages, it was perfect.

They both started talking at the same time, interrupting each other twice. Enrica laughed nervously; then she nodded her head to invite him to go first. Ricciardi managed only to put together broken sentences, expressing incomplete thoughts, and stumbling over his words repeatedly along the way. But the substance of what he meant to say was unmistakable. He told her it made no sense to go on hiding the truth.

That he'd been watching her from his window for a long, long time, but that he had some serious, extremely serious reasons to feel he couldn't live up to her expectations. He told her that he had long hoped she would find a boyfriend, a good person who deserved to be with her, and that when he had seen that German officer start to visit her home, he had assumed she was interested in him. But that he had subsequently witnessed Enrica's rejection of the man's proposal—and then he hastened to apologize for his indiscreet and uncouth manners. And so, if she didn't mind too much, he wished to inquire, that is, he'd like to ask her *why* she'd made that choice. That's right. Why had she turned down the German?

Enrica could easily have spared Ricciardi the ordeal of formulating that peroration so clear in meaning and so tangled in form, but the fact was that he was so handsome, in the driving wind and rain, with the drops rolling off his face and his green eyes, lost and despairing, that she had decided to indulge in the pleasure of letting him have his say. Then, staring into his eyes, she had declared in a quiet tone that his question made little or no sense. She went on to state that he, Ricciardi, knew perfectly well why she had turned down Manfred's proposal; not only that, but why she was bound to reject any other suitor who might step forward in the future. That she had waited for him and would go on waiting for him, however long she had to, because if two people recognized each other—at least that's what she thought about it—well, then, they had no other choice than to wait for each other, even if that meant waiting for the rest of their lives.

At that point she had smiled at him again, tilting her head to one side, her eyeglasses somewhat fogged up, her hair pulled back beneath her cap, and her begloved hand gripping the charming handle of her umbrella.

That was when Luigi Alfredo Ricciardi, in the pouring rain, standing in the dark cross street that led to the farmhouses of the Masserie dei Cristallini, finally kissed a woman on his own undertaking, for the very first time in his dark, pain-wracked existence. And when he did, he kissed the one woman of his life, the woman he'd come to love while gazing at her through a pane of glass, convinced that she could never be his.

As the rain fell, their hearts racing furiously each to the other, they'd both realized that there was no more room in their lives for reluctance and fear and conventional considerations. Enrica finally had a confirmation of what she desired and had long believed; Ricciardi left behind him the mountains of suffering that the dead heaped upon him daily.

On the way back, in a whisper, Enrica had referred to the dark passageway that led to the farmhouses as *Caminito*, borrowing the name of the Argentine tango, moody and apocalyptic, currently popular and a particular favorite of hers. And that is what they had both continued calling that place.

It was enough to mouth that word through the window, just once, to make it clear that the following day, at sunset, they would meet at that location. *Caminito*.

And it was there that he was bound, on the late afternoon of December 28th, the new and unfamiliar man that Commissario Luigi Alfredo Ricciardi had suddenly become. He was in possession of a happiness that was beyond his ability to handle or understand, but one that he'd certainly never let go of.

He turned the corner and saw her there, sitting on the bench, with a book in her hand; he thought what he'd thought a thousand times before at his window: Hello, my love.

This time though, he said it right out loud, receiving in exchange the immense reward of a loving glance.

An hour later he returned home and silently ate the meal that Nelide, his young housekeeper, had prepared for him.

His heart was still thumping when the call came in from police headquarters.

III

As they headed off toward the Teatro Splendor, Brigadier Raffaele Maione shot a glance at Commissario Ricciardi's profile as he walked along beside him.

For some time now—a little more than a month, to be exact—he had been sensing something unusual in his direct superior.

Nothing had changed in his behavior, nor had there been anything different about his working routines. Ricciardi was unfailingly present, his involvement was unreserved, and his commitment even verged on the excessive. Nonetheless, something wasn't right. Maione felt sure of it. He could sense a persistent tension, a background noise: not so much a thought or a concern—more than anything else an anxiety mixed with an expectation. A couple of times he'd even seemed to detect a fleeting smile, but when he'd looked more carefully, it was gone.

True, those had been unusual days. What with holidays and various staff members out on sick leave, the usual significant number of absences during the holidays, police headquarters was semi-deserted, which is why when the call came in from the theater, Maione had preferred to inform Ricciardi, well aware that, even after the end of his nominal shift, the commissario was sure to report immediately for an investigation. Indeed, the brigadier was now briefing his direct superior as the two of them headed toward the scene of the untimely death.

"So, then, Commissa', what happened is pretty darn odd. From what little I've understood, because on the phone the proprietor of the theater was sobbing and shouting, the lead actor of the revue, the famous Gelmi . . . You've heard of him, haven't you?"

Ricciardi shook his head decisively.

"How can you not know about him?" Maione insisted. "He's one of the most famous actors, he's even made films that they show at the movie house, and . . . Oh well, in any case, this Gelmi shot his wife on stage."

Ricciardi furrowed his brow.

"How do you mean? Was it part of the performance?"

"Yes, that is, at least I think it was. But he shot her for real. And she's really and truly dead now. None other than Fedora Marra!"

"Who is Fedora Marra?"

Maione was out of patience by this point.

"Commissa', you seriously live on some other planet, no offense, eh? Fedora Marra is one of the most important actresses in modern theater, are you kidding? And she's the victim."

Ricciardi shrugged.

"Whether it's onstage, in the dressing room, or out on the street, a murder is a murder, Maione. And that's how it should be treated, whether the victim is a worker in a steel mill or an actress of the silver screen."

Outside the entrance to the Teatro Splendor, spectacularly lit up, the usual crowd of rubberneckers had assembled. Ricciardi was reminded of the Vezzi murder, in March of last year, at the Teatro San Carlo, and the recollection made him think of Livia, the tenor's widow. And everything else that had happened afterward. For some reason he couldn't quite pin down, he felt guilty about that woman. And yet she had done much greater harm to him than he could possibly imagine having done to her.

When the two policemen arrived, the crowd parted. Camarda, the officer standing guard in the doorway, snapped a sharp military salute and said: "They're all inside, Brigadie'. Cesarano's there, too, he'll receive you."

Maione glared impatiently at him.

"He'll receive us, will he? I hope he'll serve us a glass of punch, too. This is just a happy little party. Keep your mouth shut, Cama', and don't budge from this spot. No one is to go in, and no one is to leave. Is that clear?"

The man blinked rapidly, uncertainly.

"No one, Brigadie'? Not even the doctor or the photographer? Because I heard that they're on their way and . . ."

Maione emitted a dull, worrisome growl.

"Yes, *them* you can let in, Cama'. Don't work so hard to be dumber than you already are."

The officer stiffened in another salute and said nothing.

Upon entering the auditorium, Ricciardi glimpsed a hundred or so terrified spectators, huddled in a corner, far from the stage. The commissario summoned Cesarano and ordered him to collect the personal details of every last one of them. The atmosphere was surreal, there was a silence as if they were in church, and in the background an unbroken muffled sobbing could be heard coming from the little crowd of chorus girls in costume, clustered in the corner opposite the audience. Beside the dancers, the members of the orchestra and other artists wearing their stage costumes and greasepaint stood in mournful silence, heads bowed, or else talked quietly amongst themselves.

On the stage, which was still brightly lit as if the show were still underway, stood five people. The commissario and the brigadier started forward, but a large man in tears suddenly blocked their way, red-faced, eyes bugging out of his head. He took them both by the arm, clenching tight.

"Oh, you're here at last. A tragedy, a veritable tragedy. Here of all places, in my theater, at the Teatro Splendor, I can't believe it. And right in the middle of the main performance! You have no idea of the disaster, we had to turn away everyone who already had tickets for the later show. What am I going to tell people tomorrow? Eh? What am I going to tell them?"

Maione shrugged the man's hand off of him, and with a brusque shove, he also pushed away the hand that was gripping Ricciardi's arm.

"Hey, hold on there, now. Hold on. Don't get too close and friendly, eh? Who are you?"

The man, who was about forty years old but looked much older, turned his porcine eyes toward the brigadier.

"Renzullo, Pasquale Renzullo, the proprietor of the theater! Please forgive me, but surely you'll understand that in the presence of a misfortune like this, a man can't help but lose his self-control."

Maione nodded, massaging his arm and grimly staring at the man.

"I am Brigadier Maione. And this is Commissario Ricciardi from police headquarters. Tell us what happened, Renzu'. And be clear about it, because we aren't here to waste our time."

Renzullo turned his gaze toward Ricciardi, displaying a renewed respect and slightly bowing his head in deference.

"Commissa', forgive me but this is a tragedy, a tragedy! The damage is enormous, *Madonna mia*! And there's no way to solve matters! Next thing you know, people will talk, and there's no way to put things right! Soon word will get around, and this on New Year's Day, when we normally have a full house every night!"

Many of the group of actors and artists had started to elbow each other and point at the two policemen. The commissario was fascinated by the spectacle unfolding on the stage, a sort of tableau vivant expressing the concept of despair. Of the five figures, none was moving, and two were lying on the floor; it was hard to say at first sight which was the corpse.

Maione brusquely brought Renzullo back to the matter at hand.

"Well, Renzu'?"

The man seemed to return to earth.

"Yes, yes, you're right. So, we were near the end of the middle performance . . ."

Ricciardi weighed in: "What's a middle performance?"

The other man looked at Maione in bafflement. The brigadier sighed: "The commissario isn't a theatergoer, Renzu'. Just assume he doesn't know how the theater works at all and explain it to him step by step."

The man stared at Ricciardi as if he were an animal with three heads.

"Of course. We have three performances an evening, one at 5:30, another at 8:30, which is usually the most popular, and the last one at 10:30. Toward the end of each show you have the most noteworthy numbers, the ones that the audience is eagerly expecting. The dramatized song comes right before the finale, when everyone comes onstage: actors, singers, and dancers."

Ricciardi shot a glance over at the corner of the room where the artists all stood clustered together.

"So they're not onstage the whole time?"

Renzullo once again questioned Maione with his eyes, as if Ricciardi had just spoken in Mandarin Chinese. The brigadier murmured: "Commissa', this is a revue. It's a series of different numbers, and every artist does their own number. They take turns, with a central theme running through them all. Am I right, Renzu'?"

The man nodded decisively.

"Exactly, Brigadie'. The whole show is called *Ah, l'amour!* and like I was telling you, it had in fact come to the next-to-the-last number, which consists of the dramatized song. At the end of the musical skit, Michelangelo Gelmi, the main character, pulls out his pistol and kills first Romano, his cheating friend, and then Fedora, his cheating wife. And that's when the tragedy happened, but how could it have happened? I don't understand, the first shot was fine, perfectly normal . . . But the second one . . ."

Renzullo left the sentence unfinished, pointing toward the stage with a vague gesture, not bothering to turn around. Then he mopped his brow, beaded with perspiration.

Ricciardi decided that he was unlikely to get anything more from such an upset and agitated man.

"All right, make sure we know how to get hold of you, I may have more questions for you later."

Then he approached the stage. His steps resonated on the wooden boards, in the silence that had just grown deeper. He stopped roughly a yard from the edge of the stage and stood there, observing.

On his left, two musicians looked like a pair of wax figures: an elderly man, his shoulders bowed, with a guitar resting on his legs, his eyes watery, staring at the opposite side of the stage; and a young, straight-backed man, his eyes wide open and staring, aghast, his arms hanging limp at his sides, with a mandolin in one hand.

To the commissario's right, a woman was slumped against a painted panel, in the exact same position as certain dolls that could be found propped up on beds in the homes of the middle class; legs sprawled wide, arms hanging alongside the body, head slumped onto the chest, where a large dark stain defiled the gleaming white bodice. Next to her, a young man with a mustache lay motionless, his eyes darting around as if he feared being struck by something at any moment. He too had a wet stain on his garments, but Ricciardi realized that the liquid staining the front of his trousers was not blood.

At the center of the stage, a middle-aged man was kneeling, his hair in disarray and his face heavily made up. He had a

vacant expression; his lips seemed to be in perpetual movement as if he were praying. In front of him, on the planks of
the stage, lay a gleaming pistol. It was as if everyone was, one
way or another, gathered in a circle around that object.

Ricciardi stood there watching for a few more seconds, then
he focused on the corpse. It took a moment or two before his
diseased mind visualized the ghostly image of the woman, her
chest torn open by the pistol shot, the stain spreading across
her chest. Turned toward the other side of the stage, she kept
repeating: *Love of my life. Love of my life. Love of my life.*
From her mouth and nose the blood flowed, unstoppable,
joining the pooling welter of blood on her chest.

The commissario shut his eyes and then opened them again.
Then he spoke to the young man lying on the floor: "You can
get up now. Nothing else is going to happen."

A peal of laughter came from the group of artists, but
Ricciardi was unable to identify the individual responsible for
that impertinent levity. The young man sat up, though he continued to look around him in sheer terror. Then he got to his
feet. He checked the front of his trousers and whimpered:
"Oh, my God. I need to go get changed, straightaway . . ."

This time at least three distinct sources of laughter could be
heard, though they immediately fell silent when Ricciardi
turned to look at them.

"You can get changed when I say so. What is your name?"

"Romano, Pio Romano. I'm an . . . I'm an actor, but you
already know that, I'd have to guess."

"I don't know anything. Why were you lying there on the
floor?"

The man blinked, batting his lashes. His movements were
measured and well controlled, but there were gestures he made
that betrayed a somewhat effeminate manner.

"Because I'm dead, of course. I mean to say, I'm supposed
to be dead. Signor Gelmi, here, shot me, so I have to fall down

on the ground. That's in the script. Because Signor Gelmi fires two shots, one at me and one at . . . And I don't get up until the curtain comes down, but this time . . ."

Romano pointed at the dead woman, without looking at her, before continuing to speak: "The shot, this evening . . . I could have been killed, you understand? If he'd shot her first, by mistake . . ."

And he started weeping, softly at first, and then louder and harder. Ricciardi turned his attention to the man on his knees.

"Are you Signor Gelmi?"

The man stopped muttering his incomprehensible litany and, as if awakening from a nightmare, looked up and stared at Ricciardi.

"Yes. I'm Michelangelo Gelmi and I've killed my wife. I killed her, but it wasn't me. It wasn't me."

IV

An hour later, the facts of what had happened seemed pretty clear, even though they continued to baffle the investigators.

Ricciardi and Maione were done gathering the testimony of the spectators. The various versions seemed to match, down to the smallest details. At the end of the dramatized song, a number that revolved around betrayal, as with every new performance of the show and exactly as in the show of that afternoon, Michelangelo Gelmi had pulled out the usual pistol and fired the two usual shots: one at Pio Romano, the young actor whose trousers were now stained with urine, and the other at the poor, late Fedora, who lay in a pool of blood against the painted panel.

At that point, according to what the actors, musicians, and regular attendees told them, the song would end and the curtain would come down. Then the curtain was raised again so that the performers could bask in the thunderous applause from the audience. That evening, however, the second bullet hadn't been a blank, and the curtain had remained open, revealing a variety show that had been transformed in a split second into a bloody tragedy.

The photographer had arrived; and after a few minutes, while the magnesium flashed and Fedora Marra posed for her last stage pictures, though devoid of her renowned smile, Dr. Bruno Modo also arrived on the stage. The medical examiner nodded curtly to Ricciardi and Maione, murmuring sullenly:

"You know, this habit people seem to have of getting themselves murdered late at night, when a poor hard-working wretch ought to have a sacrosanct right to an evening's entertainment, is that something you've been trying to encourage? Because it only seems to happen with you. Your colleagues, at least, have some manners, and they only call me at regular business hours. But you seem to be in cahoots with the murderers and you always call me at night. Damn you."

Maione flashed him a broad smile, thumbs carelessly stuck under the belt that supported his jutting gut, and replied:

"Ah, *dotto'*, I took charge of it personally, let me assure you. I've been working for the past two days with my friends the actors, here, and we've been laying the groundwork. Now, fellows, I told them, let's make sure it happens around eleven. Any later and the doctor is liable to move on to a different bordello, and then we'll never be able to track him down."

Modo shook his fist at Maione.

"You're right that the line of people waiting to gun you down is just too long, and I'm a stickler for the rules. I don't butt in line. I'll just have to settle for waiting to receive the late-night call to come tend to your corpses. All right, then, let's not waste any more time here. I have an appointment with a couple of young ladies and an excellent bottle of wine. What do we have here?"

Maione wrinkled his nose.

"Why are you talking about young ladies and bottles of wine, *dotto'*? It's three more days till New Year's."

"Brigadie'," the medical examiner replied, "if you're intelligent, you celebrate life on the exact days nobody else does. Because life is a special gift and there's no point in wasting it. Don't take your example from our grim young friend here, who looks like he's running a funeral parlor."

Hearing his person called into question, Ricciardi replied: "And a hearty *buonasera* to you, too, Bruno. I see that the sight of a theater stage brings out your renowned satirical vein. But what if you were to show off your own professional skills, that is, if the urge to get back to your late-night festivities isn't too overwhelming?"

The doctor threw both arms wide in a theatrical gesture.

"What is this, irony? Because, unless my ears are deceiving me, Brigadie', we've just heard Commissario Ricciardi, the Cop of the Sad Countenance, uttering a sort of joke. I must already be drunk. All right, then, let's take a look . . . But . . . but this is . . ."

Maione nodded with a sigh, as he stared at the corpse.

"Yes, that's right. Allow me to introduce you to the deceased Fedora Marra."

Modo squatted down next to the woman. As always happened in cases like this, those present murmured quietly among themselves, taking care not to look at the victim, whose sad, damaged body demanded respect, but also instilled a certain detachment. Death, Ricciardi knew all too well, is an awkward guest at the party of life.

Once the eyewitness accounts had been double-checked and the list of identities and home addresses had been jotted down, the commissario had allowed the spectators to leave the building. A few rubberneckers among the crowd would have opted to remain behind to goggle at this unexpected extension of the show, but Camarda and Cesarano made sure, with rather brusque encouragement, that they too were ushered out the doors.

The waiters, the cooks, and the bartender had all been shooed away hastily as well because they'd seen little or nothing, busy as they were with their assigned tasks. There remained only the performers and other artists responsible for the performance and the theater staff. At the actual moment of the crime, they'd all been backstage readying themselves for the grand finale which was scheduled to follow the fateful number. Onstage at the time of the shooting there had been only the five protagonists of the dramatized song, and one of the five now lay lifeless on the boards, while the others still seemed to be quite upset.

While the doctor examined the corpse, Ricciardi considered the facts. No one had heard a second shot alongside the one that Gelmi had fired. And the bullet's trajectory ruled out the possibility of a shooter firing from some other location. There were no alternatives: the lead actor had killed the lead actress by shooting her in the chest.

Gelmi was still in a state of shock. He had struggled to his feet with the support of two other artists, still wearing the greasepaint of performance, and had been conveyed out into the orchestra seating. Now he sat, eyes staring, his gaze lost in the middle distance, as his lips had resumed psalmodizing senseless words. His hands were trembling. After the first few enigmatic words uttered by the man, Ricciardi had asked him no further questions, choosing to wait a little while. And so he had instead interviewed Romano, the actor who'd been the target of the first gunshot which, luckily for him, had been free of consequence.

The commissario had immediately eliminated all suspicion of a relationship between this Romano and Marra. The trauma and tragedy of events had made blindingly clear—by shattering all barriers of self-control—the young man's effeminate nature.

Romano, gesticulating, had said: "Sweet Madonna, Commissa', I was terrified. He could have killed me. You pour your soul into your calling, and you wind up shot down like a dog onstage. Yes, that's right, every single performance unfolds in the exact same progression, the first shot at me and the second shot at Fedora. No, no disagreements, no quarrels, she was all sweetness and light, I can't believe that she's dead. Yes, I've been working with them both for years, a close and loving couple. Sure, we're theater folk, Commissa', now and then someone will rub someone else the wrong way, but nothing big. No, I hadn't seen them before the beginning of the second performance. Their dressing rooms are separate from ours, you know, after all they're the lead actors, lucky them. Or actually, I shouldn't say lucky them, should I? Not considering this slaughter. Sweet Jesus, he could have shot me. Commissa', is it all right if I change my trousers now? I feel just a bit uncomfortable, you understand."

Ricciardi had made a mental note to have another conversation with Romano as soon as the intense emotion of the moment had subsided a bit. He knew by personal experience just how many details could surface in a witness's memory in the hours following events, when a full understanding of what had befallen began to emerge in the mind. The next day, he'd be sure to question the musicians and other artists. There was something strange about this story: Why would a man kill his wife in front of all those people, eliminating any doubt about who had committed the murder, and then vociferously deny his guilt?

He walked over to the doctor.

"Well, Bruno? What can you tell me?"

Modo stood up.

"What can I tell you, Riccia'? It's a real shame. Fedora Marra was one of my favorite actresses, she was beautiful and talented, as good at playing dramatic roles as comic parts. A born actress, and a gorgeous woman. And now just look at her, a heap of bones, congealed blood, and lifeless flesh. What a pity."

Ricciardi furrowed his brow.

"Yes. It's a pity. Exactly the same as every time we find ourselves faced with this kind of thing. But what else?"

The doctor sighed.

"What else? Nothing more than what meets the eye here. A gunshot wound on in the left hemithoracic region. At a glance,

I'd guess that the diameter of the entry wound is roughly ten millimeters. No doubt the bullet severed the aortic arch, otherwise we wouldn't see blood flowing from mouth and nose. There's no exit wound, so the bullet must necessarily still be inside her. I'll be able to tell you more after the autopsy, of course. Which I'm guessing you need in a hurry, of course."

Without taking his eyes off the corpse as it continued to utter the same words, softly: *Love of my life. Love of my life. Love of my life*, the commissario replied in a low voice: "As soon as you possibly can, of course. Even though this time I don't think there can be any doubt about who pulled the trigger, when, and how. What we need to understand, though, is why."

Modo gave an off-kilter grin.

"And do you think that's a minor detail, my friend?"

Ricciardi said nothing, turned, and joined Gelmi in the orchestra seating. Maione was standing behind the man, ready for whatever events might unfold.

"Signor Gelmi," the commissario asked, "do you wish to confirm what you've said so far? Did you shoot your wife?"

The man looked up, his eyes watery. His makeup was dissolving into a sloppy grayish mass, giving the lead actor a ridiculous, unkempt appearance; now he looked every bit his age, all his years showing, a great many more years than he tried to convey onstage.

"Yes, exactly the same as I have at every performance. I shot her because that's what the script calls for. I do it three times a day. I shot her, but with a blank."

Ricciardi pointed at the victim.

"Then how do you explain this?"

Gelmi slowly shook his head.

"I have no explanation. I loaded the gun myself, and it's my own gun, and I loaded it with blanks, like I told you before. I don't own any real bullets. I don't understand."

The commissario heaved a deep sigh.

"All the same, you admit that you loaded the weapon and you pulled the trigger."

The actor nodded, slowly.

"Yes. I admit that. But it wasn't me. I'd never have killed her. She is the love of my life."

Ricciardi nodded to Maione, who gently helped Gelmi to his feet to lead him away.

The case seemed to have been solved.

V

By the time Maione and Ricciardi concluded their examination of the Teatro Splendor, it was past midnight. Despite the lateness of the hour, there was still a small knot of onlookers outside the theater; and there were even a pair of exasperated couples, objecting vociferously and waving their tickets for the last show, which had been, of course, canceled.

Several reporters approached Ricciardi asking questions, but Maione moved them away brusquely.

"Commissa'," he said to his superior officer as they headed back toward police headquarters, "the dead woman is famous, like I explained. You'll see, the newspapers are going to be a major annoyance. Let's brace for it."

Ricciardi shrugged.

"You know, Raffaele, we always work the same way. It won't be very different."

Maione made a face.

"You think, Commissa'? I beg to differ: I'm afraid we're going to spend a nasty New Year's."

Later on, as he walked home alone through the city's deserted streets, Ricciardi thought back on the strange scene of that crime, hovering somewhere between reality and make-believe, where death had burst rudely in, shattering dreams and illusions. That was why he had never much liked the theater: Ricciardi, who knew the range of human feelings and the catastrophes summoned down by their perversions, couldn't stand to see them acted out on a brightly lit stage. Especially now that the barriers he'd built over the course of a lifetime had collapsed in the presence of Enrica's smile.

He'd instinctively crossed to the opposite sidewalk after glimpsing through a distant window the ghostly image of a man dangling from a hook in the ceiling; he swung lazily back and forth, reminiscent of a salami hung up to age. The fragment of attention that he'd conceded to that scene yielded to his mind, like the buzz of an insect close to his ear, a few truncated words: *Forgive me, beloved children of mine.* Who could say what had driven that man to suicide? The last stages of some disease, perhaps, or debts, the unfortunate end of a love affair, a faithless wife.

Quickening his stride, he recalled his own stricken horror when he still believed that the German officer might succeed in his efforts to win Enrica's acceptance of his proposal of marriage. In his thoughts, he harkened back to the woman who'd been murdered just a few hours before that on the stage of the Teatro Splendor. Why had her husband killed her? Was it a betrayal, an artistic rivalry, a bitter quarrel? And why do it so openly, so theatrically, in front of a packed audience, thus eliminating any doubt and ruling out any opportunity to make good one's escape? Actors, as he'd had the chance to observe in the past, were peculiar people, possessed of strange mental processes. Make-believe, repeated day in and day out, got into their blood, persuading them that in real life tragedies could take on the same form as they had onstage.

Before getting in bed, and without turning on the light, he opened his bedroom window. The air was still warm, with the aid of that unusual tepid breeze. There was a cloying odor of dampness and mold. In the darkness, he thought he spotted a movement behind the window in Enrica's kitchen. He found himself smiling, all alone, in the dark. *Love of my life*, Fedora Marra's voice whispered to him. He got into bed, with a shiver.

The next morning, in the office, after Maione had brought him his usual espresso in a glass demitasse, Deputy Chief Garzo burst into the room.

It was a rare occurrence, because their superior officer almost never appeared in police headquarters before nine in the morning. He believed it was a prerogative of his position to arrive at work after all those who reported to him, allowing himself to garner a complete overview of the day's necessities and thereby issue all the necessary organizational instructions; or at least, so he claimed. For that matter, the fact that he was married to the niece of His Excellency the Prefect of Salerno must certainly afford him a privilege or two.

What's more, Angelo Garzo was maniacally obsessed with the formalities of his position, and whenever he wished to speak with Ricciardi, he made sure to send Ponte, the policeman whom he had transformed into his own personal valet and footman, to summon him in full pomp and regalia. Instead, this morning, there he was right in front of Ricciardi, and of course he had entered without knocking. Skinny and frail, Ponte trailed after him as usual, his eyes downcast.

Ricciardi continued to sip his espresso in utter relaxation. He knew that this nonchalant attitude got on Garzo's nerves, and he found the fact amusing. Maione moved uneasily: he'd never made a secret of the low opinion he held of the deputy chief. Maione considered Garzo to be a mere bureaucrat, an idiot into the bargain, and someone who'd used family connections to win his position, always ready to blame others for his failures and claim their achievements as his own.

Garzo blinked rapidly, irritated by Ricciardi's indifference. He was elegantly groomed and attired, as was his custom, and looked as if he was about to make his grand entrance into a drawing room for an exclusive party. His chestnut hair was combed back and the skin of his face was freshly shaved. His exquisitely tended mustache, a recent conceit that was his current pride and joy, betrayed his innermost thoughts even more eloquently than his eyes. And at that moment, that mustache was quivering with wounded pride.

"*Buongiorno*, Ricciardi. As you can see, I'm here, in case you hadn't noticed."

The commissario set down his espresso, dabbed at his lips with his handkerchief, placed it back into the breast pocket of his jacket, and calmly rose to his feet.

"*Buongiorno*, sir. Forgive me, I wasn't expecting a visit from you at such an early hour."

Ponte, who had remained in the doorway, emitted a faint moan. Maione twisted his lips into a virtually imperceptible smile and spoke: "Ah, *dotto'*, *buongiorno*. Truth be told, I hadn't even noticed that you'd come in. You were both so very silent."

The neat little mustache pursed in a snort toward the brigadier.

"Ah, Maio', *buongiorno*. Yes, I came down myself to speed things up, work waits for no one. Well, now, Ricciardi, I heard that you were summoned yesterday to the Teatro Splendor. I was informed of the fact at the home of Conte Castaldi, while my wife and I were there for a little after-dinner reception."

"Yes, indeed, sir. I've already written my report, it's a matter of . . ."

"Yes, Fedora Marra, no less, I know; no one's talking about anything else in the whole city. And I expect that starting this morning both the press and my higher-ups are going to be asking me what I know about the murder, so I'm going to need some good answers. You, Ricciardi, probably don't realize, and I see no reason why you should since it's not the sort of thing that concerns you, lucky man that you are. You have no idea of the pressures I'm subjected to. It might seem as if I pay little mind to the things that happen here in the office, but . . ."

Maione murmured: "Well, yes, in fact . . ."

The other man gazed at Maione, blankly.

"What are you suggesting, Maione?"

The brigadier beat a hasty retreat.

"I meant to say that you have so many things to do, *dotto'*. That's why we always do our best to settle matters ourselves."

Garzo continued staring at him, sternly. He had the vague suspicion that the brigadier was mocking him subtly, but he couldn't be sure. Behind him, Ponte coughed softly. Maione reached out a hand and slammed the door in the man's face. Ponte emitted a soft complaint.

"Forgive me, *dotto'*," the brigadier explained, "but there's a draft. I shut the door, otherwise we'll catch our death."

The deputy chief ignored him and once again addressed Ricciardi: "I hear that you've arrested Michelangelo Gelmi, the late Marra's husband, and that the man put up no resistance. He shot her in a theater full of people. Is that right?"

Ricciardi confirmed: "Yes, sir. It happened during the second performance, at the moment of the dramatized song. Gelmi fired two shots, one of which was a blank, aimed at another male actor, and the fatal shot, at the woman."

Garzo tacitly agreed with small, nervous jerks of his chin.

"Indeed. And therefore we can now declare to the public that, with our usual rapid efficiency, we have solved the . . ."

Ricciardi shook his head.

"No, sir. I'd recommend due caution, as far as that goes."

The other man's jaw dropped in surprise. He turned to look at Maione, as if demanding an explanation or seeking approval, but the brigadier shrugged his shoulders.

"What are you trying to say?" Garzo demanded. "Did I mishear you, or did you yourself not just tell me that Gelmi shot the woman in front of everyone during a dramatized song?"

"That is what I said. But I haven't yet informed you that Gelmi denies having loaded the handgun with the fatal bullet.

Indeed, he admits that he shot his wife, but without any intention of killing her."

The neat little mustache went back to quivering, in a mixture of indignation and irritation.

"Oh, my Lord, Ricciardi, do we want to have everyone in the city laughing at us? A man shoots and kills his wife, who is moreover a renowned actress, in front of a packed theater, and we set off in pursuit of ghosts?"

Or perhaps we should say, the commissario thought to himself, that it's the ghosts who are chasing us. *Love of my life.*

"Certainly not, sir. In fact, we've arranged to place Gelmi under arrest, and truth be told, the man put up no resistance. Still, with all due respect, I'd like to suggest that we delve a little deeper into this matter, if for no other reason than to ward off the risk of evidence being introduced at trial that might hurt our chances. Precisely because this case is of such intense public interest, you will no doubt agree that we must ensure that our prosecutorial theory is airtight and bombproof."

The neat little mustache relaxed into a brief, meditative pause.

"Yes, I see. You're quite right, Ricciardi. But make sure you move quickly and without commotion, because if anyone were to notice that we've been devoting time and resources to an investigation into an episode that's as clear as day, they'd be bound to crucify us. Do we have an understanding? Let's get this done before the start of the new year. Let's try to end the old year well and start the new one even better."

Then he turned on his heel and without warning yanked the door open, slamming right into Ponte, who'd been intently eavesdropping. The two men then moved off together.

Maione shook his head.

"What an imbecile. He doesn't even understand what idiotic drivel he's spewing. But are you really determined to continue the investigation, Commissa', or were you just saying that to keep him worried?"

Ricciardi had turned to look out the window; he stared at the city as it went about readying itself to enjoy New Year's.

"I was deadly serious, Raffaele. I want to find out what really happened. If Gelmi had really been determined to murder his wife, there are a thousand other ways he could have done it. But if he really wanted to shoot her in front of an audience, then why bother denying it afterward? I think we need to do some more digging."

Maione scratched his head.

"All right, Commissa', after all, there's not much other work to take care of right now. Nobody's going to kill anyone between Christmas and New Year's Day."

VI

Modo had completed his autopsy of Fedora Marra's corpse. The venerated, beloved, and tirelessly courted actress was now just a lump of inert flesh on a marble slab—the stone chilly and crisscrossed by the scratch marks of thousands of ineptly wielded scalpels. His colleagues after all weren't excessively careful when it came to dissecting cadavers.

Unlike them, however, Dr. Bruno Modo devoted great care to his autopsies. He like to think that he had a responsibility to devote care and attention to these bodies, too. Though they no longer possessed the vital functions of living bodies, they had once been human beings, capable of experiencing and prompting strong feelings.

And the body that lay before him truly had aroused a *great* many strong feelings.

As Modo had realized at a first glance and promptly informed Ricciardi, the bullet had made a successful journey into Fedora's body and decided to end its trip there and stay for a while. After penetrating the flesh just above her wondrous left breast, it had proceeded to lacerate the intercostal muscle and the aortic arch, then the left tracheal wall and the esophagus, finally lodging itself, by now depleted of all kinetic force, between the third and fourth dorsal vertebrae. Quite a charming excursion, occupying a mere fraction of a second from start to finish. The bullet lay before him, in a metal basin, now inoffensive, misshapen, and cold. Nine-mm caliber, judged the expert eye—the eye not of the doctor, but of the old veteran soldier.

What had caused the actress's death was the lesion of the aorta. The other damage might well have paralyzed her, left her mute, or caused an exceedingly grave respiratory crisis, but what killed her was the rupture of that major blood vessel. Staring at that waxen face, piteously cleansed of the blood that had gushed forth in such sudden abundance, Modo wondered whether Fedora had suffered. He was forced to admit that the answer was yes, and that realization prompted a vague sense of anger blended with pity, as it always did when he was brought face to face with an unmistakable case of violent death. And in this case, the death of such a lovely woman.

Fedora must have understood that she was dying. As all that blood filled the woman's chest, her thoracic cavity, her pleural cavity, as she was losing strength and struggling to breathe, she must have understood that she was dying. While her vision was growing blurred from the throttled flow of oxygen to the brain, as she ceased to feel her arms and legs, she must have understood that she was dying. Many seconds on end, perhaps as long as a minute: an enormous span of time. The intense pain, the awareness of how irreversible it all was. So many things still to say, so many things still to do. So many people to bid farewell; urgent advice, unachieved desires, and wishes to be entrusted to someone.

Love.

What might you have thought about before losing consciousness? Modo asked his mute patient. I wonder if you tried to imagine why he'd shot you in the chest for real, instead of just pretending to as he ought to have done and always had in the past. What a stunning surprise, what a miserable development. I wonder if you had the time to resign yourself. Or forgive.

He carefully stitched back up the Y-shaped incision that

he'd carved into chest and abdomen. He wasn't happy that he'd had to do a rough-and-ready suture to close the incision. If time allowed, and if the suffering of the living didn't summon him posthaste to some other dire emergency, he'd work with the greatest attention and care to ensure the body was suitable for a dignified burial. It was a matter of simple respect.

He'd just finished when Sister Luisa came clopping into the room in her wooden clogs. She was a short, fat woman of some undefinable age and possessed of boundless energy. When everyone else was dropping from exhaustion, it was none other than Sister Luisa who'd step in to make up for the shortcomings of all the others, to the casual eye, without effort and with unflagging good will; an indispensable resource for Pellegrini Hospital. Modo had a relationship of shameless intimacy with Sister Luisa, typical of the freethinker, atheist, and libertine that he was, but it was based on his profound esteem and great consideration of her as a colleague. They were friends, though they couldn't have possibly been any more different.

The nun approached the marble slab, no-nonsense and brisk as usual.

"*Dotto'*, where are we? Are we done playing?"

Modo chuckled.

"Sister Luisa, you're the usual party pooper. Just as I was finally settling in to enjoy the company of a woman who can't deafen me with idle chitchat."

The nun turned a sad glance to the corpse.

"Poor thing, so young and so pretty. She was a famous actress, wasn't she?"

The doctor nodded.

"Yes, you should have seen her . . ." Then he turned to look at the nun and managed to put on a smile. "You need to get out more often, Sister Luisa. One of these evenings, let me take you to the movies: just you and me. You can take that dish towel off your head, and I assure you, you'll drive the men wild."

She compressed her fat lips, displaying a funny grimace.

"Ah, that's for sure, *dotto'*. There aren't many real women around these days. If I hadn't met a certain Someone before this . . ."

And she pointed at the cross hanging on the wall of the autopsy chamber.

Modo snickered.

"That guy always seems to get the finest ones. It's obvious that He has pull of some kind, connections in high places. Anyway, Sister Lui', tell me why you've come downstairs. Has something happened?"

"Certainly, otherwise you'd never see me down here in the midst of all your corpses, poor souls. There's someone upstairs who wants to talk to you. She's wearing a cape and a cowl; it's hard to understand what she's saying, but I certainly made out your name."

Modo heaved a deep sigh.

"It must be one of my lovely admirers, they're obsessed with me. I'll be right there."

Once he reached the hospital lobby, the doctor managed to make out with some difficulty a figure waiting, seated on a chair in the shadows. The figure was off to one side, away from the steady flow of people entering the building or leaving after having paid a comforting visit to a patient.

Modo narrowed his eyes: at a first glance, the figure, bundled up against the cold, looked vaguely familiar. He couldn't have pinned down exactly what it was, in part because whoever it was sat slouched to one side, but a vague recollection was starting to bob to the surface in his memory.

He stepped closer, pushing his way through a group of people who were engaged in a lively discussion with a young doctor. He could perceive the difficulties being experienced by his younger colleague as he tried to explain to a crowd of kin and relations why he was going to have to detain a certain Giuseppe, suffering from diphtheria, and thought to himself that he really wouldn't have wanted to be in his colleague's shoes, though he had been in the same situation himself thousands of times before. Family members often reacted badly to unwelcome news.

By now he was close enough to his mysterious female visitor to guess at the reason for her off-center unnatural position: she must be suffering from a sprained shoulder, and perhaps a wrist fracture as well because of the way she was holding her forearm. What's more, she had shifted her weight onto one buttock, as if the other half of her body were in some considerable pain.

He sped up his pace and practically broke into a run for the last few yards that separated him from the woman. When he stood before her, he glimpsed a number of dark stains on the fabric of her garment; this was certainly not looking good. Who knows why, the thought occurred to him that he'd have to give Sister Luisa a good ribbing for having failed to notice any of this.

"At your service, Signora. What seems to have happened?"

Extremely slowly, the woman raised her head to look at him. The doctor furrowed his brow and squinted to see better; and then, swept by a nasty hunch, he reached out and pushed the hood aside.

The face that was thus revealed was horribly swollen and puffy. One eye was swollen shut entirely, the white of the other eye was badly bloodshot. One cheekbone looked fractured and was certainly enlarged, and likewise the nasal septum; the lower lip was split and bleeding. The open mouth was gulping down air with a painful effort, allowing him to glimpse several shattered incisors.

The doctor held his breath as he wondered how that poor

thing had managed to drag herself all this way and whether she had arrived alone. This was hardly the first time he'd been confronted with the aftermath of a savage beating, but someone had really taken it out on that face with an extra measure of cruelty.

From the woman's lips, there came a hoarse whisper.

"Bruno. Forgive me, Bruno. They can't know about this. No one can know."

Modo shivered; there was something familiar in the timbre of that voice.

Suddenly he recognized her.

"Lina? Is that you, Lina? Why, what . . ."

He didn't have a chance to finish the question, because she collapsed into his arms.

VII

That Michelangelo Gelmi had shot his wife was an undeniable statement of fact, and Ricciardi decided to start with that. He wanted to know whether the man would stick to the same story after a night left to brood over what had happened. "I killed her, but it wasn't me," he had said in the moments of grim panic following his wife's death.

Now the actor found himself in a cell at police headquarters, awaiting his transfer to prison. Before summoning the man to his office for a further interview, the commissario—who really knew nothing about show business—asked Maione to brief him about the couple's fame. The brigadier threw both arms wide.

"Well, Commissa', I'll admit that what with the kids to raise, my work on the police force, and the general shortage of time, it's not as if I spend that much time at the movies or the theater. But everyone knows Michelangelo Gelmi and Fedora Marra; or, I should say, nearly everyone, forgive me."

Ricciardi invited him to continue.

"Well, it was Gelmi who discovered Fedora, before anyone else even knew who she was. They're both from this town, but I think they first met in Rome. She was originally working as a seamstress, I seem to remember, and he persuaded her to start acting. They performed together, they took a liking to each other, and they were even married. At a certain point, she started making movies on her own, and there was less and less talk of Gelmi. Then this revue arrived in the city. More I couldn't say."

The commissario nodded, lost in thought. Then he told Maione to bring the prisoner into the room.

Gelmi appeared, accompanied by two guards. He was a wreck. His complexion was ashen, his hair was askew, revealing his thinning hairline, his eyes were blank and his shoulders bowed. Though onstage he looked no older than forty or so, he now seemed older than sixty.

Ricciardi ordered the guards to leave the room and asked the brigadier to help the man to be seated. During his interrogations, he didn't like to take advantage of the discomfort instilled in suspects by being forced to remain standing. It wasn't just pity, either. He did it partly to instill a positive attitude toward himself, the suspect's questioner.

But the actor remained indifferent to that act of courtesy. He seemed immersed in a world all his own, lost in who knows what thoughts or memories. From time to time, his gaze turned incredulously to the shackles on his wrists, after which he would slowly shake his head, as if replying to some mute question he had asked of himself.

Ricciardi waited for a few seconds, then began speaking: "Well, Signor Gelmi, you've had the whole night to think things over. I wanted to talk again because yesterday, at the time of your arrest, you uttered these words: 'I killed her, but it wasn't me.' You were upset, and you didn't seem to be in any state to explain what you meant by that. Now, though, before you're transferred to prison, I'd like to ask what you meant by those words."

At first, the other man didn't seem to have heard, and then, with an infinitely slow motion, he looked up at Ricciardi.

"Ah, it was you. Please, bear with me, I didn't remember you. But I can perfectly recall those words, because it's the truth. I shot her, that's true. It was my finger that pulled the trigger, and everyone saw it. But I'm not guilty of her murder, I was only the physical perpetrator. That's the wording you use, isn't it?"

For some indecipherable reason, a strange smile appeared on the man's face, as if he'd just uttered an amusing line. Ricciardi waited for him to go on talking, but the man remained in silence.

The commissario prompted him to speak: "I'll ask you again: could you explain more clearly?"

The actor started and spoke.

"I load the pistol, with blanks. Just shells with some gunpowder, in other words. No bullet. Just the noise, boom, and the smoke. The actor falls down, apparently dead, and the audience goes: Ooohhh. Then the musicians end the song, the curtain falls, and the audience clap their hands. The dead get to their feet, they join hands with the living, we all take our bows to a roar of applause. That's how it goes every day, three times a day. Always the same . . ."

Maione weighed in, with a calm voice: "Yes, but this time your wife actually died. That strikes me as a pretty big difference. It's not as if someone muffed their line, or slipped on the floorboards, or broke a guitar string. A person was murdered here."

Gelmi turned in astonishment toward Maione as if the brigadier had said something unthinkable.

"That's right, it's exactly the point. And I continue racking my brains to understand how it could have happened. I've thought about it all night long, and I can't set my mind at rest."

Ricciardi sighed softly.

"All right, then. Let's start over from scratch. Describe for me exactly what you did, starting from the moment that you loaded your pistol."

The actor furrowed his brow.

"Fedora and I have two dressing rooms, separated from the rest of the troupe. The others change into their stage costumes in one big room at the end of the backstage corridor. The dressing rooms are shut and locked, and I always carry the key to my dressing room in my pocket. I ready my pistol, a 1915 Beretta semiautomatic. I used it when I was in the army. I held the rank of captain, you know that? I fought on the Piave in June of 1918."

He broke off as his gaze once again began to wander in the middle distance.

"And then what?" Ricciardi persisted.

"I do my makeup, I get dressed, and I go onstage."

"What do you mean by, 'I ready my pistol'?"

The other man shrugged.

"I clean it, I check it to make sure it won't jam, and then I load it. Five shells in the clip, one in the chamber. Two shots a performance for three shows."

Ricciardi nodded.

"That means that, taking into account the fact that the fatal shot was fired at the end of the second performance, three shots had already been fired before it. Is that right?"

"Yes, that's right, three shots. Including the shot fired at Romano, the other actor who performs in the dramatized song."

Ricciardi stopped to think. Then he asked: "Try to remember. Were you ever separated from the gun?"

"Commissario, I have three numbers in the revue, and it's only in the last one, the one in which . . . Only the last one requires the use of the pistol. The rest of the time, I leave it in my dressing room, where no one can get in unless I let them. Aside from Fedora, of course. Aside from Fedora . . ."

Maione broke in: "So, onstage, does the order of the shots ever change? You don't sometimes shoot *her* first, and then *him*, do you? Or else . . ."

The actor vigorously shook his head.

"How obvious it is that you don't know much about the theater, brigadier. There's no improvisation in theater. Theater is the product of study, commitment, and concentration.

Nothing is left to chance. The sequence of actions is prepared down to the smallest detail, and it has to be that way. I always shoot my treacherous friend first, and then my faithless lover. She must die last, after begging my forgiveness, hands extended, eyes rolling in desperation."

He started to imitate the gestures of the actress, but the chains on his wrists prevented him. He stared at his hands, aghast, and then dropped his eyes again.

Maione replied, sarcastically: "That said, it seems to me that something unexpected did happen, this time. And someone must have put the live bullet in there, in amongst the blanks, wouldn't you have to agree?"

The actor nodded, grimly.

Ricciardi tried to run back through the events.

"So, since the last time you used the weapon, there was the interval between the two performances, and then the two numbers you did during the performance in which your wife died. Who could have made their way into the dressing room to replace the blank with a live bullet?"

"No one, commissario, let me say it again. That's what's driving me crazy. Sitting between Fedora's and my dressing rooms and the big dressing room used by the rest of the troupe is Erminia, and no one can get past her without being seen."

Ricciardi looked up, jutting his chin.

"Who's Erminia?"

"She's the dresser, a member of the theater's staff. Even if someone had tried to make their way to my door—and let me tell you one more time that it's always shut and locked, and that I carry the key—she would have stopped them or else she would have come to knock and ask if I wished to receive them."

Maione concluded: "So you loaded the bullet."

"But I don't own any real bullets. All I have are the blanks, I buy them ready-made, that way I don't have to go to the trouble of making them myself."

Ricciardi changed the subject.

"How were your relations with your wife?"

The actor looked up at him again. Suddenly his expression had turned wary.

"I loved her with all my heart, from the minute I met her the first time, and I love her still, even now that I'm sitting here talking to you both about her death."

"And did she love you?"

Gelmi hesitated ever so slightly, a detail that didn't escape the attention of the two policemen.

"Why, of course she loved me. It was I who discovered her, a diamond in a heap of charcoal. I made her great, a titan of the theater: she could have had whatever she desired, she could have worked in America and with the finest directors, but she chose to perform in this revue, just so she could stay with me. And believe me, I never demanded it of her. This is what she wanted. Don't you think that might have meant that she loved me?"

Ricciardi piled on.

"No disagreements, in the recent past?"

Now Gelmi seemed to be on the defensive.

"What couple on earth doesn't have disagreements? I think it's normal for a husband and wife to have different points of view, especially when they are in the same line of work. Fedora is . . . *was* a strong, determined woman. She had her opinions, naturally. She was fiery and full of pepper, and when she was convinced she was right, it was a struggle to get her to change her mind. But it was nothing serious. Just artistic differences."

Maione persisted: "So, no arguments?"

"No, brigadier. No arguments, no fights. And I would never, never have dreamed of hurting her. I've never hurt a soul in my life. Except on the battlefield. And even now, after all these years, I still have nightmares about those kids, those young men, on our side and on the enemy side, dead in a hail of grenade fragments, run through in agony by bayonets. And I wake up with a start. I swear to you, for what my word of honor is worth, that I never put that damned bullet in the magazine. I fired the gun, but I'm an innocent man."

Ricciardi leaned forward.

"Then who could have had the motive, and the opportunity, to murder your wife by using you? Because if we theorize that you're telling the truth, and you'll understand that all the evidence is against you, we're going to have to come up with a different scenario."

Gelmi fell silent, his eyes wide open, staring at Ricciardi, his lips trembling. At last, in a sighing voice, he said: "Commissario, I don't know what to tell you. Believe me, I desperately want to help you: not for my own sake, not to win back my freedom, because I stopped living the very same instant I realized that I'd killed my own wife. It's certainly not to free myself of these," and he rattled his shackles, "that I hope you catch the murderer. But I can't stand the thought that whoever murdered that wonderful woman through my own cursed hands should go on living happily in a world that they deprived of her. No, that's something I can't dream of tolerating. So I beg you with all my heart: find them. Leave me behind bars for the rest of eternity, but find Fedora's murderer."

The actor had just stopped talking when tears of sorrow rolled down his cheeks. Or perhaps they were tears of rage.

Before the eyes of the two policemen, the man seemed to age by the minute.

VIII

Once the guards had taken Gelmi away again, Maione and Ricciardi remained in silence for a few minutes. Then the brigadier murmured, as if speaking to himself: "Certainly, they're all still actors, and what they say might turn out to be a big fat performance. And then this one in particular is talented and renowned, even though in the recent past, as I was telling you, he'd started to fade a bit from the public view; that said, it sounded to me like he was being sincere."

Ricciardi stood up and went to the window.

"What we know for sure, as your good friend Garzo would say, is that he pulled the trigger, and he did it in front of a theater full of witnesses. And he can't explain how anyone else could have placed a real bullet in amongst the blanks."

The brigadier, as was always the case when he was at his most intense concentration, looked as if he was about to fall asleep.

"That's not all. Whoever did it would have to have been something of an expert, in order to know exactly where in the clip the bullet needed to be inserted. I examined the pistol myself, Commissa'. There were still two cartridges in the magazine, both of them blanks, just like the other three that had been fired before the shot that killed poor Fedora. That's clear, isn't it?"

Ricciardi half turned around.

"Yes, unless we consider that there might have been an

error in calculation and that the real target might have been the young actor, that Pio Romano. This hypothesis should be checked out, too, don't you think?"

"Anything is possible. Maybe the bullet wound up in among the others by accident, and it was just a tragic twist of fate. Or else we're just wasting our breath, and Gelmi really was the murderer. By the way, I don't know if you noticed, but when we asked him if his wife loved him, Gelmi was pretty evasive."

His superior officer nodded.

"It seemed that way to me, too. More than evasive, though, he seemed to be on the defensive, as if he were offering a response to some kind of gossip. Maybe we should talk to someone else from the troupe to get a better understanding. And there's one other thing: the bullet was fired with remarkable precision. When you're acting, it's hard to aim so accurately. The doctor told us that the woman died instantly, didn't he?"

Maione rubbed his chin.

"Yes, even though he hasn't yet given us the autopsy results. Maybe I should swing by the hospital before heading home to see what he can tell me. In any case, there was a substantial age difference between the two of them. Marra wasn't yet thirty-five, and Gelmi is well over fifty. I'm sure that gratitude and affection are wonderful things, but a woman like her, married to an older man, must have faced considerable temptation."

Ricciardi turned back to look out the window. He reflected for a little while before talking again.

"It all points back to the Teatro Splendor and the troupe of actors. Let's admit, if for no other reason than sheer logic, that Gelmi really was exploited by some mastermind and never planned out cold-blooded, premeditated murder. In that case, either someone took the pistol after he loaded it and replaced a blank with a live shell, carefully counting the number of shots that would be fired before the fatal one, or else they did it immediately before the gun was used, during the second performance."

Maione was perplexed.

"What difference would it make, Commissa'? Doesn't it amount to the same thing?"

"In such an elaborate plan, every detail is important; the margin of error must be reduced to a minimum. All that is needed is for the gun to jam, or Gelmi to make a mistake, or for his hand to shake, or sweat blur his vision, and the next thing you know the real bullet has killed or wounded the actor Romano, or it plows into the painted backdrop, or it gives Fedora nothing more than a flesh wound. And maybe that explains why the third and final performance was ruled out: he would have been tired, he could have missed the target, he might already have wasted one of the previous shots, thus altering the order of the bullets. What we need to understand, then, is why they didn't choose the first performance."

Maione shook his head in astonishment.

"*Mamma mia*, Commissa', then that imbecile Garzo is right when he says that, if you want to understand criminals, you need to think like them! Still, and forgive me for saying so, if I were Gelmi and I'd murdered my wife, I'd be hoping that we would reason exactly this way."

Ricciardi twisted his lips in a grimace.

"Maybe we should just stop worrying about it now, and put Gelmi on trial for murder. After all, he did fire the fatal shot. Still, I'd be in favor of going to take a walk, just a quick walk, around the backstage of the Teatro Splendor, to see how the show works and how the actors move from their dressing rooms to the stage, as well as to hear what they have to say about the relationship between husband and wife. That way, we can put our consciences at ease, what do you say?"

The brigadier broke into a broad smile.

"That'd be great, Commissa'. I really love the theater. As a young man, before the disaster took me," and here he raised his hand with the wedding ring, "I went to the theater regularly. I even dreamed of becoming an actor myself, so I could kiss all the actresses. Let's go to the theater. That way we can set our minds and our consciences at ease."

IX

D r. Modo; with the woman passed out in his arms, called loudly for help. In spite of her stoutness, her short legs, and her long skirts, Sister Luisa was—as always—the first to arrive.

"What's happening, *dotto'*?

"Hurry, Sister Luisa. She's badly hurt."

In a flash the nun took it all in and took off at a run toward a hallway, while the doctor supported the unfortunate woman, careful not to hold her too tightly: she was clearly having difficulty breathing and was emitting hoarse gurgling noises.

Modo prayed to himself that there was no irreversible damage.

"Dotto', there's a new young woman. You have to believe me, she's spectacular."

"Donna Wanda, that's what you always say. There's a new young woman, she's spectacular, and then every time it's just the same old bowl of reheated soup. The truth is that there's no one else like you."

"No, no, Dotto', this time it's true. And after all, you're far too gallant, but the truth is that I've gotten old. And this young woman here, trust me, is a worthy successor."

"All right, let's hear it, what's she like?"

"Well, as far as pretty goes, she's pretty, Dotto'. But she has something extra, I couldn't tell you what. You know it, I'm ignorant. But she . . . she's intelligent. The kind you like, in other words."

"Oh, all right, let's have a look at her. I have just half an hour before my shift starts. What's her name?"

"That's something special about her, too. She doesn't want to use a stage name. Her real name is Lina, and that's how she wants to be known."

With the help of a male nurse and Sister Luisa, Dr. Modo laid the woman gently down on a stretcher.

The pain caused by this change in position brought her to with a start and a long, bloodcurling moan. The doctor was accustomed to suffering, and he saw it on a daily basis. Still, that doleful groan raised goose bumps on his arms. While the wheels of the gurney squeaked as they rolled her toward the emergency clinic, before the curious eyes of both patients and their family members, Modo mentally reviewed the urgent care procedures.

Lina, Lina, he thought to himself. What have they done to you?

"Tell me about yourself, you never tell me anything at all."

"Dotto', you know that I'd rather listen to you. You say such interesting things."

"Interesting, seriously? The work I do is nothing but pain and suffering. That's all I can tell you."

"Well, as for that, my line of work isn't all that different, believe me . . . You can't imagine how much pain and misery I see in these men who come up to see me. In theory, they come here to have a good time. In fact, though, they come here to forget the anguish that they carry with them."

"Really? And how do you know that?"

"There are times when they actually start crying. If their wives could see them the way I see them, they'd feel pity instead of hatred."

"And why do you speak of hatred, Lina?"

"Because women hate men. And men hate women every bit as much. Don't you know that?"

In the clinic, the doctor and Sister Luisa removed the clothing of the woman as she lay, partially conscious.

She presented numerous wounds and contusions. Bluish bruises were spreading and darkening almost everywhere on her body . . . The expert eye of the ex-military doctor, who'd done his training on the field of battle, had seen clearly, and his initial diagnosis found immediate and stark confirmation. The shoulder was dislocated, and the wrist was fractured: the ulna showed white through the flesh of the forearm. Then there was her cheekbone, her eyes, her lips, and her teeth.

Her face was unrecognizable. Swollen, shattered. Blood flowed from the badly cut eyebrow.

That face, once so lovely.

"Don't talk nonsense, dotto'."

"What nonsense do you mean? You're very beautiful, and you know it."

"If I was very beautiful, I could be an actress, and not in this profession."

"Let's leave aside the fact that a great many actresses also practice this very same profession, are you sure that you're not acting every single day?"

"Oh, now you're really trying to make me laugh. I understand what you're talking about, dotto'. But the truth is that in here, in these rooms, acting doesn't do any good, in fact, quite the opposite. The barrier has to fall."

"What barrier, Lina?"

"The barrier that we all raise, every day, to keep from being recognized by other people."

"And what is your barrier?"

"My face, dotto'. My barrier is my face."

For sure she had at least four broken ribs. And the compound fracture of the ulna would have to be reduced through surgery. For her face there wasn't much to be done, except to apply ice.

What worried him more than anything else was her cranium. At the back of the head there was an enormous bump, and Modo had felt a slight depression, detectable to the touch, above the left temporal lobe. All the same, if she really had arrived at the hospital under her own power, on her own two legs, as it had appeared—however incredible it seemed—at least it meant she was able to walk.

He was worried about her abdomen as well. For now, it appeared treatable and didn't seem to be swollen from any powerful hemorrhaging, but there could be any number of complications, as was also true of the lungs. Her breathing was rough, with the occasional wheeze, and the blood that was filling her mouth might have a number of sources.

Who did this, my friend? Who did this to you?

"How long have we known each other, Lina?"

"Oh, dotto', for a long time. Too long, perhaps. What are you going to do with an old woman like me?"

"You were just a girl and now you're a young woman."

"And you've always been the most captivating customer I have, Bruno. And that's not all."

"What else?"

"Well, you talk to me, we talk to each other. Do you think that's a given? It is not. There are times that men don't even say so much as buonasera."

"Well, frankly, I'd come here just to talk, think of that. I like women, and you know that: but you, you're special."

"And what's so special about me?"

"You're intelligent, you're sensitive, and you're sweet. You take one look and you understand things."

"It's just that after all these years, we understand each other instantly, you and I."

"I remember when Wanda told me that there was a new girl. It was you. I thought you were gorgeous, and I still think the same."

"Here we go again with the beauty, huh, dotto'? Beauty is gone in a flash. And women like me never even get a chance to grow old."

"Don't be silly. Poor old Wanda was ancient when she died."

"She seemed ancient, but she was actually younger than you. No, trust me, we don't get a chance to grow old."

"You will, I'm sure of it, you'll grow old. And if you ever want to leave this place, you only need to ask."

"Really, and who would take me? Come here, close to me. Talking about the future makes me sad. And now I feel like tickling you."

The woman had lost consciousness once again. But her suffering must have been unspeakable, because every time he touched her, she emitted lengthy groans.

The doctor decided to sedate her and gave her an injection of morphine. Then he tried to clear his head, sweep his mind free of memories, and focus on what to do next.

The lacerations hadn't been produced by a blade. These were not stab wounds. The margins of the wounds spoke clearly, and so did the ecchymoses: someone had beaten Lina with their bare hands. It was easy to make out the clear signs of punches and kicks. Whoever it was must have inflicted that punishment upon her for quite some time, even after she'd fallen to the ground. Perhaps she'd passed out: at least Bruno hoped she had. Maybe her attacker had believed her dead.

Still, even if she was in critical condition, she was still alive. Lina was a strong woman.

*

"It's one thing to be sensitive, it's quite another to be weak. You're sensitive, but you're not weak, Linarella."

"What do you know about it, dotto'? Are you so good that you know how to judge a person by seeing her only once every fifteen days for half an hour? Everyone has the strength they need to survive. What about you, for example? Are you strong or are you weak?"

"If you do the work I do, you have to have a heart of stone. Otherwise, you can't go on."

"Well, I happen to think that you need a nice soft heart, full of blood, a heart that beats even for people you've never met. It's the work that I do that demands a heart of stone."

"Why is that?"

"Otherwise, the worst disaster that could possibly happen will befall you. You'll fall in love."

"And then what happens?"

"Do you ask me that because you've never been married, dotto'?"

"What does that have to do with anything?"

"I'll tell you why: there are hearts that are just too big to let us live with just one person."

After pulling tight the last stitch of her sutures, the doctor looked out the window and realized how much time had passed, given the dim light he saw outdoors.

Now Lina's breathing was regular, even if she was still making that nasty wheezing sound. Her heartbeat was healthy, but he still couldn't rule out the risk of internal bleeding. And he didn't like that depression above her temple one bit.

Modo recoiled at the thought of what Lina must have gone through. He couldn't dismiss from his mind the picture of her on the ground, in the shadows, with someone beating her ferociously. He was convinced there must have been at least two attackers, if not more.

But what had she been doing out and about? Women like her weren't allowed out until sundown, they were even obliged to have other people purchase their personal linen for them, at the cost of a surcharge, because they were forbidden to be out on the streets while the shops were still open. Where had she been going? Or where had she gone?

Then he was stunned at the thought that she'd managed to drag herself all the way to the hospital. The pain must have been atrocious, but she'd thought about him.

He lightly touched her forehead to check for a fever. That swollen, unrecognizable face registered no reaction.

Modo didn't even notice that his cheeks were bathed in tears.

X

Maione had done some digging and was able to report to Ricciardi that Gelmi's and Fedora Marra's troupe, now bereft of both their lead actors, had gathered at the Teatro Splendor; they were trying to decide how to put on the show, by modifying the numbers in the revue, and for how much longer they could do so.

Commissario and brigadier together therefore decided to head over to the theater. As they exited police headquarters, the December sun was starting to sink into the west.

They were greeted at the theater, as they had been the evening previous, by Renzullo, the proprietor. His manner was less frantic, but he remained quite pessimistic concerning the near future.

"Certainly," he said, "the first few days there will be crowds. You can just imagine, the curiosity to see where it happened: the newspapers, the city, and perhaps even the nation as a whole are talking of nothing else. But then, things will start to go downhill. Without Fedora and Michelangelo, who do you think will want to come and pay to see the revue? It's a disaster, Commissa', an enormous disaster!"

Maione grew uncomfortable. That foolish man annoyed him.

"What kind of disaster are you talking about? You're keeping the revue in rotation until January 15th, aren't you? Between one thing and another, you'll have a full house from now till then, and you come out smelling like roses."

"No, indeed, Brigadie'. Not a bit. Because the show, *Ah, l'Amour!* is a joint production, ours and Gelmi's. We put it together ourselves, and most of the artists are from here. It was scheduled to end on the 15th, that's true, but then it was scheduled to travel on to Rome for a month and return here. Fedora was a star attraction, topping the bill at even the most important theaters. And instead now . . ."

Ricciardi grew attentive.

"And instead now?"

Renzullo sighed.

"To be truthful, Commissario, the big draw was Fedora. She was who people came to see, and her name was internationally renowned. She was wonderful, a formidable actress; she could sing and she could dance. She was born for the stage, and she died, sadly, on the stage. I still can't resign myself to the fact."

Maione said: "Gelmi was a big name, too, wasn't he?"

Renzullo shrugged and his double chin wobbled in a comical fashion.

"Michelangelo? Sure, sure, of course. He certainly was a big name."

"What do you mean, Renzu'? Speak clearly, if you don't mind."

"Michelangelo was a genuine star, no doubt about it. But every star, you know, eventually sets. As things stand now, Michelangelo is only, or *was* only, Fedora Marra's husband. His fame was dying out. A man is only handsome as long as it lasts; then his hair starts to thin, wrinkles arrive, false teeth . . . If you liked him when he was young, then you no longer want to see him now that he's old. That would just remind you that you're getting old too. And the audience no longer wants to think about things like that."

Ricciardi weighed in: "Was he jealous of his wife?"

Renzullo's eyes opened wide.

"No, no, Commissa'. Michelangelo was extremely grateful to Fedora, who could have had whatever her heart desired and had instead chosen to help him to stay in the limelight and go on filling theaters. In the business, her kindness, her devotion to her husband, her gratitude for his having discovered her, were all cited as exemplary. Michelangelo always told her so. Everyone had witnessed it. There was no envy between them, far from it. That's why I can't understand why he would have shot her. It kept me up all night."

Maione spoke up: "What do you mean?"

"I can't understand why a man would kill his goose that lays the golden egg. Without Fedora, Michelangelo would have been washed up in the theater, let's be clear. Finished. No one would dream of casting him alone. For that matter, he was starting to lose his voice, so he's not much good even as a singer anymore. He would have had to accept a steady downgrade; smaller and smaller theaters, and cheaper and drearier. If you only knew how many I've seen wind up like that. *With* Fedora, Gelmi was still a big name. But now he's a dead man."

Maione snorted: "Truth be told, she's the one who's dead. Take us to see the artists, Renzu'. We want to talk to them."

There was something strange about the hall of the Teatro Splendor. Ricciardi wondered just what it was. It wasn't the fact that he was seeing it without an audience. Nor was it the silence, only slightly disturbed by the chatter and laughter of the working staff, which reached his ears, muffled, from the distant kitchen.

Suddenly, the commissario understood. It was the light; it poured down from above, through the skylight. A subdued glow that gave the large room the same atmosphere as an empty church. On the stage, someone had placed a rose at the exact spot where Fedora Marra had slumped to the floor: the star, the prima donna, the unquestioned protagonist. A red rose, naked, with a long stem, no longer really fresh, because a few petals had already broken off.

Ricciardi stepped closer, attracted by the ghostly image that revealed itself only to his eyes, and no one else's. The rose, the petals, the dark leaves, the curtain gathered off to one side of the stage. Fedora's corpse, drooling and spitting blood from its mouth and nose, with a large stain on its chest, all the while staring sweetly at the far side of the stage, murmuring: *Love of my life. Love of my life. Love of my life.*

Those were the exact same words that Michelangelo Gelmi had used in his declaration of innocence. The love of his life, the woman whose very existence on this earth he had cut short with a bullet to the heart. Suffocating her in her own life's blood, but still giving her time enough to give back that final thought.

Love of my life. What right do I have to condemn you to all this, Enrica? What madness, even greater than my own lifelong madness, could persuade me to think I might be able to share my life with you? How can I hold your hand on a sunny morning in the midst of the dead that I see while they remain invisible to you? The dead who call me, unheard by you? Wouldn't it be better, far, far better, to leave you to your life? Why did you reject the offer of that German officer, making me responsible for your solitude?

Ricciardi's heart began to race, pounding louder. *What about your own happiness?* a voice whispered to him. *What do we have to say about the fact that for some time now, you've been waking up with a smile on your face?*

He went back to focusing on the murder. He turned to Renzullo and said: "If you please, alert the troupe and tell them that we are here and ready to interview certain individuals among them. First summon Romano, and then the musicians who were onstage at the moment of the murder. After that, we'll go backstage to take a look around."

Pio Romano had a very different appearance from the one he'd displayed in the circumstances—quite mortifying for him—in which they'd first met. If it hadn't been for his somewhat ashen complexion, he would have seemed exactly what he hoped to seem: a handsome, well dressed, and nicely groomed young man, determined to be a successful actor.

He walked toward Maione and Ricciardi with a smile.

"Commissario, what a pleasure it is to meet you again! I'm sorry about yesterday, it's not every day that you see a fellow actor and colleague murdered right next to you, especially not immediately after having allowed yourself to be shot by the very same pistol, luckily in my case firing a blank. I'm entirely at your disposal."

When he fell silent, he could still fool you, but the minute he opened his mouth there was no concealing his tendencies. He reminded Maione of Bambinella, the *femminiello* he regularly turned to for information about everything and everyone. The two of them could have passed for twins, if you ignored the attire.

Ricciardi asked: "How long have you been working with this troupe, Romano?"

"Oh, from the beginning. Three seasons. There were fifteen or so of us at the auditions and, modestly, I have to say that they chose me."

Maione interrupted: "*Who* chose you?"

"Signor Gelmi in person. He's the one who chooses the actors."

"And did you always play the same part?"

The man was nervous; he avoided even looking at the stage, doing everything he could to keep his back to it.

"The role of the faithless best friend, you mean? Well, not just that role. We all perform in more than one number in the show. I'm also a very good singer, I have a fine baritone voice. I play the fiancé who can't seem to close the deal in *Quanno mammeta nun ce sta* and the young suitor in *E allora?* I don't know if you're familiar, it's the one that goes: *Nel tram di Posillipo, al tempo dell'esta'* . . ."

Maione grew impatient.

"Roma', this isn't an audition, you know. Why don't you tell us, instead, whether you had witnessed any arguments between Gelmi and his wife in the recent past."

Ricciardi shot him a glance. Maione wasn't usually this brusque, but the brigadier replied with an imperceptible nod of reassurance. Don't worry, Commissa', it clearly meant, I'm taking care of this.

Romano put on a vaguely guilty expression.

"Forgive me, Brigadie'. I tend to wander. Yes, there were certainly some arguments between Michelangelo and Fedora. He was . . . well, nothing serious, eh, don't get me wrong, but a little bit jealous, yes, that he was. Maybe he could sense that everyone liked Fedora, because she was a wonderful woman, inside and out. As for him . . . well, he was charming, you've seen him for yourselves, he's a good-looking man, and talented. But he was getting older, Brigadie'. He was certainly getting older."

Ricciardi broke in: "Was he jealous of you, too?"

Romano looked at him with a strange glitter in his eyes. He seemed somehow gratified by that question.

"Jealous of me? Certainly, he would have had plenty of good reasons. I'm a man with a pleasing presence, Commissa': a very pleasing presence. That's why I decided to become an actor, because of my appearance. I know that I'm quite attractive. Just think, my mother, God bless her soul . . ."

Maione stepped forward and snarled: "Roma', I'm going to say this once, and I won't say it again: Answer the commissario's questions. It's in your best interest, trust me."

The actor ran his tongue over his lips. A faint beading of sweat appeared on his forehead. His voice suddenly became high-pitched and a little screechy: "Certainly, forgive me. No, he wasn't jealous of me. He trusted me, I'd have to imagine. And then, Fedora was like a sister to me, we spent lots of time together; she even asked me advice about her onstage costumes, her makeup . . . I take an interest in those things, as well, you know, and . . ." His gaze came to rest first on the brigadier and then on the commissario. "In other words, it's not as if women and I . . . Gelmi trusted me, you see."

Ricciardi nodded. He understood full well that people with Romano's tastes needed to be quite cautious. He decided that he'd heard enough, for the moment.

"All right, Romano. We're done. One last thing: in your opinion, was Gelmi's jealousy based on reasonable suspicion or was it the fruit of an obsession? And do you think the victim had been, or might have been involved in an illicit relationship?"

Romano thought it over and then smiled.

"Commissario, if you had asked me that question when both Gelmi and the poor, late Fedora were present, I would have said no without a moment's hesitation. I like my job; the wrong turn of phrase would have turned one or the other of them violently against me, and I would soon have been fired. But Gelmi is in prison, isn't he? And Fedora . . . So if I have to tell you the truth, I'd say that there was something on her mind. From the way that she dressed, the way that she talked . . . Even in performance, when someone is happy, you can tell. And Gelmi was a bit jealous, like I told you. But not obsessed, no; and there have never been scenes between them. Perhaps it was partly out of concern for his reputation: he didn't want to stoke the flames of gossip. And he knew he depended on his wife for his profession. In any case, they were in love. Perhaps it was not the kind of love affair that sweeps you away, but still, it was full of tenderness and kindness."

Tenderness, thought Ricciardi. *Love of my life*, Fedora's ghost kept saying, on the stage behind the rose.

XI

As agreed, Ricciardi and Maione also requested a private interview with the two musicians who were onstage when the fatal shot was fired; the guitarist and the mandolinist who had huddled, appalled, at one corner of the stage, motionless as a pair of props, spectators with some of the best seats in the house for an event that was the talk of the entire city.

Before going to summon them, Renzullo provided the policemen with a bit of information: "Commissa', they're first-rate musicians. Gelmi and Fedora were very selective in their choice of cast and crew. The guitarist is named Elia Meloni; Aurelio Pittella is the mandolinist. They were *posteggiatori*: strolling musicians who played in trattorias or did the occasional serenade; and they rounded out their earnings by playing in the street, part-time buskers. They were starving, all things considered. Gelmi and his wife first heard them, in fact, playing in front of a restaurant, and they fell in love with them. It was a sound hunch: their presence in the revue became a truly fundamental element. This is the first revue they've performed in; they were scheduled to tour all of Italy, and this was the opportunity of a lifetime. For them and for the others. Who knows what will become of them now, poor guys."

Just like Pio Romano, the new arrivals also turned their backs to the stage, doing their best not to look at where Fedora had slumped to the floorboards and where the rose now lay, almost withered and sad. It seemed as if no one wished to remember that final, tragic image.

Ricciardi, however, wanted to delve into the witnesses' memories.

"Did you notice anything out of the ordinary yesterday, say, before the show? Did Gelmi and Marra have any disagreements or quarrels?"

The answer came from the elder of the pair, Elia Meloni, the guitarist. He was well over fifty. His slick black hair grayed around the temples, producing a strange, two-tone effect; the skin was slightly reddened around his cheeks, and fairly wrinkled. His back was bowed, his hands were large, his voice was low and deferential, and he had a tendency to put a tense smile on his lips that his eyes, watery and sad as those of a hunting dog, failed to echo.

"No, Commissario. We both talked it over, between us and with the others as well, and no one remembers any such thing. The lead actor—Gelmi, I mean—and his wife seemed happy and untroubled, focused on the show, like always. And so were we, as far as that goes. Nothing unusual, otherwise we would have noticed it."

The two men wore clothing that was far more humble and threadbare than the costumes they wore onstage. Their jackets and trousers sagged shapeless at knees and elbows, their lapels shiny with wear, their shirts a dull gray from too many trips to the washtub. It was clear that they hadn't yet begun to enjoy the benefits of a salary in a successful revue: and, at this point, who could say if they ever would.

From time to time, the tall, skinny young man turned around as if some irresistible force were drawing him toward the stage. Then he'd turn back to look at his colleague and the two policemen.

Maione spoke: "Tell us what happened."

The guitarist turned to look at the brigadier. There were no doubts about which of the two was the spokesman.

"We were doing the very last number of the revue, a

dramatized version of the song, *Rundinella*. You know it, of course? The lyrics are about a man whose wife leaves him. She runs off with his best friend. It's a lovely song, and we perform the musical accompaniment. When it's necessary, Aurelio, here, who's a virtuoso, emphasizes with the mandolin. It's not a difficult piece, but it has the breadth and dimension of a story. It's practically a short novel, a *romanzo*."

Ricciardi spoke to the mandolinist.

"And at what point does Gelmi fire the gun?"

The young man turned to look at his colleague, who urged him on: "Aure', answer the commissario."

Pittella's voice came out deep and sonorous.

"At the end of the song. Then we bring it to a close. Elia runs through the chords and I repeat the melody from the introduction, but in a higher octave, as if the mandolin were taking the singer's place. The lead actor wasn't able to hit that high note for the whole duration, so I . . ."

Meloni interrupted, brusquely.

"But not because there's anything wrong with his voice, eh, Commissa', it's just that the time in question is too long. That's the only reason. He has to shoot the two faithless lovers who fall dead at his feet, portray his extreme sorrow and pain, and then throw the pistol away . . . In other words, it's no simple matter."

Maione butted in: "Renzullo told us that you were both hired by Gelmi. Did you know him and his wife well? Did you spend time with them outside of working hours as well?"

The guitarist shook his head.

"Oh no, Brigadie'. We only met the lead actor and his wife last summer. They were dining with friends at a trattoria in Mergellina, where Aurelio and I were playing, hoping for a tip or two. He started singing too, and we shifted key to match his voice. We always do it, it makes our customers happy. Gelmi liked what we'd done, and he suggested we come to the theater the next day. We auditioned all morning, do you remember, Aure'?"

Pittella nodded and worked up the nerve to speak.

"Signora Fedora was happy with us, too. They told us to come in on the following Monday, because there was something we might be interested in. But we've never seen them outside of this theater, we wouldn't dream of it."

Ricciardi remained silent for a few seconds as he thought. Then he asked: "By any chance, did you get the impression that yesterday Gelmi fired his gun any differently than other times? Did he just aim the pistol in Romano's and Marra's direction, or did he take careful aim?"

The mandolinist heaved a sigh, shuddering at the recollection, while Meloni replied: "I'd say not, Commissa'. Certainly, we tend to our playing, we keep our eyes on our instruments, we're not like those audience members who enjoy the revue with a glass in their hand, but I don't think there was anything different."

Maione weighed in: "What about you, Pitte'? Did you notice anything?"

The mandolinist turned once again briefly in the direction of the rose. From the shadows of the stage, Fedora's ghost spoke softly to Ricciardi: *Love of my life. Love of my life. Love of my life.*

"What was different was the blood. All that blood," the young man murmured.

The phrase, uttered as if to himself in that bass voice, was a gust of icy wind on a winter day without a chill. From the skylight came a dwindling shaft of light.

Meloni resumed: "We weren't on personal terms with the lead actor and his wife, Commissa'. We just tried to do our best at what we know how to do, because this was a huge opportunity and we were hoping it would offer us a living that until recently we couldn't even have dreamed of. As you can see, however, that dream has ended. The show is shutting down and everyone is back out on the street, to fend for themselves; in our case, we're back where we've been all our lives. It looks like that was fate."

Everyone fell silent, each of them following the trail of their own thoughts.

In the end, it was Maione who broke the silence.

"If either of you happens to remember any new details, let us know."

Meloni coughed sharply.

"Excuse me, but what else is there to figure out? Isn't it obvious what happened?"

The brigadier shrugged his shoulders.

"This is standard practice, Melo'. We still have to ask these questions."

Pittella opened his eyes wide, suddenly revealing the naïveté of his twenty years of age.

"But the answer never changes. Gelmi killed his wife. We were there."

Ricciardi and Maione exchanged a glance, each thinking that that was the only solid, incontrovertible fact of the whole affair.

XII

When the dread dinner hour approached, Enrica prepared to submit to the unfailing assault with stoic patience.

Not that she had any shortage of that quality. Indeed, patience was one of her most noteworthy traits, perhaps the most intimate and evident quality she possessed. It could be sensed in everything she did: the tone of her voice, her gaze, the gestures of her hands. Enrica was patient, and everyone said so.

Patient but also stubborn.

Since the two characteristics were in sharp contrast, they could lead a person to misjudge her. Her gentle sweetness, the fact that she was a young woman of few words the smile that she presented to anyone she encountered, and her good manners were not, in fact, evidence of a submissive nature that someone thought she had glimpsed in Enrica.

Someone whose maiden name had been Maria Tritone, before taking Colombo as her married name. In other words, Enrica's mother.

The last two months had been difficult for Enrica. Scenes and tantrums were followed by long, sulking silences, cascades of innuendo, sarcastic asides, and hidden resentments lurking behind every allusion. A small-scale domestic and private inferno, and one that was a real burden to tolerate. At first Enrica had been forced to bow her head and place her hopes in her father's feeble but heartfelt support. Even though he had few enough arguments to deploy, her father had done his best to defend her.

But this time, objectively speaking, Maria was right. Manfred was a perfect catch. A young and handsome gentleman, charming and well-to-do; loving and thoughtful, gallant to his future mother-in-law and respectful to his future father-in-law; merry and amusing with the children, likable and comradely with her sister's husband; careful not to run afoul of Enrica's father on political matters. Her father, after all, was an old-fashioned liberal, with little patience for Fascism and the Nazis, the German cousins of the Italian Fascist party, increasingly close, a movement to which the major, in fact, subscribed enthusiastically. Manfred, a Prince Charming out of a fairy tale, the ideal man that any young woman could only dream of finding.

Any young woman, but not Enrica.

And in fact, on the very day of her twenty-fifth birthday, she had had the nerve to reject him, as if he were an unwelcome gift, thereby officially sanctioning her transition from eligible blushing bride to intractable old maid. She was no beauty, the Colombo family's firstborn daughter. She was tall, unbecoming, and she wore spectacles. She had no interest in makeup and she stubbornly refused to have her hair styled in a pageboy, the fashionable cut. She also avoided the fashionable brightly colored line of modern apparel. What's more, when night fell, she had no interest in going out with groups of her girlfriends to the theaters and movie houses that were so popular with soldiers, successful professionals, and bachelors as a group.

Enrica heaved a deep sigh and made her entrance into the kitchen. As usual, the conversation then underway came to an abrupt halt, leaving not even a shadow of doubt as to what the subject had been. Alongside her mother, those present in the kitchen and frozen in the act of gossiping about Enrica, were her younger sisters: Susanna, already married and the mother of a son, even though she was two years younger than Enrica, as Maria never failed to remind her on a daily basis, and Francesca, who might have been just a teenager but who made it more than clear that she had no intention of reaching Enrica's advanced age without finding a husband. At the stove was Fortuna, the elderly housekeeper who had raised her and who was the only one, aside from Enrica's father, willing to defend her from that tribunal of hostile women.

Enrica approached the table and put on her apron. Among the tasks she was responsible for in those days leading up to New Year's Day was the preparation of the sautéd broccoli: a recipe that might seem simple at first glance but remained crucial and not without its challenges. Somewhat like Enrica herself.

There was a massive quantity to prepare, because this dish wasn't just eaten during the New Year's Day dinner, but also in all the meals that preceded it. Her sister Susanna sighed, and stared at her: "You'd think that broccoli was easy to make, but no one cooks it like you do, Enri'. My husband says that you have golden hands in the kitchen, whereas whenever I'm the one cooking things, he makes a face and says nothing."

Enrica smiled as she drained the vegetables.

"Oh, no, Susi, you know he's just teasing you. You're a good cook, too, in fact, you're an excellent cook. Plus you're a mother, too, right? It can't be easy."

Turned toward the stove, as if keeping an eye on Fortuna's cooking, Maria said: "There you are, in fact: a mother. And someone like you, who loves children, spends time with them, and helps them with their lessons, ought to have children of her own."

Francesca, who had sliced the garlic and was pouring olive oil out of a large tin and into a glass, burst out laughing.

"It's true, though, Enri'. You of all people, the way you are with children, you'd think you'd already have a dozen of your own. In another home, though, because we're already full to bursting here. But I think there's no real problem, because you'll be living with Mamma and Papa for many long years to come."

Fortuna scolded her, roughly: "Shut your mouth, France', and worry about yourself. People do things in their own good time."

Enrica ventured one last, desperate attempt at changing the subject: "I bought these from Tanino. That young man has turned a little strange, has anyone noticed? He seems less cheerful lately, and who knows . . ."

Her mother turned, stung, to look at the housekeeper.

"Don't talk to me about people's own good time. I'm the only one who knows how much work it is to raise a respectable young woman, teach her all that she needs to know in order to become a good wife and a good mother. And all that, just to find her still here at home, a grown woman now, without so much as a prospect on the horizon, and most likely bound to remain an old maid for the rest of her life."

Enrica sighed.

"Mamma, you have no idea of what life might bring. It's true, I'm alone now, but . . ."

Maria glared sternly at her and hissed: "You know how badly you hurt me on the day of your birthday. An enormous wound. And you did it on purpose."

"Oh, don't be ridiculous, Mamma, I had no intention of causing you pain."

Her mother slammed her hand down on the table, making a cutting board bounce into the air.

"Oh, you didn't? Then would you explain to me why you rejected the most eligible bachelor you could have hoped for? That poor major was deeply hurt!"

Francesca chuckled:

"He turned red as a chili pepper and kept muttering who knows what in that language of his . . ."

Maria glared daggers at her.

"Don't you dare, young lady. We don't joke about serious matters in this household!"

Enrica shook her head, eyes turned downward at the vegetables ready to be popped into the pot.

"Mamma, we've already discussed this. I never thought he was going to pop the question, it was the last thing I was expecting . . ."

"What do you mean, you weren't expecting it? Do you seriously think that a man asks for an invitation to dinner on the day of your birthday, brings flowers and presents, and dresses up in his fine uniform just because he thinks of you as a friend? And anyway, even if you hadn't been expecting it, why did you turn him down?"

Beneath the full weight of her sisters' eyes, and face to face with a fiercely inquisitorial mother, Enrica behaved no differently than ever: patient but stubborn.

"Mamma, I didn't feel up to it, that's all. Maybe it wasn't the right time, maybe . . ."

"But now you've had the time to think it over. And what do you say now?"

What can I tell you, Mamma? That I'm in love with the kindest and most handsome man on earth? That I've waited and waited for him, and precisely because of that refusal you criticize so fervently, I finally had the joy to see him come to me? That we spent time together, telling each other the stories of our lives? That we stood, holding hands, in a narrow lane not far from here, an alley that's become our secret paradise? And that as I gazed into his green eyes, I envisioned my future with him, even though we haven't yet spoken of it?

"I don't know, Mamma, maybe . . . I don't want to make anyone suffer."

"Then would you explain to me why you were so decisive that you didn't even leave him a glimmer of hope?"

Because there never really was any hope, Mamma; that's why. If a woman is in love, she can't even think of shaking hands with another man, much less kissing another man's lips.

"Mamma, please, stop torturing me. I'm not in love with Manfred, and it hardly seems fair to him, either . . ."

Maria slammed her hand down on the table once again. Susanna's and Francesca's heads both bowed at the same moment.

"Who's talking about love? A woman needs to get settled, she needs a home and children! Love comes later, the important thing is to find your place in the world! Your father and I aren't going to live forever. When we're no longer around, would you tell me who's going to take care of you, look after you, protect you and keep you?"

He will, Mamma, because I know that he loves me. He just needs time to find the courage to come here and ask Papa for his permission to take me out, unaccompanied. Then he'll kiss me in the movie theater, just like what happens to all the other girls and . . .

"In any case," Maria went on in a decisive tone, "the important thing is that you understand what a foolish mistake it was. That it was only because you weren't expecting it, as you've confessed, and that you understand that a catch like Major von Brauchitsch doesn't come along every day."

Susanna stared at her mother blankly.

"Well, anyway, Mamma, what's done is done. Enrica has already turned him down."

Maria replied while staring at her eldest daughter with a defiant glare.

"That's absolutely not the case. I've written to the major myself, explaining that Enrica's words were dictated by a high state of emotion, that she never meant to turn him down, that

I know my own daughter, and she's not the type to turn him down. That all she needed was a chance to think things over, and that now she's ready to see him again."

Enrica couldn't believe her own ears. She stared at her mother's mouth in disbelief, as if she were speaking some alien, incomprehensible language.

"I don't understand, Mamma: you wrote to Manfred? You've . . ."

The woman replied, firmly: "That's exactly what I've done. I've invited him here to dinner on the last night of the year, and I'm delighted that I've done so."

Enrica felt herself die inside.

XIII

Renzullo accompanied Maione and Ricciardi backstage at the Teatro Splendor, as the commissario had requested. There were two doors leading to the theater's backstage area.

One led in from outside, a door at the back of the building, which immediately opened onto a short flight of steps that ended in a narrow hallway lined by a bathroom and the large room that served as the collective dressing room for the rest of the troupe; that dressing room was split in two by a wooden partition: on one side the women, on the other side the men. The hallway then continued for a few more yards, curving along the line of the stage and then finally opening out into a larger space, a sort of antechamber for the dressing rooms of the lead actor and lead actress.

The second entrance, from within the building, through which the policemen and Renzullo now passed, was set at the back of the stage. Once they'd made their way past the coiled ropes and cables of the curtain and the materials used for the backdrops, including the painting of the Milan cathedral and the Venetian lagoon, the three men found themselves standing in the antechamber in question.

There, sitting on a chair with a badly worn straw seat, pushed up against a tiny table, a middle-aged woman was knitting in the dim light. She had an unkempt head of reddish hair, and her face was covered with freckles; a threadbare blanket was wrapped around her shoulders, like a tattered shawl.

Renzullo pointed at her.

"This is Signora Erminia. She does a little of everything: she mends costumes, makes ersatz coffee, distributes the fan notes that the spectators send to dancers and actresses, and occasionally even to the musicians. But her most important task is to make sure that no one bothers the lead actors. Anyone who wishes to reach Michelangelo and Fedora's dressing rooms must necessarily pass by her."

The woman turned her porcine, mistrustful gaze from Maione to Ricciardi, and then back to Maione. The uniform seemed to make a special and unpleasant impression upon her, but it certainly didn't intimidate her. The brigadier recognized in her manners the age-old aversion felt by the lower classes of the city toward the police, and it annoyed him.

He touched his fingers to the visor of his uniform cap and spoke: "*Buonasera*, Signo'. We'd like to ask you a few questions, about yesterday evening, just to get a better idea . . ."

The woman half-shut her already small eyes and interrupted him: "What is there you'd want a better idea about? Everyone saw exactly what happened."

Maione took a deep breath.

"Of course. But we'd still like to ask those questions. As long as it's not an inconvenience for you, ma'am, of course."

Erminia didn't seem to pick up on the irony and unfurled a smirk of indifference. Her hands had never once stopped moving the knitting needles.

"If you want to waste your time, please, be my guests."

Ricciardi weighed in, in part to soothe the tension: "You said that everyone saw it, Signora. Including you?"

The woman replied without once taking her eyes off Maione, almost as if she were engaging him in a silent duel: "No, not I. From here, as even you must understand, I can't see the stage. But I heard it. I heard the song and the shots, as usual."

Maione, meeting her gaze, asked: "And was there anything different from the usual sequence of events?"

This time the woman spoke to Ricciardi, and in such a way that it couldn't be missed.

"When Signora Fedora falls, it usually makes no noise at all because she drops slowly. But last night there was a loud bang from the stage backdrop, the one with the monuments. Then the music stopped short, and the audience started to scream."

As if nothing had happened, Maione went on: "And at that point, what did you do?"

Erminia continued staring at Ricciardi.

"Nothing."

The commissario furrowed his brow.

"You didn't so much as move?"

The woman shrugged her shoulders.

"My job is to stay seated on this chair. Whatever's going on out there," and she waved in the direction of the stage, "doesn't concern me. They don't pay me to watch the show. In the theater, you have to pay if you want to watch."

All at once, she turned toward Maione and smiled, putting on display a mouthful of rotten teeth and blackened gums. The policeman maintained his composure.

"So you're saying that you understood something very serious had happened, and you just remained seated? You weren't even a little bit curious?"

The woman seemed to consider those words for a moment, while her hands ever so briefly fell still with the knitting needles. Then she said, in a low voice: "Brigadie', I'm from San Giovanni. Where I come from, it's an everyday occurrence to notice that something's happened out in the street, in front of our apartment, our *basso*, something that might be healthier not to have seen or heard. In San Giovanni, unless you learn early to mind your own business, you won't live long. My job is to keep anyone else from entering the dressing rooms of the leading actors. And that is what I do."

Ricciardi nodded.

"So you never left your post, not even between one performance and the next? I'm interested to know whether anyone could have slipped into Gelmi's dressing room, even if only for a moment, between the end of the first performance and the musical sketch in which Signora Marra was killed."

The woman showed no sign of hesitation.

"No, no one entered the dressing rooms."

Maione persisted: "Are you sure you never stepped away, not even for the briefest moment? I don't know, to grab a quick cup of ersatz coffee or to see to some personal need . . ."

"No," Erminia replied in no uncertain terms. "I leave my post only if Signor Gelmi or Signora Fedora asks me to. You can't begin to imagine how many people try to worm their way into the dressing rooms, even during the performance. They show up there," and she jutted her chin toward the far end of the hallway, where the door to the outdoors stood at the end of the short flight of stairs, "or here, from the stage, bringing bouquets of flowers and fan letters. Sometimes other members of the troupe try to get by, to talk about their own matters or issues concerning the revue. But I have strict orders not to let anyone through, and no one gets through. I only go to the restroom after everyone has gone home."

Renzullo broke in, struggling to stifle a laugh: "Signora Erminia is better than a guard dog, believe me. I pay her salary, and even I can't get free access to Michelangelo's and Fedora's dressing rooms. She's a tough nut, Signora Erminia is."

Maione nodded his head, acknowledging the valor of his adversary. Ricciardi asked: "By any chance, did you see whether Gelmi or Marra left to go anywhere else?"

The woman hesitated briefly: the first time. Her eyes darted from Renzullo to Maione.

"I mind my own business."

The brigadier shot back harshly: "Signo', today let me tell you what your business is: answer our questions, otherwise you're bound to get in that very same kind of trouble that you've always been so eager to avoid. Do I make myself clear?"

Clearly unimpressed, Erminia shut up in an obstinate silence until Renzullo exhorted her to speak: "Ermi', don't be stubborn. This is important."

At last, she made up her mind. Speaking in a low voice, she almost seemed afraid that the two actors could still hear her from their dressing rooms.

"Before the beginning of the second performance, Signor Gelmi went to see Signora Fedora."

She fell silent again, as if she had nothing more to add. Ricciardi and Maione exchanged a glance and waited for the rest, but the woman seemed determined to waver no further from her vow of discretion.

"Perhaps I failed to make myself understood," the brigadier persisted aggressively. "You must tell us everything you saw and heard."

Unwillingly, Erminia went on: "Signor Gelmi stayed in his wife's dressing room for a few minutes, perhaps five minutes. I could hear their voices, even if it was the intermission: that's when everyone's talking and it's hard to hear what people are saying behind closed doors. But they were arguing loudly. Then he went back to his own dressing room."

Ricciardi asked her one last question: "When he walked past you, how did he look?"

Erminia opened her mouth to reply but immediately shut it again. She looked at Renzullo and he smiled at her reassuringly.

So she said, in a whisper: "He was crying. Signor Gelmi was crying."

XIV

As he led Ricciardi and Maione toward the dressing rooms of the two lead actors, Renzullo, referring to Erminia, said in a low voice: "You have to understand her, Commissa'. She's been with us for two years, it was Michelangelo who recommended I hire her. She really loves and needs this job. Her husband is an invalid from the war and can't leave home. She's afraid of losing her position. That's what makes her so mistrustful. But believe me, she's honest and scrupulous; a very hard worker. If she tells you no one got in, then no one did."

Maione murmured: "Still, the fact that Gelmi went to speak to his wife before the second performance is important news. And when he left, he was in tears. Renzu', you knew him well, didn't you? What do you think could have happened in those five minutes?"

The impresario seemed uncomfortable.

"It's true, Michelangelo and I had been friends for years. When I decided to start a theater of my own, he helped me out. Then Fedora arrived, with her sudden dazzling fame and her popularity with the public . . . But let me reiterate, they were by no means in competition on the stage. Quite the opposite. As for matters of the heart, though, I can't help you; Michelangelo wasn't prone to spilling certain types of secrets."

Ricciardi insisted: "But you must have had some idea . . ."

Renzullo had stopped in front of a door upon which a sign

had been posted with the words: "Signor Michelangelo Gelmi." He thought about it for a moment, then went on talking.

"Commissa', I don't think that he was really jealous. I presume that he knew that Fedora, so young and beautiful, was being courted hand and foot. And I imagine—though I can only imagine it because I've neither seen nor heard anything to flesh out my belief—that he cared deeply about respect and decorum. The actor's profession is a special one, and they live and die on fame. Gelmi still had a name, a reputation, and a few followers. If he became nothing but a . . ." and here he stopped short and simply raised the pinky and forefinger of one hand in the universal symbol of the cuckold, "then he might as well retire. All that Michelangelo cared about was his name and his art."

"So yesterday's quarrel . . ."

A grimace appeared on Renzullo's face.

"These are things that happen between a husband approaching old age and an attractive wife still in the bloom of her youth. If they ever fought, they were very discreet about it. Only Erminia could hear them, and she would never have told a soul. You saw for yourself how devoted she was to both of them. Then Michelangelo must have gone back to his own dressing room and . . ."

As if continuing the discussion he opened the door with the sign on it. Inside, only the dimmest of light arrived from a small, high window. The impresario turned on the light switch and a bare bulb, dangling from the ceiling, faintly illuminated a makeup mirror surrounded by small spotlights, a tabletop crowded with cans of greasepaint, brushes, and combs, and a clothes cupboard with a single door, standing ajar. Inside were Gelmi's stage costumes. Completing the furnishings were a chair, a small sofa, and a coffee table on whose surface lay a newspaper.

Renzullo also turned on the lightbulbs surrounding the mirror, which emitted a spectral glow. Then he walked over to the wardrobe and confidently put his hand in, reaching behind the costumes. When he pulled the hand out, it was grasping a bottle of brandy that contained nothing more than a puddle of amber-colored liquor at the bottom, like some tiny reservation of a guilty conscience.

"Here you have it, Commissario: Michelangelo Gelmi's true best friend. It's a sad and nasty miracle, given his bad habits, that last night he was able to shoot Fedora right in the heart, from that distance."

It was chilly in the room, colder than out on the street. A stale odor of cigarette smoke, alcohol, and lavender hovered in the air. On the mirror, wedged into the lower corner of the frame, was a flyer for a show, *Il principe dei sogni—The Prince of Dreams*—featuring Gelmi's name, in large letters. Ricciardi leaned closer to check the date of the performance: March 1924. Nearly nine years earlier. The year was not even followed by the Roman numerals of the Fascist calendar.

The commissario looked around. Loneliness. Disillusionment. Weariness. Resignation. There was no need for a talking ghost, he could recognize those emotions easily.

He shook himself with a shiver and nodded his head to Maione. Together they followed Renzullo into Fedora Marra's dressing room.

The victim's dressing room was quite different than her husband's. Nothing grim or gray. The room was filled with a cheerful, colorful, variegated messiness. Various articles of clothing were scattered all over the place; a charming dressing screen concealed a full-length mirror, while the surface of the vanity was cluttered with all sorts of cosmetics. There was a blend of scents and odors that reflected the jumbled heap of hats and ostrich plume boas, skirts, and bodices; a sweet and penetrating perfume wafted off the numerous bouquets of flowers, displayed with coquettish pride. But there was also a bitter after-scent, perhaps the faint trace of a manly cologne.

It was as if one might expect Fedora to return any moment, overheated and smiling, from her time onstage. It all seemed suspended and timeless, awaiting the actress's brilliant and flighty persona. The space between those walls must have been the woman's true home, much more so than any apartment she may have slept in at night.

Here, too, there were flyers and postcards wedged into the corner of the frame around the makeup mirror, but these were for recent shows, and there were also photographs of well-known celebrities. Ricciardi recognized the face of a cabinet-level minister, features frozen in an atypical smile, as well as other leading figures of the regime. A rising star, then, Fedora. A setting sun, instead, Michelangelo. Their respective careers were diverging, and now death had parted them once and for all.

In front of the vanity table stood a gracefully designed chair. Ricciardi found himself staring at it, lost in thought. The chair's position, standing at a diagonal with respect to the surface piled high with makeup and cosmetics, and with its backrest turned to the door, would be useless in terms of applying that makeup, since it wouldn't afford a full view of the reflected face. Nor was it compatible with the movements of someone about to leave the room. The commissario followed the hypothetical line of sight of a person sitting in that chair and his eyes came to a halt on a coatrack from which hung a dressing gown, alongside several elegantly cut dresses, garments that she would certainly have worn after the evening's last performance: the dressing gown was the only article of clothing that could neither be worn onstage nor outside of the theater.

The commissario stepped forward. Renzullo, who up until

that point had observed him curiously, intervened: "Wait, Commissa', what . . ."

Maione hushed him with a brusque wave of the hand, as if he wished to keep him from articulating aloud a silent thought process. Ricciardi extended his hand into the pocket of the dressing gown and extracted a folded sheet of paper.

He opened it and read.

My love,
Again, tonight, I'll wear your embroidery before falling asleep, and in my heart it will be the last thing I hear.
Don't worry, I belong to no one but you. I'm yours, yours and happy! Till tomorrow.

F.

He handed the note to Maione, who read it in silence, moving his lips. Renzullo, too, peeked over the brigadier's shoulder and blushed.

"Commissa', it doesn't seem right to rummage through the belongings of poor dead Fedora."

Ricciardi replied, decisively: "This isn't rummaging. This is a murder investigation. A murder that has an appearance and a substance, and the further we move ahead, the less the two aspects seem to match up. Now let's meet with the rest of the troupe, before the show begins."

XV

In the café, while everyone else was watching Livia, Livia was watching Manfred. Who was looking into the middle distance.

Paradoxically, during the period between Christmas and New Year's Day, restaurants, bars, and taverns tended to be more crowded than usual. It was a singular phenomenon, because that was a holiday period and it would have been logical to suppose that people would rather spend time with their families; professional offices were shut for the holidays, boarding schools ended lessons, and students returned home. As a result, loneliness became even harder to tolerate, and those who had no one to sit down to a meal and sing Christmas carols with tended to seek their company elsewhere.

Livia knew that sensation well. Far too well. She had discovered loneliness and made it her friend long before becoming the widow of the great tenor Arnaldo Vezzi, worshipped by many during his lifetime and even more now that death had deliriously enlarged his fame; a genius of bel canto and a thoroughly awful human being. And loneliness had become her prison after she lost her young son, her only child.

Of course, she'd had no shortage of suitors. She was always surrounded by would-be lovers just hoping for a sign, an encouraging smile, a single word. Because she was more than just lovely, lithe, elegant, and feline. Livia was magnetic. A woman who appeared in full, living color in the general setting of a black-and-white world of women.

When she entered a crowded room, she instantly attracted the gazes of all the men, captivated by her allure, as well as the women, who instantly recognized a rival against whom, they instinctively knew, they wouldn't have had a chance. The power that she exercised had something mysterious about it, and it emanated the sensation that no one could ever conquer it entirely. And so she represented a challenge to any and all.

Now, too, at the bar Gambrinus, at the hour of the final aperitifs, when the customers were loitering, waiting for the theaters to start their shows or for dinnertime to roll around, the lonely people clustering around the café tables couldn't take their eyes off her. In a subtle but detectable manner, the men in the room had all turned their chairs to ensure they could admire her, pretending to gaze out onto the street, leaf through the newspaper, or chat with the unfortunate female interlocutor sitting across their table. Sometimes, beneath their hats a vague smile could be detected, a desperate attempt to attract her attention.

But she had eyes for no one but her companion, the most envied man in the café, who however, for some inconceivable reason, seemed to be utterly indifferent to the delights of his privileged position.

It also should be said that Major von Brauchitsch had a pleasing appearance, so much so that the ladies, irritated by the indifference of their male companions, had decided to focus their interest upon him. The exotic uniform of the German army, the blond hair and blue eyes, the considerable height, the athletic physique and large hands combined to form quite an attractive figure. And the faint limp that he had displayed as he walked to reach his table, chivalrously pulled back Livia's chair as she took a seat, and then sat down in his turn, seemed to bespeak a war hero. And yet the handsome military man had then proceeded to down three glasses of beer in rapid succession, and now sat staring in blank silence at a vague point in the middle distance, his only motion being that of occasionally running his hand through his hair.

Livia decided to go ahead and break that silence. For that matter, patience had never been a gift of hers.

"Are you planning to sit there like a bump on a log just drinking the whole evening? If you wanted to get drunk before dinner, we could have just skipped seeing each other entirely."

She didn't dislike Manfred one bit.

She had begun to see him at the behest of Falco, who was blackmailing her in accordance with his usual practice. That indecipherable individual, an employee of some secret structure of the government, was interested in the German officer's activities, and he had asked her to get to know him and gain his trust. That request had been couched in the velvety terms of a veiled threat.

Falco had also made it clear to her that she could venture so far as to become his lover; in fact, he had suggested to her, without ever stating it explicitly, that this might be the best strategy if she wished to extract indiscretions from the man. Suddenly she had felt as if she were the leading character of a French novel, a sort of modern Milady caught between a handsome foreign officer and . . .

The thought suddenly filled her with sadness, but she pushed that feeling away decisively.

Manfred shook his head.

"Forgive me, Livia, you're right. I'm not very good company today, I shouldn't have accepted your invitation."

She smiled.

"On the contrary. It's on days when you feel that way that you shouldn't be alone. Trust me, I know what I'm talking about. If you start down a certain slippery slope, you start to slide downhill, and the next morning you wake up with a colossal headache, more alone than before. But why don't you tell me why you chose not to go back to your home for the holidays?"

The major shrugged.

"I didn't much feel like it. My mother lives in Prien. She's in good health, but her mind is less than clear, and to see her in that state . . . And I had some business to take care of here."

Livia tried to test the ice.

"What sort of business does the cultural attaché to a consulate have between Christmas and New Year's?"

Manfred waved his hand vaguely.

"Nothing especially interesting. Forms to fill out, for the most part. But I preferred to stay here."

Livia feigned indifference. Falco had told her that during this short period, in fact, two Italian navy ships with experimental equipment would be sailing through the city's bay and that for security considerations they would anchor well offshore and far from the wharfs. But that wouldn't keep anyone who happened to own a pair of powerful binoculars from spying on them, from a safe distance.

"Then what's bothering you?"

Instead of answering her, Manfred reached into his jacket pocket and pulled out an opened envelope, laying it on the table in front of him. Livia heaved a sigh of annoyance: "That's the third time you've shown me that damned letter. Do you mind telling me why?"

He gave her a bewildered glance.

"I don't know what to do."

The situation in which Major von Brauchitsch found himself triggered conflicting emotions in Livia. On the one hand, she felt stung in her pride, because any man's obsession with a woman other than her, especially when flaunted in her presence, was an unusual event that she didn't care for; on the other hand, the specific circumstance allowed her to nourish one final and fleeting hope about tender feelings she was not yet willing to give up. If this Enrica—whom, incidentally, Livia had had a few opportunities to lay eyes on and decided that she lacked any charms or attractions—had actually found in Manfred the man she desired, that is, a husband and a father for the numerous family she no doubt wished to produce for the fatherland, be that Germany or Italy, it could only mean that Livia would have a new shot at her intended prey.

Because Livia was certain that Ricciardi, who was the real reason she was still living in this city, would sooner or later give in to her love. She had no doubt about that. Even if that unbecoming young woman, who dressed so drably and wore eyeglasses, must certainly possess some special quality if she had cast her spell on other men. Or those two, at least.

"What do you mean, 'I don't know what to do'? You need to go, that much is obvious. They've invited you, she wants to see you again, and you don't have any other plans for the last night of the year. It all adds up, you ought to be happy about it."

Manfred grimaced dubiously.

"That letter isn't from her. It's from her mother. If she'd really wanted to see me, she would have come to me, she would have told me: 'You know, I wasn't expecting that, and I was scared, and that's why I turned you down.' But instead . . ."

Livia considered the man's weary face, his slurred speech, and his vaguely whiny tone of voice. No one could ask her to console a drunken German. Not even Falco.

She was tempted to get to her feet and leave him sitting there without another word; then she remembered a pair of green eyes and she decided to persist, sweetening her voice: "Sometimes women don't have the courage to go back on their word, even when they realize they've made a mistake. In those cases, they turn to the aid of someone else, an . . . envoy, an intermediary. And who better for that purpose than a mother?"

The German furrowed his brow.

"You think so?"

"Certainly. Perhaps she saw her daughter in state of despair, shut up in her room weeping over what had befallen her, regretful but too proud to admit her error, and like a good mother, she simply took the initiative. Whatever the case, it's an opportunity, and it's worth taking advantage of it."

Manfred replied sorrowfully: "But she rejected my offer, don't you understand? You don't know how embarrassing it was. I found myself there, in that drawing room . . . And the father, the father didn't even dare to look me in the face. I've never felt so humiliated in all my life. And yet I felt certain that she wasn't indifferent to me."

Livia heaved another sigh of exasperation.

"Now you tell me, are you or aren't you a soldier? You've faced up to enemies in open battle, you suffered the pangs of your late wife's death, and now you're afraid of a young woman you have a crush on?"

Those impatient words produced a few indiscreet smiles at neighboring tables. Manfred got a grip on himself.

"You're right, I need to react: I'll go. I'll send my reply today and accept the invitation. Thank you, my good friend. Thanks for helping me to make this decision."

Livia smiled.

"But now it's time for you to stop drinking. You promised to take me to the theater. You know that Fedora Marra, the actress, was murdered, right? It was her husband who did it. A friend of mine was there that night and this morning she called me and told me over the phone that it was one of the most exciting things she'd ever witnessed in her life."

The major grimaced.

"Believe me, Livia: there's nothing exciting about seeing another person murdered. Take it from someone who's seen more than his share of corpses."

"Still, you're going to take me to the Teatro Splendor, I'm

very curious to understand just what happened. It must have been jealousy: men lose their minds when faced with the slightest doubt."

With a still slightly slurred voice and a melancholy smile, Manfred concluded: "It's not jealousy. It's betrayal. It's betrayal that makes men lose their reason. That's what can drive men to kill."

Without there being any logical connection, in front of Livia's mind's eye there appeared Falco's indecipherable face.

She shivered.

XVI

By now it was almost time for the show to begin, and from the auditorium came a buzz of voices from the audience, accompanied by the sound of clinking glasses.

Nonetheless, there was none of the cheerfulness so typical of an expectant crowd. No laughter and no catcalls. It was clear that today the spectators were going to devote a different type of attention to the stage. They had come to see where Fedora Marra had been murdered at her husband's hand: the hand of the famous Michelangelo Gelmi.

Before they entered the big collective dressing room used by the other artists in the troupe, Renzullo explained to Ricciardi: "Commissa', I know that we ought to have shut down the show out of respect for Fedora, and also for Michelangelo, who is no doubt living through a hell on earth, but it's December 29th, these are the days of the year when we sell out the house, and the rest of the troupe and I have talked it over and we've decided that we can't afford to reimburse the tickets that have already been sold. If we were to stop the performances, it would mean missing everything until after New Year's Day: and by then— forgive me if I say it, and believe me I'm ashamed to be thinking about such things—the effect of everything that's happened will have vanished. What's more, we thought that the best way to remember Fedora would be to make sure the show went on."

Maione asked: "So how did you handle things with the lead actors' routines?"

Renzullo turned to look at him.

"They appeared in six out of ten numbers, including the grand finale with everyone onstage. We decided to eliminate the dramatized song. No one felt up to that. And after all, at this point it was difficult to get our hands on the gun and the blanks. For the other performances we have Romano, whom you've met, and who's very good. We entrusted Fedora's two roles to one of the younger actresses, Memè Montuori, who's pretty and talented, but a little short on experience, and a dancer, eliminating her lines. That way she'll only need to dance around the singer, who will of course be Romano. Fingers crossed . . . I mean, the Lord only knows, it won't be the same thing, but we feel confident that for today's performances, the audience won't be worrying about the quality of the revue."

"Well, well, well, so you're taking advantage of the murder. That's how it is, isn't it, Renzu'? The dead are forgotten . . ."

The impresario snapped out a retort: "Hey, no, Brigadie', that's one thing you should never have said to me! Who's going to pay me back the money I paid to feature Michelangelo and Fedora? And what are we supposed to do about the box office over the next few days, when the public's curiosity starts to diminish and we have more and more empty seats in the house? Do you have any idea how much it costs to keep this theater running? You have no right to accuse me of . . ."

Ricciardi interrupted him, impatiently: "All right, all right. Enough's enough. Now let's finish talking to the others."

Red-faced, and savagely glaring at Maione who was snickering as if he'd just told a joke, Renzullo ushered them into the large, shared dressing room of the artists, where the wooden partition wall offered the women a scant minimum of privacy. The impresario clapped his hands.

"Ladies and gentlemen, if you please, gather round."

A few at a time, all the while tying ribbons and inserting buttons in buttonholes, the troupe showed up, full force: about fifteen people, including the musicians of the orchestra, the actors, and the dancers. Many of them were already familiar faces to Ricciardi and Maione, especially Romano and the two musicians, Meloni and Pittella, whom they had already questioned.

Their faces reflected conflicting, alternating emotions: excitement that they'd soon be stepping onstage before an eager audience and the fear they might not be up to the challenge. The lead actor and the lead actress—the two stars whose names appeared in large type at the top of the attractions, the two people who had directed them as a troupe and behind whom they had been able to shelter from the critical darts of reviewers and opinion leaders—were gone now, but their audience, at least for the remaining scheduled shows, were still around, and they wouldn't hesitate to launch resounding boos and shrill whistles of derision whenever they perceived even the slightest difference from the original production. The tension was unmistakable. The faces of the younger performers were reddened, the expressions of the older actors were somewhat bewildered. Eyes darted here and there, avoiding contact with anyone else's. And the presence of the two policemen, a chilling reminder of last night's tragic event, just minutes before the curtain was about to be rung up, certainly didn't help.

Renzullo spoke in a stentorian voice.

"Friends, I realize that you're focused on the performance, and I have no doubt that you'll give it your all, and then some. But I'd like to ask you for a few minutes of your time to answer a few questions for the commissario and the brigadier, here, to whom we are required to provide our full cooperation."

There were four dancers, selected by hair color in order to satisfy each and every taste. They were dressed like little peasant girls, but the skirts with their ample flounces made it easy to glimpse the fishnet stockings and garter belts that would soon thrill the viewers in the front rows.

The brunette spoke first.

"What do you have to ask us? Everyone saw with their own eyes that that crazy old man murdered Fedora."

The violinist, a skinny beanpole of a man in his early sixties, upbraided her: "Why, didn't you hear what he said? Someone replaced the blank in his gun with a live bullet."

Meloni, the guitarist, said in a subdued voice: "But he couldn't say who."

Pittella, the mandolinist, replied: "Because there was no way that anyone could have done it. The only one who had a chance to get into the lead actor's dressing room, where he kept the pistol, was the lead actor himself."

The violinist weighed in again, reinforcing the idea that he was a loyal follower of Gelmi's.

"I believe him, all the same. Someone framed him."

Another member of the orchestra, a big strong man with enormous hands, backed him up.

"I believe him, too. Do you all really think that if a man wants to murder his wife, he's going to do it like that, in front of everyone?"

The dancer with the red hair, possibly the most attractive of the lot, hissed: "Precisely because it made no sense, it must have been him. He's an actor, isn't he? There's no difference for him between theater and reality. And so he chose the betrayal scene to highlight the point."

Ricciardi butted in: "Is it the only one on the subject of betrayal?"

Pio Romano replied, almost sweetly: "Yes, yes, Commissa'. There are other love songs, but they don't mention infidelity. And the pistol appears only in that number. *Rundinella* is the tragic number. Aside from that, there is a serenade, a comic sketch, a . . ."

A slightly older actor, dressed in a badly worn tailcoat and a dented, dinged up top hat, mocked him: "Come on, Pio, what are you doing now, the entire summary? The truth is that

Italia," and here he pointed at the red-headed dancer, "is right. For people like us, there is no difference between the stage and life. Michelangelo killed her, full stop."

The violinist attempted a strenuous defense.

"But the pistol . . ."

The man in the top hat had a retort: "It was his pistol and he loaded it himself. Perhaps when he saw her lying there dead, he might have repented. That seems possible."

The blonde dancer, a young woman with a nice body but a longish nose, sighed: "Oh my God: that blood, the makeup smearing and melting . . . I'll never be able to sleep again."

Everyone fell silent. Maione glanced at Ricciardi.

The commissario put on an almost solemn expression.

"I have a question. And I would remind you that withholding information in a murder investigation might very well result in charges. But I don't want you all to answer me right away. I'll be sitting waiting in Signora Marra's dressing room, with the door open, for the entire duration of the revue. Each of you, and I mean all of you, drop by as you leave the stage. If you have nothing to say to me, then you can just wish me good evening and be on your way: otherwise, I need you to speak. Is that clear?"

Astonishment took possession of all those present. It seemed that Ricciardi with his stark, dramatic tone had met the spirit of the place.

Romano nervously ran his tongue over his lips.

"What's the question, Commissa'?"

The detective gazed at him fixedly.

"Do any of you know whether Marra had a secret lover, even if you can't tell me their identity, and whether her husband was aware of the fact?"

After those words, a profound silence settled over the room, until Renzullo interrupted with a cough: "It's time, people, we need to go onstage. Give it your best. Raise the curtain."

XVII

When the music announced the beginning of the show, Ricciardi and Maione withdrew into Fedora's dressing room and prepared to wait in that sweetly perfumed air, surrounded by bouquets of flowers and feather boas.

Renzullo excused himself: he needed to go and make sure that the revue, operating without its protagonists, was functioning decently all the same. Before leaving, he couldn't help but express a hint of satisfaction, however melancholy: "Sadly, we've had to turn down requests for tickets from a hundred or so people. If it goes on like this, and if we do at least as well, we'll have a sold-out house until the middle of next month. Let's hope so, Commissa'. Let's just keep our fingers crossed."

After the impresario left them alone, Maione partly shut the door and said: "Now I'd like you to explain, Commissa', because I'm not sure I understand. First of all: Why do you want to see the artists one at a time? Wouldn't it have been enough to just talk with those who were on close terms with Gelmi and Marra? What do you think the others know about them? Second: Why is it important that they come talk to us in this specific room? Third, and this is the most important thing of all: Why are we still investigating? At this point it seems obvious to me that we've already arrested the guilty party, and we have further confirmation from the sheet of paper that you found in the dressing gown."

Ricciardi responded with a faint smile. Even if he acted a

little put out, deep in his heart he was always happy when Maione asked for an explanation. Those requests helped him to straighten out his thoughts.

"It was, in fact, the note that convinced me that it's worth my while to dig deeper. In the meantime, the place where we found it already tells us something: Fedora kept it in the pocket of an article of clothing that, in all likelihood, she wore between one change of clothing and another. That means we can assume that she had no intention of taking the message outside of here, and that the recipient was someone whom the victim regularly frequented here in the theater, which narrows the field."

Maione tapped his hat, in place of his head.

"That's why she wrote: 'till tomorrow.' She knew for certain that she'd see the person again the following day . . ."

"Exactly. And the correspondence must have been conducted on a daily basis, and in fact she added 'again, tonight' and 'don't worry,' as if bidding them farewell prior to a momentary separation."

The brigadier was perplexed.

"Yes, Commissa', but what is this embroidery that the actress was going to wear at night? A gift?"

"That we still don't know, but it's fundamental to find it out, if for no other reason than to discover whatever motive her husband might have had. And since I'm convinced that none of the artists would ever talk about such a sensitive matter in front of their colleagues, I chose to give them all a chance to meet with me alone. That way, they can avoid reciprocal accusations and all sorts of malicious gossip. Have you noticed that there's already a division between those who maintain Gelmi's innocence and those who believe that he's guilty?"

Maione threw both arms wide.

"I'll say. But I think that's relatively normal, given the environment. There are those who're just grateful to have been cast or hired, who're thinking to themselves, 'Now we're all going to be fired,' and those who want to take advantage of this opportunity to get their moment in the spotlight."

As the performances unfolded on the stage, the audience warmed up in its enthusiasm. Propelled by the force of desperation or perhaps by the desire to seize an opportunity, the troupe was giving its all, and the audience seemed to sense the fact.

At a certain point, actors, dancers, and musicians began filing past the two policemen. Their discomfort at finding themselves among the clothing and possessions of the dead woman was easy to discern. Their faces looked warm and uncomfortable, their eyes darted evasively. They mostly recounted the same basic concepts, each in different words: Commissa', I barely ever crossed paths with Signora Fedora, at rehearsals or onstage. We almost never spoke; she was kind and always had a smile on her face, but she never confided in me. No, I never heard anything about any illicit or secret love affairs. Did I know whether she was on normal terms with her husband? I really couldn't say. I mind my own business. I'm just here to work.

There were a few though who really did have something to say. The first was the tall, skinny violinist, the one who had defended Gelmi in front of everyone.

"My name is Franceschelli, Commissa'. Renato Franceschelli. I've known Michelangelo for thirty-five years, we started out together, and since then each of us has taken his own, very different path. Still, every chance he's had, he reaches out to cast me. Or at least, he did until now. Commissa', he's innocent, I'm sure of it; he wouldn't hurt a fly, he's a gentleman, a kindhearted person, the finest lead actor you could imagine. Did Fedora have someone else? Truth be told, I have no idea: she was young and beautiful, and there were plenty of men buzzing around her, in part because they assumed that Michelangelo, at his age . . . Well, you follow me, right? But I've never seen her in any compromising situation with anyone else. She certainly never mentioned anything to me about a secret lover, nor do I think that she said anything of the sort to anyone else."

Franceschelli's version was more or less the same as that put forth by the most experienced artists, the ones who'd worked with Gelmi the longest.

There was a more varied array of opinions among the younger artists.

The dancer with the chestnut hair simply spoke her farewells and left.

On the other hand, the blonde dancer with the prominent nose, still out of breath from the cancan that she'd just performed, threw restraint to the winds: "Gelmi is a drinker, Commissa'; he's a heavy drinker. There are days during rehearsals when he can barely stay on his feet. When a person wraps his arms around a bottle, he'll start to see phantoms of all kinds, and maybe he imagined something. I don't know whether Fedora was seeing another man; whatever the case, if she was cheating on that old drunk, I can hardly say that I blame her. We're women, and we need human warmth: gratitude is surely a fine thing, but life is life. He killed her because of some deranged fixation, trust me."

Pio Romano took a softer line.

"Let me tell you, lately Fedora seemed different, but I can't swear on a bible that she was being unfaithful. Sure, Gelmi was . . . a bit distracted, and the more time went by, the further apart they grew. Sooner or later, perhaps they would have split up, but to think that he might have murdered her . . . Perhaps he wasn't himself, Commissa'. It happened at times."

Two dancers, the brunette and the redhead, came in together to save time and avoid missing their entrance onstage. Their versions failed to match up entirely.

The first one introduced herself as Clelia and said: "I don't think Gelmi was happy. He was afraid of losing her: she was a diva, she had hordes of admirers. When she walked out onto the stage, none of us counted for a thing anymore."

The other one, Italia, took a harsher approach: "That's what bothered him most, if you ask me: she alone existed for the audience. They adored her, and even outside of the theater, out on the street, men couldn't stop looking at her. Maybe he was jealous."

Ricciardi asked: "Is it possible that Fedora had a special bond with someone else in the troupe?"

The two young women exchanged a glance of surprise. It was Clelia who answered the question: "You mean with someone here, in the Teatro Splendor? I'd rule that out, Commissa'. We would have noticed, wouldn't we, Ita'?"

"Yes, of course. Also, why would any of us risk their career like that? No, if she had a lover, he wouldn't have had anything to do with the revue."

Among those who established a certain distance were Meloni and Pittella. As usual, the spokesman for the duo was the guitarist: "We were the last ones hired; we owe everything to the lead actor and it would be best for us if we just mind our own business. Yes, we knew that he liked to take a drink now and then. We could smell it wafting off him during rehearsals; we sat close to him. His voice would sound a little slurred, too, even though, thanks to his professional training, he always managed to keep on key. We had fewer interactions with Signora Fedora, because she didn't sing as often. Let me say it again, we never spent time with them outside the theater."

The young man had little to add, but what he did say was rather harsh.

"He's an old man who drinks too much and sleeps the day away. She was beautiful and full of energy. If you ask me, there was nothing wrong with her deciding that she wanted a new lease on life. But the lead actor was jealous, and so he killed her."

Meloni hushed him up with an angry glare, and the mandolinist shut his mouth like a mousetrap.

The last one to enter the dressing room, after the comic number ended, was the actor with the threadbare tailcoat and the dented top hat. Third only to Gelmi and Marra, he was the best-known name in the cast, at least in the city: his name was Vincenzo Zupo, stage name Zuzú, and he specialized in the *macchietta*, those humorous songs rife with double entendres that brought out belly laughs from the part of the audience made up of young men and soldiers.

To see him onstage, he looked like a sort of marionette; he was capable of simulating awkward, disconnected movements that were bizarre and hilarious. When not in his onstage persona, his presentation was that of a sarcastic and melancholy man, with big sad eyes that stood out over the greasepaint.

"Commissa', we actors are strange people. Over the years, out of the habit of depicting all sorts of exaggerations, because that is how you might best describe the emotions we portray onstage, we eventually start to exaggerate offstage as well. And we talk ourselves into believing it's all true: the tears and the shouts, the laughter and the betrayals. Perhaps poor Michelangelo fell victim to a dream and forgot the difference between reality and imagination. Fedora was an actress, too, and she too made believe for a living. Perhaps she dreamed up a great love of her life and believed in it. This sort of thing happens in the theater world. Outsiders don't understand it, they think that we're normal people who practice an unusual profession. In fact, it's the other way around. We're unusual people who practice a normal profession."

Ricciardi took the time to study that sad and asymmetrical face, as if it were a metaphor for the words that the man had just uttered: comic verve on the outside, subdued melancholy on the inside.

"But Zupo, could this dream, this illusion of love actually lead someone to commit a real-life murder? After all, by now whatever success Gelmi still enjoyed depended on Fedora."

The actor displayed an unhappy smile.

"I told you, Commissa'. We stage people tend to get a bit confused. We think we can transport our acting into life, thereby transforming it into a sort of revue. But life rebels against that. And after all, there isn't just one kind of love. There can be many types, and when they get mixed together, they can become dangerous."

To emphasize his point, he performed a movement with his hands and shoulders, miming the act of mixing. Maione chuckled and even Ricciardi couldn't keep a look of amusement from appearing on his face.

"One last question, Zupo. In your opinion, could there have been an embroidery that Fedora wore at night as a sort of promise of love?"

Zuzú opened both eyes wide. He took his time to think it over, and then, at last, he spoke.

"We embroider continuously. A poem, a song, even a comic sketch, if it's well executed, resembles nothing so much as an embroidery. It might be a lovely undergarment, a nightgown, but even a glance, a word, a sequence of notes. We embroider, Commissa'. No matter what."

After the comedian left the room, Maione sighed: "He was the last one, Commissa'. To judge from the applause, it strikes me that Gelmi's and Marra's orphans have managed to pull it off. Whereas *we're* back at square one."

Ricciardi massaged his temple.

"Who can say, Raffaele. We've gathered information that may turn out to be useful later. As far as I'm concerned, I learned what I needed to know, and I'm even more convinced

134 · MAURIZIO DE GIOVANNI

that we need to investigate Gelmi's motive. No one has really figured out why he pulled the trigger, or at least, no one has said why."

Maione lifted his hand to the visor of his cap.

"Agreed, Commissa'. With your permission, I'll let you head back to the office to finish up your day, and I'll swing by the hospital to see the doctor and find out whether he can give us the findings of the autopsy. Then I'll head home, again, with your permission: when New Year's is in the offing and she has a banquet to cook, Lucia becomes a real wild woman; I've got to go rescue my poor children. Do you know what she told me yesterday? She said: 'You're off gallivanting around at the theater all day, and I'm stuck in here slaving away.' Have you ever heard of such a thing?"

XVIII

Maione immersed himself in the city, as if preparing for the impending night, experiencing a pleasant sensation of warmth as he did so.

That year, the winter had decided to play hide-and-seek. The distinctive atmosphere of the days between Christmas and New Year's Day, with the shops always open, offering every sort of foodstuffs and delicacies, and an endless assortment of fireworks ready to go out into the world and live for only an hour or two, lacked only one thing: the cold. The brisk, chilly air that pushes you to stay inside and bedeck your dining room table. There was a distinct lack of raised coat collars and umbrellas; the carefully mended overcoats and blankets wrapped around the shoulders of women waiting outside the shops.

An almost springlike temperature, Raffaele thought as he hastened his step toward Pellegrini hospital. A slight warmth that left people baffled, wandering around with their overcoats draped over their arms, peeking up at the sky to figure out if there was even the faintest threat of rain. If for no other reason than to justify it being December.

The policeman nodded a brusque greeting to the man at the front desk, who was working to persuade a drunk that he'd survive even though he'd vomited, and headed down the hallway in the direction of the morgue. But Modo wasn't there. An attendant told Maione he'd find Modo in the clinic; he was caring for a patient in serious condition.

In front of the clinic door, the brigadier found Sister Luisa, the petite, greatly feared nun who assisted the doctor in his work. Maione and the nun had seen each other frequently, and Maione had developed the belief that, if it came down to it, that short, stout *capa di pezza*, or raghead, inflexible and energetic, would have been far more effective than two experienced police officers.

He greeted her in a confidential tone: "*Buonasera*, Sister Lui'. Do you know where our mutual friend is?"

The woman turned around, and as she did so, he was petrified: he'd never seen her in such a woebegone state. Her eyes were bloodshot, her lips were quivering; an anguished grimace crossed her face.

Maione was worried.

"*Mamma mia*, Sister, what's happened? Some catastrophe?"

The nun nodded, conquering her anguish.

"I hadn't noticed, Brigadie'. She seemed so . . . normal. I didn't notice the way she was bent over, her wounds . . . I just left her there, may the Good Lord forgive me. I told her to wait, I started giving instructions to a nurse, and I wasted at least ten minutes before calling the doctor. How could I possibly have been such an idiot?"

Maione stared at her, perplexed.

"Sister, either you calm down or I won't be able to understand a thing. Who was it that appeared normal? And what was it you hadn't noticed?"

Instead of answering him, the nun knocked softly on the clinic door, opened it, and entered the room. Maione followed her and immediately recognized Bruno Modo, with his back turned, bent over a gurney with two nurses beside him; he was busy medicating someone.

Sister Luisa murmured: "Dotto', it's Brigadier Maione. He wanted to see you. I thought that . . ."

Without turning around and without taking his hands off the roll of gauze he was winding, the doctor hissed: "Of course. The brigadier wears a uniform, so if he asks, he gets an answer, while a woman who's badly hurt can just wait all day long."

The nun bowed her head in humiliation. Maione felt the need to weigh in in her defense.

"Dotto', now you're being unfair. You know how devoted Sister Luisa is to those in need. Show some patience, it's not like you to humiliate her in this manner."

Modo straightened up, though he still kept his back turned to the policeman. He said nothing for a moment, then said to the nurses: "That'll do. You can leave, thanks, and if I need anything I'll call you. You, too, Sister Lui'. And please forgive me, I didn't mean to hurt your feelings."

The nun's voice came out in a whisper.

"No, *dotto'*. I'm afraid you were right. Excuse me."

Once they were alone, Modo gestured for the brigadier to step closer, moving aside so that Maione could now see the person on the gurney.

Laid out on a white sheet was a woman's ravaged body. Her skin was covered with bruises and her right arm was bound up with a splint. Bloodstains were spreading through the gauze bandages that mercifully wrapped her. Her face was swollen and unrecognizable: from her lips, parted to reveal bleeding gums and shattered teeth, there came a terrifying, rhythmic groan. Even though Maione was hardened to the sight of the results of human violence, he felt a stab of pity pierce his heart.

He clamped his jaw to stifle his fury.

"Who did this . . . this thing?"

Modo shook his head; his white hair tumbled messily over his forehead. There was no trace in his gaze of the good-natured irony that normally resided there. He had the face of an old man.

"She's a friend of mine, her name is Lina. I don't even know her last name, as I've just realized. Whenever we met, I was so busy talking about myself, my life, my useless thoughts, that I never bothered to ask."

His eyes filled with tears. Maione coughed in embarrassment and the doctor regained his composure.

"I don't know if she'll make it, Brigadie'. She's strong by nature, otherwise she'd already be dead, but right now I'm not capable of evaluating the potential lesions to the internal organs. I've sedated her. She was suffering terribly, so I haven't had a chance to ask her what happened and who it was. She shouldn't even have been out on the street. She's one of Mamma Clara's girls, from La Torretta."

Maione nodded. He knew the house, a fairly refined establishment.

"And you have no idea of whether someone had it in for her, or was living off her back . . ."

Modo stared at the poor woman's devastated face.

"No, not Lina. She never let anyone exploit her. She's intelligent, and strong . . . And beautiful. Take my word for it. I . . ."

He ran his hand over his eyes; Maione thought he might be giving in to tears again, but instead Modo went on talking in a more determined tone.

"Brigadie', I've never asked you for anything. I don't much believe in the law, as you know. Even though you and Ricciardi did help me when I found myself in serious trouble, putting your own liberty and jobs at risk by doing so. I'll never forget that, I can assure you."

The policeman protested: "Dotto', you shouldn't even say that, you . . ."

Modo interrupted him, grabbing his arm.

"Listen to me, Raffaele, you have to help me track down whoever perpetrated this brutality. Without any official reports or warrants, without involving police headquarters or even

Ricciardi; he's working on Marra's murder, and I don't want to distract him from his work. What's more, he knows very little about the circles Lina moves in. In contrast, you are a man of the world, and you're a friend of mine. I'm begging you, consider this a personal favor that I'm asking."

Maione scrutinized the doctor with a sidelong glance and a half smile.

"Are you trying to insinuate that I have practical experience of the brothels of La Torretta? You should understand that the fact that I know Mamma Clara and a few of her girls is strictly on account of my own professional duties, eh? Not theirs."

Modo too put on an expression that seemed to contain a hint of irony.

"I've never doubted the fact, Brigadie'. Never doubted the fact."

The policeman scratched his ear.

"Okay, all right. After all, it's probably better to go on working, rather than going home and looking after those devils. Later you can tell me all about Lina, and then I'll run by and see Mamma Clara; and tomorrow, if it's useful, I'll ask Bambinella for some information. For now, though, bear with me and tell me what you found out while examining the actress. That's why I came here in the first place."

The doctor took a breath.

"It's all confirmed, Brigadie'. It's all just as it appeared. The bullet penetrated the left hemithoracic region and took a nice fast trip through Fedora's lovely body: intercostal muscle, aortic arch, trachea, and esophagus; then it found a comfortable little perch between the between the third and fourth dorsal vertebrae. It's at your disposal, somewhat the worse for wear, but intact. The report is in an envelope down at the front desk. As I had ventured, the fatal wound was in the aorta; hence the blood from her mouth and nose. I'm afraid she suffered: nearly a minute went by from gunshot to death."

Maione turned his gaze to the woman fast asleep on the gurney.

"Certainly less than this poor thing is suffering. I really want to identify the cowardly bastard who reduced her to this state."

Modo nodded, grimly.

"So do I, Brigadie'. So do I."

XIX

Through the large sound horn of the gramophone, the music was spreading through the dim light of the living room, distorted only slightly by the rustling of the needle; and perhaps that very imperfection rendered it even more captivating.

Looking out at the thousand glittering lights of the distant city and the sea that extended, black, dotted with the gleams of lamps from fishing boats and running lights on ships passing through, the woman sprawling comfortably in the armchair thought to herself that the finest thing about life is its very imperfection, the imprint of diversity, the richness of the original traits that stand out against the drab gray of convention.

In contrast, the man lying on the sofa across from her continued to look at her with eyes by now well adapted to the partial darkness, thinking to himself that this woman was just perfect. Perfectly beautiful, with a perfect soul and a perfect sensibility. Perhaps *too* perfect.

When Bianca Borgati di Zisa, the Contessa Palmieri di Roccaspina, paid a call on Carlo Maria Fossati Berti, the Duke of Marangolo, this is how the hours passed. She would join him a little before sunset in his magnificent home on the lofty floor of the palazzo that overlooked the waterfront, stepping out of the chauffeured car that he had sent for her, and she'd find her friend already reclining on the sofa, a woolen blanket draped over him, two soft pillows propping up his head.

Each time, the nobleman apologized for receiving her in

that fashion, and told her that unfortunately the day hadn't been a good one for his health. Each time, she would lean over to kiss him on the cheeks and reply that actually she thought he looked much better, and that they'd soon go back to strolling along the seafront. Each time he pretended to believe her and every time, both of them, behind the smile they each wore as a mask, felt themselves die a little bit inside, ravaged by nostalgia.

Then Bianca would put a record on the platter of the gramophone, something she had selected from the duke's vast collection. Usually she chose one of the American records; Marangolo arranged for them to be brought to him aboard one of the large trans-Atlantic ocean liners that docked in the nearby port at least once a week. The warm, despairing voices of wonderful, ebony-skinned singers, accompanied by the lamenting wail of saxophones and amorous trumpet, surrounded the two friends' silences, filling them with emotions and sentiments far more than thousands of empty words might ever have done.

As they listened, the two of them gazed out at the vast mass of salt water framed by the large windows as if it were a sequence of a film in a movie theater, only in full, living color. The street below was, so to speak, offscreen. It almost seemed as if they were aboard a plane flying at low altitude, capable, as if by magic, of stopping at a given point in space and hovering in the empty air. The sea repaid their attention kindly, offering an ever-changing spectacle, glowing at sunset, dimming to darkness in the embrace of night, teeming with boats or displaying itself both deserted and boundless.

The third guest in the room, the one that most strongly made felt its disagreeable presence, was melancholy, the only one present that chattered endlessly, making loud demands and dredging up hostile memories.

Most of the inhabitants of that miserably poor metropolis,

who struggled day by day to carve out even a fragment of human dignity, would have wondered what damned reason there could be for sorrow to prevail in a living room occupied by a man wealthy beyond all imagining and a woman so lovely and refined as to intimidate any ordinary person. And yet there was not a place, in the entire city, where that emotion predominated so powerfully and so unrivaled.

Carlo Marangolo was a sick man. His liver was damaged beyond repair, and the doctors had not been able to do anything more than prolong his suffering. The duke's immense wealth had still not been enough to buy him a little health; his darting, intelligent dark eyes were the only element still ferociously alive in that waxen, wrinkled, jaundice-yellow face, framed by straggling, disorderly locks of lank, unhealthy-looking hair.

As always, he was totally focused on the woman sitting beside him; the true wonder for him was being able to look at Bianca as she looked out at the sea.

Bianca was much younger than him. He had always loved her and because of that love, he'd never been able to imagine anyone else beside him.

Bianca, whose melancholy came from a long way away.

Her husband, Romualdo, was in prison. He had claimed responsibility for a murder, putting an end to a social life in steady decline, oppressed by the vice of gambling that had led him to squander every last penny to his name, including his wife's inheritance, and culminating in an arrest that had made the rounds of gossip in the city's most exclusive drawing rooms for months and months.

The woman had experienced the worst kind of poverty, the kind that follows wealth. She had also been shut out of the higher ranks of polite society. Her relatives had shunned her and her closest friends had promptly abandoned her. All except Carlo. He had remained a close and steadfast friend.

For some time, he had secretly underwritten the husband, until it became clear to him that access to money only fed the demon.

After Romualdo's arrest, Bianca had shut herself up in a home emptied of all furnishings, a house that was falling apart, just like her life. That was when Marangolo had decided to devote his last remaining years to a mission: he wanted to bring back to life the woman he had always loved from afar. He had spoken with her at great length, explaining what fun it would to be to flip the condescending pity of the ladies of high society into scalding envy. In order to bring her around, he had taken advantage of an opportunity that then and there had struck him as ideal: she could help that green-eyed commissario, so mysterious and intelligent, who had liberated her of her husband's obsessive tyranny, but who was now in serious trouble.

What he hadn't foreseen, though—he mused inwardly for what seemed like the thousandth time, as he admired his good friend's exquisite profile—was that the cure might prove more deleterious than the disease. Though he, of all people, ought to have suspected that.

My heart is sad and lonely
For you I sigh, for you, dear, only
Why haven't you seen it
I'm all for you, body and soul . . .

This voice from across the ocean mingled with the sound of the waves, braiding together their thoughts and heartbeats—two hearts, so close and yet so distant. Carlo wondered where Bianca's mind was wandering, and he was terrified at the thought of the answer. He also questioned himself concerning the nature of that strange sentiment of his, locked up inside a body that would never again be able to dream of love, and yet nonetheless so blind and selfish that it still demanded it. He felt sorry for himself.

"What's wrong, friend of mine?" he asked in a whisper.

Bianca turned around. Her long neck, her hair gathered high, a shade of blonde that caught the sunlight with flecks of copper, her eyes an incredible, extraordinary violet hue, her small, upturned nose. Even in the dark of night, even in the flickering glow of the candles lit on the low table between them, even just in his mind, Marangolo would have been capable of describing every single square centimeter of that flesh that had never belonged to him.

The contessa's deep, warm voice made its way through the song.

"Nothing, Carlo. I'm just resting. I'm letting my mind go where it pleases without any defense, at least for a while. And how are you feeling?"

The man waved his hand in the air, dismissively.

"My state of health is a long and boring topic. A sad novel, published in installments, and without a happy ending, I'm afraid. Let's leave it aside, I won't allow anything to ruin the perfection of the hours I have you here."

She responded dismissively.

"But you know I come here every day. By now, people are probably starting to come up with strange ideas of their own."

The duke snorted impatiently.

"I am beyond any and all suspicions. But tell me about yourself. How is the fake relationship with your smoldering dark policeman going?"

Bianca turned to look out at the sea with a slow toss of her head, displaying to the other man the elegance of her features, like something out of a cameo, and at the same time revealing the innermost nature of the sentiment that was oppressing her heart.

"He thanked me. A few days ago he came to pay a call on me, he sat down in my drawing room with a smile, which is a genuine rarity for him, and said that he harbored a boundless gratitude toward me for having freed him—by pretending to be his lover—of the odious accusation of pederasty that was hanging over his head."

Carlo listened attentively.

"And so?"

"And so," she went on in a neutral tone of voice, "he told me that, for personal reasons, we could no longer be seen in public together, that he no longer wished to go on pretending, and that for me, too, this would be a better way forward."

The song ended. Bianca stood up and went over to the shelf full of records next to the gramophone.

"Would you care to listen to something more lighthearted? Cole Porter, perhaps. *Love For Sale . . .* That would be fun, don't you think? You go into a store and instead of a new hat, a dress, or a loaf of bread, you buy yourself some love. Whatever color you like, whatever weight you please."

The notes of the music filled the room without transmitting the cheerfulness that had been promised.

Carlo's voice took on a dark timbre.

"And why did he tell you that? That's not the behavior of a gentleman: to thank you and dump you."

Bianca stepped close and tucked in his blanket, solicitously, then went back to her seat.

"Instead it's an act of profound sincerity, typical of him. He's an honest man, and he can't stand deceit. After all, unmasking lies is his profession, as we saw with Romualdo."

The duke coughed and then wiped his mouth with a handkerchief.

"What would be the truth, the frankness, behind this declaration of his?"

The woman shrugged and sat there, staring out at the night.

"I asked him that. After all, I'm still a woman. I lacked the tact required to feign indifference."

"And what did he say?

"He replied that, as I was well aware, his heart belonged to another. As long as this person was distant, he didn't find it inappropriate to socialize with me in public, but now that the two of them have begun to see each other—something that, by the way, he was revealing only to make the situation clear to me—he no longer thought it was right to pursue the farce. But you know what the best part of it was? That he had the tone of voice of someone who was freeing me of his presence. Basically, he believes that he's been a burden to me. Don't you find that hilarious?"

She laughed, in fact. But sadness throttled her.

Marangolo considered inwardly how the people he could least tolerate were those who were honest to the point of being obtuse.

"You ought to tell him."

"Tell him what?"

"That his presence was anything but a burden. That his company and his friendship were more than welcome, as far as you were concerned. And that you care nothing for your reputation, for what others might say about you, about the two of you, least of all the opinions of that flock of plucked hens in the drawing rooms and clubs."

She replied after a brief silence: "In fact, I had considered having a conversation with him. Or at least letting him know that he can consider me a friend, and confide in me if there's anything bothering him. And I can think of the perfect occasion for that talk. Princess Vaccaro di Ferrandina—do you remember her?—is going to be holding a New Year's Day reception the day after tomorrow. She's invited me, but of course I'd never go on my own. I can ask him to accompany me. I don't believe he has any other plans."

Marangolo felt a surge of joy mixed with the pang of jealousy that he'd learned to recognize so well over the years. There's my Bianca, he thought. Sweet and combative.

"An excellent idea. But you'll need a new, magnificent outfit for the event. Let me take care of it. We don't have much time: tomorrow morning I'll have Gustavo drive you around to the shops. You must be the loveliest one there, even lovelier than you usually are."

She scolded him, tenderly.

"Carlo, stop spending all this money on me. You know that it makes me uncomfortable."

The duke's laughter pealed out hoarsely.

"Stop it with this nonsense. I possess a useless mountain of cash that will soon enough belong to you anyway, since I plan to name you my universal heiress; you'll become by far the wealthiest woman in this city. What's so bad about now starting to dip into that wealth already?"

Silence fell. Then Bianca murmured: "Don't say such things, I don't want to lose you. You're my one point of reference. More than a father. My life would be nothing without you."

The duke momentarily concealed the depth of his emotion behind another racking cough.

"For now, I'm here. So let's make the best use of this time and prepare a fine strategy. For the hat, what color did you have in mind?"

Outside, the night, comfortably resting upon the sea, smiled.

XX

D oubts. He was full of doubts. Doubts that drowned him and clawed at him.

His thoughts, whichever way they turned, wound up slamming into a solid brick wall.

Sitting in an armchair, with the radio playing dance music in the background, while the housekeeper Nelide cleaned an already immaculate kitchen, Commissario Luigi Alfredo Ricciardi faced up to his own uncertainties.

That murder case, simple though it seemed to be, was unnerving him. It seemed obscure to him. He couldn't grasp its aim or its mechanics, he couldn't penetrate to its essence.

If Gelmi had planned out the murder, he'd have done it in such a way as to avoid being the only possible suspect; whereas if his act was the result of a momentary burst of rage, it would have taken place during a quarrel, the most recent one having taken place, according to the devoted Erminia, just before the second performance.

Instead, this was a hybrid, with the distinctive characteristics of premeditation shown by the order of the bullets in the clip, but also with the typical traits of an angry and flagrant act carried out during the theatrical performance of a betrayal.

The comic, Zuzú, had told him that actors confuse make-believe with reality, and perhaps that was true: but in real life betrayal certainly dictates an immediate reaction, it is much less likely to inspire a laborious, clear-eyed process of revenge. What's more, there were two aspects in direct contrast with each other: Gelmi had pulled the trigger and Gelmi had declared his own innocence.

For the umpteenth time, Ricciardi summarized the statements of the witnesses and the fellow artists, colleagues of the two lead actors. There was no solid evidence, but the overall picture fit well with the hypothesis of the victim's being involved in a secret love affair, as confirmed by the billet-doux they'd found in the pocket of her robe. But the real question was: did the husband know? And what had been the purpose of his visit to Fedora's dressing room, from which he had emerged in tears?

That note deserved to be studied more closely. "Again, tonight, I'll wear your embroidery before falling asleep," Marra had written. What embroidery? An article of clothing? A gift? And why "in my heart it will be the last thing I hear"? That odd mixture of tactile and auditory perceptions baffled Ricciardi. What's more: "Don't worry, I belong to no one but you. I'm yours, yours and happy!" What was the meaning behind that invitation to remain calm? Was her lover jealous, too? Of who? Everyone knew, as far as he could tell, that Gelmi no longer had intimate relations with his wife.

Last of all: "Till tomorrow." That meant the woman was certain that they'd be seeing each other again. This excluded the possibility that the lover, or presumed lover, was extraneous to the group of artists because, as had been perfectly clear during their interviews, when the show was on, the members of the troupe were confined to the theater, engaged in rehearsals and the three daily performances. That said, who could it be? And in any case, why go to the trouble of devising such a complicated murder?

No one could possibly have sidestepped Erminia's sharp eye and made their way into Gelmi's dressing room. What's more, the woman was loyal to the death to Michelangelo, who had arranged for Renzullo to hire her in the first place.

Therefore, if she'd known anything about evidence that might serve to clear him, she would certainly never have kept it to herself.

It all led back to the most obvious interpretation possible: Gelmi had murdered his wife in a fit of jealous rage, professional envy, bitter resentment, or possibly because of some sort of indecent behavior. Perhaps Fedora had decided to leave him and had communicated that fact to him prior to the second performance. At that point, Michelangelo had made his decision, and in keeping with his intrinsic nature, he had acted out that intention on the stage, before an audience.

Still, there was something troubling Ricciardi. Something he'd seen or heard. It was an all-too familiar sensation: like a puzzle piece out of place, a detail out of focus, apparently normal but, in reality, anything but.

On the radio, the orchestra completed its performance with a flourish, and the announcer informed the listeners that the next piece would be a song. The radio then produced the opening bars of a melody that had enjoyed a special place in the commissario's heart for some time now.

The warm intonation of Carlos Gardel's voice warbled out *Caminito*.

Instinctively, Ricciardi shot a glance at the clock in the corner of the room. It was roughly 10 PM, the hour at which, by a tacit but ironbound understanding, he would make himself seen at his bedroom window, keeping the light off. Enrica would do the same, stepping close to her kitchen window in the building across the way, half a story lower. The two of them would smile at each other, now freed of the veil of reserve and secrecy, at this point without fear and instead reveling in the joy of beholding each other.

Caminito que el tiempo ha borrado,
que juntos un día nos viste pasar,

he venido por última vez,
he venido a contarte mi mal.

(Little street that the years have forgotten
Where she and I once walked together so happily,
I've come here just one last time,
To tell you about my sorrow and pain.)

But that was the evening of doubts, and Ricciardi was once again assailed by a wave of hesitation that came from another corner of his troubled soul.

The eagerly awaited evening appointment had a less agreeable collateral aspect. On the fourth floor of Enrica's apartment building, shrouded in a vague luminescent glow, a sight displayed itself to his cursed and inward vision, the spectral image of a woman who had hanged herself. The disproportionately long neck, stretched by the traction of rope and body weight, her bulging eyes, blackened tongue protruding from the mouth in a perennial, ghoulish smirk, and her despairing voice continually repeating: *You damned whore, you took my love and my life.* One last, chilling invective.

Dead out of hatred, dead out of misery, dead amidst suffering.

Usually, in a matter of months, those apparitions would dissolve. And yet there were certain phantoms that, for unknown causes, persisted in infesting the place of their passage into the world of the dead, and they lingered, incessantly spewing out their last thoughts, their extreme sentiment.

To see that presence hovering over Enrica's smile was, to Ricciardi's mind, a ghastly oxymoron, a mocking contradiction in terms that called everything else into question. His love thrived and grew day by day, gaining in bulk and mass and solidity; but if a part of him labored under the illusion that he'd be able to live a normal life, there was also an aspect of his awareness that clearly glimpsed the selfishness of a bond rooted in a lie.

Because concealing his true nature from Enrica meant lying to her. Nothing more and nothing less.

Caminito que entonces estabas
bordeado de trébol y juncos en flor,
una sombra ya pronto serás,
una sombra lo mismo que yo.

(Little street, you were lined with clover,
And flowering reeds were in bloom along your way,
Very soon you'll be just a shadow,
A shadow the same as I am now.)

The sorrowful verse of that song rang out like a menacing wave of grief; Ricciardi shuddered. Lies . . . Fedora had concealed the truth and now she was dead. What would become of him? And to what degree would his own condemnation fall on Enrica's head?

That was why he had never made any mention of the future the few times they had actually gone out. He was still struggling with himself and with his own fears. What would be the right thing to do? Speak to the young woman's father, that good and unceremonious man, so similar to his daughter, who had actually come to talk to him when he realized what was happening to Enrica with Manfred? Ask his permission to spend time with his daughter, saying nothing about the fact that their frequentation might very well lead to nothing at all? Or tell Enrica: Listen, my love, I want to spend every minute of the rest of my life with you, but I can't and I won't and I *must absolutely never* become a father?

As he stood up, at the first stroke of the hour from the wall clock, his mind flew to Bianca; the undecipherable expression, hovering between sorrow and sweetness, that had appeared on her face when he had told her that she should consider herself free of any obligation to see him. Perhaps, unintentionally, he had hurt her. Like Livia, whom he hadn't seen in quite some time now, but whose actions were the clearest possible symptom of the pain he had caused her.

Caminito que todas las tardes
feliz recorría cantando mi amor,
no le digas si vuelve a pasar
que mi llanto tu suelo regó.

(Little street, every afternoon,
I walked the length of you singing my love.
Don't tell her if she comes by,
that my tears watered your ground.)

He stepped over to the window with the customary tempest raging in his soul. Across the street, behind the glass panes of the kitchen window, Enrica was standing there, waiting for him.

She wasn't smiling, though.

The young woman looked up and met his gaze. Two floors further up, the hanged woman murmured: *You damned whore, you took my love and my life.* Behind the commissario, Carlos Gardel sang:

Desde que se fue
triste vivo yo;
caminito amigo,
yo también me voy.
Desde que se fue
nunca más volvió,
seguiré sus pasos
caminito, adiós.

(Since she went away, I live in sadness.
Little street, my friend, I'm leaving too.
Since she went away, she's never returned.
I'm going to follow her, little street, goodbye.)

As if she were listening to the same piece of music, Enrica mouthed the syllables *Ca-mi-ni-to*, communicating an appointment to meet the next day.

Ricciardi noticed that her lower lip was quavering: she had either been crying or was about to. What had happened?

The radio underlined that instant:

Caminito cubierto de cardos,
la mano del tiempo tu huella borró;
yo a tu lado quisiera caer
y que el tiempo nos mate a los dos.

(Little street covered in weeds,
the second hand erased your footprint.
I would like to fall down next to you
and let time kill us both.)

Ricciardi reached out his hand.
But Enrica was already gone.

The old man's story resembles a dream. The young man feels himself being drawn into a world that seems real but isn't. At least, that's what he thinks. At least, that's what he hopes.

Maestro, is it a sure thing that he murdered her, though? I mean, he shot her in front of everyone, the musicians, the other actor . . . Couldn't it be that at that very same instant, from backstage or the darkness of the audience . . . No, says the old man, and his voice betrays no emotion, not even a flutter of torment. No, he fired the gun. No one ever had a shadow of doubt about that. Well then, the young man asks, what are we talking about? Certainly, it's strange that it should happen onstage, I understand that, but still . . . The old man listens to the swallows outside; they've started singing their high piercing songs just as his hands stopped running up and down the instrument's neck, caressing the strings with the pick. He turns his ear to listen, his head tilted ever so slightly, as if he were searching in that noise, so subtle and chaotic, for a tone or a melody. The young man falls silent and waits. He's learned that a story like that one, a third-person account, not unlike a memory belonging to someone else, or an article in a dusty old newspaper extracted at random from the teetering pile next to the bedroom door, might well just cut off midway through.

They'd talked about it during their previous meetings. A song is a story taken from life, you don't just dream it up at the drawing board to stick it in a novel; it might even lack an ending, it might be about a single fleeting instant, a kiss or a gaze, a regret or a hope. Then why does it become a song? the young man had asked one afternoon, while it was raining incessantly outside, and there was nothing to be seen but the rainwater pounding furiously down at the window. Because, the old man had replied, these are moments that are important to the author, that count more than anything else to him and to his life. They have an unbearable weight and, even though they last no more than an instant, they wound deeply and leave their mark. A song is the story of a scar.

And so the young man knows: what the old man has started to tell him, executing in masterful fashion the first verse, might already be over; a faded photograph as it emerges from a rusty metal box.

Instead the story goes on. And the old man, having discovered the key of the swallows' song, starts speaking again.

The policeman, he says, already possessed the solution. He just didn't realize it yet. It lay concealed in the chaos and confusion, because in disorder there is everything. Look at this room, it looks like a storeroom chockablock with trash and old junk. Before long, after I've left this world, when Concetta finds me here with my instrument in hand and my jaw sagging open, my blind eyes turned to the window and the sea, and perhaps to the swallows, they'll load all this rubbish onto a van and haul it off to the dump. But buried among the books and newspapers, the scores and the records, there's a meaning, a sense to things, a purpose that I alone understand. A thread that runs from my birth to my death. And even though it's been snipped, it will continue to exist even after the objects have been thrown away, tossed willy-nilly into and among the traces of lives of who knows what other people.

The same thing was happening in the policeman's mind: a broken web needed to be knotted back together. But what he needed to know? He already knew it.

The young man asks, softly: What about the song? Couldn't he just focus on the song?

The old man smiles and his face wrinkles up like a crumpled handkerchief. I've taught you well, *guaglio'*. Very well indeed. Yes, if he'd concentrated on the song, perhaps he'd have figured it out earlier. But he didn't have anything to do with our art. For him, for most people, and even for many musicians, songs are just words and music, and maybe they're a useful way to remember or preserve a thought, as if they were some kind of gelatine. He certainly could never have imagined that they were alive. Only people like us know that.

The young man senses a surge of proud warmth filling his chest. People like us . . . So in the end, I've received it, my diploma, he thinks. The old man goes on: For us it's normal that certain things can only happen during a song. Because we know the stage, whatever form it may take, even if it's just the street. It's the place where a dream, every dream becomes real, infecting and invading life. There is no way out, there's no place to run.

What do dreams have to do with it, Maestro? That man really fired his gun.

The old man struggles to his feet and goes to the window. His back is straight, his long thinning hair moves in the wind. The young man senses a flutter of wings nearby. Springtime or not, the swallows have returned.

The dream has everything to do with it, *guaglio'*, says the old man. Oh, it matters, that's the only lesson you have yet to learn, and it's the last one. I'm absolutely going to have to teach it to you, if I hope to protect you.

Protect me? What do you mean, Maestro? From what?

The other man turns around, his instrument grasped in his right hand, hanging at his side, like an extension of his arm. A dream, he replies, is a damned fog that envelops you and strips you of all your points of reference. It reduces your eyesight, it tangles up your emotions, it leaves you alone with the little you can see and nothing more. A dream is a perversion, because it tricks you about its reality. And it triumphs in sleep, when you close your eyes and the world that you have around you vanishes. A dream is like quicksand, like a lake with its treacherous still waters, like the sea at night. It swallows you up, and it never lets you go. That's why I told you that swallows have only one dream, and they believe that life is that dream: returning and returning, over and over. Who can say how many of them die, flying away and flying back. By the thousands, or even by the millions, along the path that they travel. And yet they care nothing at all, stubborn as they are, because their damned dream, in those tiny, obtuse heads, is always the same: to return, to return.

His tone is angry, and his phrases come out chewed off and broken. The young man, peering into in the dying sighs of the sunset, sees the sprays of saliva as the old man speaks, backlit, and thinks to himself that this is an ancient rage, that it might perhaps come from some other fragment of the story. He doesn't interrupt, but he's dying to ask.

The old man drags himself to the armchair and lets himself drop into it; his eyes remain shut, and he pants to disperse the fury that's filling his body.

Then he speaks again: in a dream, though, there's nothing we can do. We can't reach out our hand to defend ourselves, or to grab what we want. We're just dreaming and our hand refuses to move. And we can sense our frustration, our sense of ineptitude. There we are, trapped, the protagonists of all that happens and, at the same time, helpless spectators, the only ones who cannot act.

As if guided by a mind of its own, the instrument suddenly snaps into position. And without playing the introductory chords, the old man sings another verse.

Vulanno pe' città nove e stramane,
tu no, nun puo' sape' che te ne vène ogge o dimane.
E si nun truove maje chi te vo' bene quanto te ne vogl'io
ll'amice 'o ssanno
che faje vulanno?

E torna rundinella,
torna a 'stu nido mo' ch'è primmavera.
I' lasso 'a porta aperta quanno è 'a sera
speranno 'e te truva'
vicino a me.

(Flying through new and distant cities,
no, you can't know what will happen to you today or tomorrow.
And you'll never find anyone who loves you like I do,
Your friends know it,
what are you doing, flying like that?

Come back, little swallow,
Come back to this nest, now that it's springtime.
I'll leave the door open, when it's evening,
hoping to find you
next to me.)

The young man is breathless. Love, innocence, and pain, hope without hope, even madness. The passions concealed in the song—not only had he never heard any of them before, but he didn't even believe that they existed. My God, he murmurs. My God.

Yes, says the old man. That's exactly right. And while the policeman was searching for the broken thread, everyone else was a prisoner of their dreams. Each in thrall to his own dream. Blinded by that madness, they thought they could get away.

The young man feels his heartbeat pound in his ears; he sits waiting, but the old man's mouth emits no sounds. He waits and waits, and then he asks: Maestro, what about the swallows? He points at the window, his finger leveled as if in some act of accusation. Dreams come true, don't they? If they stick together, they achieve their dream. Certainly, a few of them fall by the wayside over the course of the trip, but the others arrive here, and they rebuild their nests here in your rain gutter. And as many are born as die, and perhaps even more. Isn't that a dream come true?

The old man shakes his head. Yes, but among themselves they know they're different, they're not all the same, the way they might seem to us. And perhaps the ones that die leave a memory among the others. Not all swallows return, *guaglio'*. That's the truth.

In a low voice, the old man resumes his story of dreams and flights without returns.

XXI

Even though his shift at the office didn't begin until noon, Maione left home early, and was therefore one of the first in the city to notice the unusual atmospheric phenomenon.

There was fog in the air.

In a city where even the climate liked to exaggerate, where there was a regular alternation between the ferocious heat that seized you by the throat and the damp chill that insinuated its way into your bones, where the rain slapped down furiously for a few minutes at a time and the hot wind gusted the scents of Africa and the insanity of the sea, tossing skirts high and making off with hats, well, even there that kind of mist—capable of dulling the senses and transforming a person into the only inhabitant of a world closed in on itself—was virtually unknown.

At the threshold of his front door, Maione looked around, confused. At least the unseasonable heat had a cause, or rather, an effect. A stray dog went past, hugging close to the wall and looking up at the brigadier as if in search of a little comfort, and then continued his way up the street. Maione heaved a sigh and stepped out into the mist.

Lucia had grumbled a bit: she was counting on her husband for the traditional dinner the following day. Not any direct assistance, let that be understood; the cooking was the exclusive domain of Lucia and her two eldest daughters, whom the woman was instructing in the art of preparing both main and side dishes. But Raffaele could take care of the littler ones: take them out to play or entertain them with a fairy tale or two.

Her objections, however, subsided immediately, after Maione told her a story far more appalling than any made-up one. At that point, it was she who urged him to go, and to waste no time in tracking down the bastard or bastards who had savagely beaten that poor young woman. Lucia, thought the brigadier, as he narrowed his eyes to better make out the street ahead of him, was an intelligent and discerning woman, always attentive to the importance and seriousness of his work.

The evening before the policeman had ventured as far as La Torretta, to talk to Mamma Clara. The elderly madam had welcomed him with her usual attitude, at once rough and affectionate: "Brigadie', what an honor! Are you interested in having some fun? I have a brand new *guagliona*, a Venetian, who's a delectable pastry. Come right in."

Maione had shaken his head, and then he'd given her the bad news. The woman had listened in silence, and tears had started running down her cheeks, even as her face maintained its initial expression of flinty impassiveness. Then she'd said: "Lina is a young woman who's good as gold, she's like a daughter to me. She has a kind thought for everyone, the customers adore her and even the other girls love her like a member of their own family; they take shifts on a fifteen-day basis, but she's full time, a regular. I don't have family and in my head I've always assumed that she'll take my place when it's my time to go. This morning she let me know she was taking a day off and left, saying: 'Till tonight, Mammà.' That's what she calls me: Mammà. Ask anything you need to ask, and if there's anything I can do to help, consider it done. No doubt about it, consider it done."

Unfortunately no information emerged from the conversation that might amount to a promising lead. The young woman who'd been attacked had never mentioned enemies to Mamma

Clara, much less personal problems with customers who might have threatened her; and at work she had never been involved in arguments or disagreements.

"Brigadie', you know it well: this isn't an easy line of work. But Lina is special. She understands people. She talks to them. Certain clients, such as Dr. Modo, come to see her for that very reason, and they never even take their clothes off. None of them would have even dreamed of laying a finger on her. Not a chance . . . not a chance of anything like this."

Then Maione had asked her whether she had an address or name for any relations. At first the woman had shaken her head, but then her face had lit up and she had waved for him to wait. And she'd headed off through a small door. She'd reappeared minutes later waving a folded sheet of paper.

"Here you go. The girls always give me an address I can turn to if anything happens; I don't know, an accident of any kind. She'd given me one, too, but she's been with me so long I'd completely forgotten about it. But I never throw anything away."

Maione had taken the sheet of paper and put it in his pocket. As he was about to leave, Clara stopped him: "Brigadie', forgive me. I wanted to ask you . . . I mean, I can go to the hospital, right? The doctor wouldn't be ashamed, would he? I want to be close to Lina, tonight. Like I told you, she calls me Mammà. And if something bad happens to a daughter, a mother needs to be near her. What do you say, can I go?"

The policeman suddenly felt a knot in his throat, and all he'd managed to do was nod his head affirmatively.

He hadn't slept well. The sight of that ravaged body had persecuted him, appearing before his eyes every time that sleep dared to venture near. It hadn't been a normal beating. He'd seen plenty of them in his time, and this one was different. Whoever had had it in for the woman wanted to see her dead, and if that was in the midst of indescribable suffering, so much the better.

And so, before going to the address indicated on the sheet of paper, which was on the far side of the city from the brothel, he had decided to meet with someone who might, perhaps, know more about this matter even than Mamma Clara. He had no doubts about the sincerity of the proprietor of the cathouse, but he had learned that sometimes people choose not to confide in those they love best; in part to keep from placing burdens on their shoulders that can prove tiresome, or worse.

He started his long walk up the hill, which the fog made even longer than usual. He put one foot ahead of the other, steeped in a dreamlike dimension; from time to time the cobblestone paving tripped him up. Irregular and pothole-riddled as it was, it required sharp eyesight from even a practiced pedestrian. Perhaps due to the recently past Christmas, or the imminently impending New Year's Day, the narrow lanes, or *vicoli*, seemed empty of life. The brigadier felt a twinge of melancholy at the sight of all those abandoned, deserted streets, drained of desires and passions, where solitude reigned unopposed.

Suddenly, somewhere nearby, a man began singing. Perhaps it was a bricklayer at the start of his workday, or even a lover launching into the previous night's last serenade or else the first of the coming day.

Si duorme o si nun duorme, bella mia,
siente pe' 'nu mumento chesta voce:
chi te vo' bene assaje sta mmiez'a via
pe' te canta' 'na canzuncella doce . . .

(Whether you sleep or don't sleep, my lovely,
Listen to this voice for a moment!

The one who loves you so much stands here in the street
To sing a beautiful song for you.)

The refrain was nicely modulated by a fine tenor voice, and
Maione, with a smile, felt himself once again the master of his
city.

Once he reached his destination, he became suddenly
aware of the early hour and wondered whether the person he
was going to see would be up and about, resigning himself to
the likelihood of a wait; but as he reached the top of the stairs,
panting as usual and slightly dizzy as the blood rushed to his
head, he found the door left ajar. The song that he'd heard
coming from who knew what obscure corner of the neighborhood came to a halt, and a familiar voice spoke: "Brigadie',
come right in! Make yourself comfortable!"

Maione made his way inside through the myriad items of
Chinese furniture and bric-a-brac that furnished the small
apartment and found himself in a small room whose existence
he had never suspected. The room looked out upon a narrow
balcony.

"Bambine', what is this place? I didn't know you actually
had a terrace."

The muffled atmosphere gave the personage seated out on
the tiny balcony in a small armchair an even more surreal
appearance than usual. She looked like a ghost of indetermi-
nate gender in the midst of the Amazonian jungle. Her long
hair was bound up in a high bun, with just two curls dangling
over her ears; her earrings dangled alongside them, undulating
back and forth, accompanying every small movement of her
head; her long, slightly equine profile; her large, liquid eyes,
which accentuated the resemblance to a purebred horse; all of
this bundled up in a red satin robe with embroidered flowers,
tone on tone, from which extended a pair of hairy, skinny,
gracefully crossed legs.

Maione sighed, wondering to himself as he always did what crime he had committed to deserve having to put up with that sight.

"Eh, Brigadie'," said Bambinella, "there are many things you don't know about this girl, and let me assure you, many of them are things that yours truly would gladly make available to you, if you wished to find out more; I'm quite sure that they'd make you a happy man. I never let anyone see this room; I come here when I want to spend some time alone, and I'm happy to tell you that that's not a common occurrence."

The policeman looked around. The furnishings here were different from the rest of the apartment. Sober, almost spartan. A table, two chairs; a photograph on the wall depicting a smiling priest surrounded by several children dressed in smocks with bows at the collar. Then the little balcony, which looked out from the back of the building.

"Why are you sitting out here? And how did you know I was climbing the stairs?"

Bambinella sighed theatrically.

"But have you seen it, this fog? Isn't it the strangest thing, Brigadie'? It's lovely. It seems like a dream to me, some kind of magic. Suddenly everything is gone: the buildings, the alleys; there aren't even any people. And with the new year just arriving, you realize that? Perhaps the end of the world is coming, and we're all about to die."

Maione replied by making the ancient sign of the horns, with extended forefinger and pinkie, a gesture thought to ward off bad luck: "Or maybe it's just the end of *you* that's coming, and about time, too. But why are you saying all these things that bring bad luck today of all days?"

The *femminiello* shrugged her shoulders, with a graceful movement.

"I mean, a girl can't entertain a serious thought. Anyway,

it's not as though the alley telegraph stops working just because there's fog. And, respectfully speaking, you're quite the sight this morning, with that uniform and those fine broad shoulders of yours that make me think certain naughty thoughts . . ."

"Do me a favor, Bambine', continue your philosophical line of thinking, that way maybe you can save your life again today. Listen, I need some information."

Bambinella turned to look at him with a spark of interest.

"If this is about what happened at the Teatro Splendor, why don't you tell me all about it, because nobody's talking about anything else in the whole city. What happened? Did Fedora have a boyfriend? Who was it? *Mamma mia*, how I like that Michelangelo Gelmi, what a powerful, captivating man. I can still remember in that film, what was it called? *The Ride of the Bedouin*. I must have seen it at least ten times, I've seen it! And I'd give him a ride, oooh, such a ride . . ."

The policeman threw both arms wide: "It's just no good. There's no way to have a decent conversation with you, the older you get the worse it becomes. We're working on the theater, but we still don't know anything specific. In any case, you're the one who needs to give me information, not the other way around. I need you for something else, though. I should tell you that a woman came in to Dr. Modo's hospital and she . . ."

Bambinella leapt to her feet.

"Ah. So this is about Lina from La Torretta?"

Maione sighed in resignation.

"And how do you know about that, now? That's fresh news, from yesterday. Who on earth told you about it?"

The *femminiello* leaned against the railing, tugging her robe around her neck. Her large eyes darted this way and that, in an attempt to penetrate the layer of mist. But it was no good.

"A couple of friends told me, one of them a customer of

mine. They found her at a street corner. They drove her over to just next to Pellegrini hospital. She had asked them to take her there."

Maione instinctively lowered his voice.

"And where did the beating take place?"

Bambinella had a moment's hesitation.

"Brigadie', I can tell you about this thing, but I have to be certain that you're not going to bring the law into it."

The policeman clenched his fists.

"And how do you expect me to make you a promise like that? Do you remember, who I am? Don't play hard to get or I'll throw you behind bars in the blink of an eye."

In contrast to his expectations, Maione saw Bambinella glare at him defiantly.

"Then I'll get dressed and come with you, Brigadie'. Because this time my mouth is stitched shut."

Maione couldn't quite wrap his mind around it.

"Why, what's come over you? That poor woman is at death's door. She's not out of danger yet, that's for sure. Modo is pessimistic; don't you feel even a twinge of pity?"

Bambinella whispered: "Precisely because I'm capable of pity, I won't talk to you, unless you can assure me that the law won't be brought into this thing. Otherwise I'll clam up even if you take me to prison and torture me there, the way you always do with criminals."

The uniformed man was shocked.

"You think we torture . . . Have you lost your mind? Who do you take us for, you idiot?"

"It's one way or the other: either you promise and you'll find out, or you don't promise and you don't find out."

The brigadier seemed like a steam locomotive on the verge of exploding. He took a long deep breath and hissed through clenched teeth: "I give you my word of honor, damn it all to hell. Now talk."

Bambinella smiled sweetly and sat on one of the two chairs indoors, gesturing for Maione to make himself comfortable as well.

"Brigadie', Lina is a friend of mine. We've known each other for a very long time, from long before you can even begin to imagine. Among those of us who practice this profession, in brothels or as freelancers, she's an institution, a saint. Ours may be a profession of sinful women, but if the Lord Almighty was able to forgive Mary Magdalene, then I'm sure that Lina, too, will go straight to heaven."

"Yes, so I've heard. But I'd say that not everyone agrees with you, if what happened happened, right?"

"It's not quite such a simple matter, Brigadie'. It's not so simple." The *femminiello* appeared to hesitate, and then she began: "My friends sell fish and they were on their way back from Pozzuoli. During the holidays they go there twice a day, because there's considerable demand, and that's why she's still alive today, otherwise she would have died on the spot."

"Where did they find her?"

"At the Masseria del Campiglione, the farmhouses."

That was the same place as had been marked on the sheet of paper that Mamma Clara had given Maione.

"Go on," said the policeman.

"I don't know much more than that. They spotted her from a distance, and she was already lying flat on the ground. There were two men pounding away at her, but they took to their heels when they saw the delivery van approaching. My friends lifted her up and Lina told them: 'Please, take me to Pellegrini hospital, to Dr. Modo.' They had to ask her to say it three times, because it was impossible to understand."

Maione thought back to that ravaged face, and the fog that lay in wait outside the little balcony suddenly seemed more menacing than before.

"Bambine', you know who did it. Otherwise, nothing that

you've told me so far required that promise. If you love your friend, give me the names."

The *femminiello* met the policeman's gaze.

"Brigadie', precisely because I love her, I can't do that. I know those names, I can imagine them, but I can't tell you."

The policeman shook his head.

"I don't understand, damn it."

Bambinella's eyes filled with tenderness.

"Listen to me. Everyone has dreams of their own. Even a whore, otherwise she'd never be able to put up with this life. And Lina had her dream, in fact. Or, I should say, she has her dream. She's had it for sixteen years. A dream she's worked very hard to attain. And who are we, you and I, to take that dream away from her? I'm sure that she'd rather die than lose that dream. And that's the whole story."

After that, she got back to her feet and went back outside to stare at the fog. She cleared her throat and in her wonderful light tenor voice began to sing again:

'N cielo se so' arrucchiate ciento stelle
tutte pe' sta' a senti' chesta canzone,
aggio 'ntiso 'e parla' li ttre cchiú belle,
dicevano: 'nce tene passione . . .

(In the sky a hundred stars have gathered
All there to listen to my song.
I've heard the three most beautiful stars talking,
And they said: "His passion is real!")

She turned around and saw Maione standing there, mouth hanging open. She shyly put a hand in front of her mouth, coquettishly covering the laugh that emerged, resembling nothing so much as a horse's neigh: "I dearly love to sing," she said. "But I only sing here, on my secret little balcony. You wouldn't have thought it, would you? All the things you don't know about me. Some time I'll have to give a nice little private lesson. *Arrivederci*, Brigadie'. And if we don't talk before then, have a happy end and a happy beginning."

THE FOG

And then, Brigadie', there's the fact of this fog.

Up till now, perhaps, we were fighting but equally matched, don't you think? You were searching, and I was hiding. And you were stumbling around in the dark; you need to know something to find it. What you had received, and what the commissario had received, were just scattered words without meaning.

And the idea of bringing everyone into Fedora's dressing room, what sheer absurdity: as if sitting in the middle of all that bric-a-brac would make it possible to capture the meaning.

Instead, there was fog the whole time. A fog made up not of vapor, not water suspended in the air, but fragments, objects that served to construct an illusion of truth. Objects for pretending, the way she pretended.

Because Fedora pretended, Brigadie'. That's something you need to understand.

Obviously she did, you might say, after all, she was an actress. That was her job. But it's not obvious by any means, believe me. Generally speaking, if the artists' dreams arrive on the stage, it's only for a moment; then they get their feet back on firm ground. Instead, she used her talent and her beauty, because she was certainly talented and beautiful—no two ways about it, that much is certain—to befog people's minds.

Which is why this thing about the fog is so strange. Almost symbolic, really. It represents what Fedora did in life, and not only onstage: pumping smoke in people's eyes.

Take a woman, Brigadie'. A normal woman, one like all the rest. Give her a talent, the talent of make-believe, and give her the tools: the clothing, the makeup, the perfumes; striped stockings and high-heeled shoes. Cut her hair in a bob, put the most fashionable little cap on her head and a fur stole around her neck. Then watch her smile, with those dazzling white teeth that make your head spin just to look at them, or laugh with a voice that sounds like pearls falling onto the floor. A woman like that has no limits, Brigadie', let me tell you. If a woman like that wants a man, she'll just reach out and take him.

Yes, fog conceals the truth, but it doesn't change it. If you search carefully, it pops out in the end.

Instead, Fedora and people like her change the truth, and then some. Because they are the lie. Because they're smugglers of dreams.

A dream and a fog, my dear brigadier, each works in a different way. Dreams poison you, and fog convinces you. So I thought I could get away with it, make off scot-free, when we all woke up in that strange fog. I believed that it had descended around us specifically to conceal my dream, to save it.

It seemed like a good omen, that fog.

But you already know how it turned out. The fog wasn't enough, and I was forced to defend myself.

If Fedora was no longer among us, that was because I had chosen to make it so.

As if I were God, as if I were the Lord Almighty.

She was no longer among us, with her incessant charades, with the constant playacting that she introduced into everything she ever did. With her betrayal, in other words.

Because betrayal isn't just having a lover, Brigadie'. Betrayal is also allowing others to believe that you're one thing when you're actually another. It's a betrayal to be short and become tall. It's a betrayal to be pale and seem tanned. To be ordinary and appear beautiful.

Everything that women like Fedora do is a betrayal.

The venom they inject into your blood is a betrayal. Dreaming of possessing them is a betrayal. No longer looking at women at all is a betrayal.

When you betray and when you're betrayed, Brigadie', then you start to dream.

The reality that you have no longer pleases you, so you cherish your damned dream and you think you can conceal it.

And the fog helps you.

The problem is that, sooner or later, that fog is bound to lift.

And indeed that's what happened.

I realized that, with the new beginning, the turn of the year, my dream had dissolved, so I shot Commissario Ricciardi.

XXII

Ricciardi forced himself to collect his thoughts in order to organize the work that lay ahead, while waiting for Maione to start his shift around noon.

The brigadier was indispensable to him, and both men knew it, even though he behaved so unfailingly respectfully that he never crossed the boundary between their respective ranks. Actually, Ricciardi relied on his direct subordinate's good-natured, empathetic manners, knowing that with his instincts, Maione was capable of cutting through the emotions that made up murders; a gift that the commissario, an introverted man little inclined to shows of emotion, lacked entirely.

That morning, in the office, he was having difficulty concentrating, because Enrica's state of upset, which he had glimpsed the evening before through the window, continued to claw at his mind. What had happened? He would have to wait until the afternoon to find out, when he would see her at the appointment set for the narrow street that they had dubbed *Caminito*; until then, he'd only be able to formulate the vaguest of conjectures.

He didn't want her to suffer. The mere thought, the simple possibility brought with it a stab of pain that had hitherto been unknown to him: a sort of latent migraine, like a disagreeable toothache, something impossible to ignore, which kept him from paying attention to anything else, unless it was with the greatest of effort.

If you truly loved her, he told himself for the umpteenth

time, you should let het go. You should blow up every obstacle into outsized barriers, dream up new ones, choose never to see her again. Make her believe that you have another woman in your heart. Lie to her, and even to yourself. Lie for her own good.

He looked out the window. How strange, to see fog in the city. In the Cilento mountains where he had been raised, that was a common, recurring phenomenon. The sudden transition from the heat of the sun to the chill of the night gave long hours to that creeping mist, as it slowly rose from the countryside and enveloped the world in a breathless silence. He remembered that, as a child, when he looked out the large picture windows of the castle where he lived with his mother, he liked to imagine fantastic animals hunched in the mists and great battles between armies of knights and hordes of dragons. Fog is a wonderful sheet to accommodate dreams.

The ghostly images of the dead, however, still reached him even through that compact white curtain. In particular, a man who had been run over just two days earlier by a truck as he was distractedly crossing the street. Nearly sliced in two by the wheels of the vehicle, he continued leafing through documents, repeating these words: *Thirty-five plus three makes thirty-eight, plus seven makes forty-five. Thirty-five plus three makes thirty-eight, plus seven makes forty-five.*

Your accounts were all straight, Ricciardi told him silently. I wonder if that was money you were hoping to collect or promising to pay. In either case, you won't be able to take care of that transaction. For you, there will be no new year.

So these are my friends, he thought to himself, the merry band with whom I'll spend the rest of my life: I'll never be able to free myself of this madness. It will hunker down there, murmuring its stories of death and damnation to me for all time.

He tried to review the evidence that he'd assembled concerning the murder of Fedora Marra. He could sense a persistent sour note in the chorus of voices that he'd listened to thus far, but he couldn't have pinned down exactly which one it was. He was certain that the woman had had a relationship with someone at the Teatro Splendor. Proof of the fact was the note that he'd found in the pocket of the robe in the dressing room. He wondered when Fedora had meant to deliver it to the intended recipient, and whether she'd planned to do so in person or by means of someone else.

As he was following that line of reasoning, the door swung open and Deputy Chief Garzo burst into the room, accompanied by Ponte.

"Ah, Ricciardi, so you're here. Excellent, I just wanted a quick confab with you."

The commissario turned, slowly, and stared at him, expressionless.

"*Buongiorno*, sir. Forgive me, I didn't hear you knock. Perhaps I was lost in thought."

His superior officer's face reddened ever so slightly. Behind Garzo, Ponte coughed as he stared at the wall.

"And yet I'm sure I knocked," Garzo lied. "Whatever the case, I'm here for some clarifications about the Fedora Marra case. No matter where you turn, no one's talking about anything else. Yesterday, for instance, at the Piscitelli residence, where I was attending a tea party, they told me that we were supposedly skeptical about how things had actually gone. They even told me about witness interviews held during the performance. An actor supposedly revealed these details to friends of his, one of whom brought the news directly to the marchesa."

Ricciardi nodded, calmly.

"That is correct, sir. As I had previously advised you, I will be moving forward with discretion . . ."

The deputy chief halted him with a brusque hand gesture.

"And this would be your concept of discretion, Ricciardi?

Hunkering down in the theater, in the middle of a performance, and questioning the artists? Are we trying to get the
whole city to laugh at us behind our backs? I can already see
the banner headlines: *Backstage Investigation. The Police
Attend the Revue, Surrounded by Actors and Dancers.*"

The commissario sighed.

"Sir, events are anything but clear-cut. I need to continue
my . . ."

The other man turned a meaningful eye toward Ponte, who
was just now gazing fixedly at the ceiling, and once again interrupted Ricciardi: "What on earth is there about this case that
you find unclear, damn it to hell? Gelmi shot his wife in front
of a theater full of people. What does a person have to do
before we can ship him off to prison on charges of murder?
Chew off bites of the victim until they've been devoured
whole?"

Ricciardi fell silent, gazing impassively. He knew by bitter
experience that this was the best possible tactic. Garzo, red in
the face, shouted: "I'm besieged by a tidal wave of anxious
questions from the city's collective aristocracy. Would you be
so kind as to tell me how you intend to proceed? Or must I go
on pretending to know what's going on, and hiding behind a
shield of investigative confidentiality?"

The commissario pretended to display an awed admiration.

"My heartfelt compliments, sir. You've identified the most
appropriate attitude: this is a sensitive case and it demands a
special duty of secrecy."

The deputy chief hesitated ever so slightly: "Yes,
but . . . How exactly is it that you're proceeding?"

Ricciardi decided to feed the bureaucrat's curiosity with a
few crumbs of information; after all, he felt he owed it to him.

"It would appear that Marra was conducting an affair. We
have a number of pieces of evidence that confirm the fact.
This, as you can well understand, might constitute a motive.

Even if Gelmi was lying, and no one had introduced the fatal bullet into the magazine without his knowledge, the premeditation would have quite a different probatory weight."

The other man's eyes bulged and a lascivious smile appeared on his lips.

"Seriously? Marra was having an affair? So Gelmi was a cuckold! And with whom was she cheating on him? There are people who would pay good money for the details!"

The commissario struggled to conceal his disgust.

"We don't know that yet, but as soon as we are able to determine it, and I feel quite confident that we'll succeed quite soon, I'll inform you."

Garzo seemed satisfied. Ponte's sigh of relief, as he stood studiously examining the floor, practically echoed through the room.

"All right, all right. Just keep on working then, in that case. And make sure that you keep me posted on even the slightest development. In any case, and this bears repeating, in any case, you absolutely must complete your investigation by the end of the day tomorrow. I cannot justify, in my monthly report to the ministry, the continuation from one year to the next of an investigation that features such an obvious perpetrator."

"Certainly, sir. We are in agreement."

Garzo's neat little mustache twitched in a gossipy little jerk.

"It was obvious that a woman like Fedora had to have a lover. Gelmi was too old for her. Have a good day, Ricciardi. Come, Ponte, we're late for my espresso."

XXIII

The New Year's Eve dinner, as it was understood in that city, refused to penetrate into Nelide's mind.

During the far-too-short period in which her aunt, Zi' Rosa, had instructed her, bestowing lessons from the elevated perch of her many years as a native of Cilento in the big city, the matter of the Christmas festivities had never yet been addressed. And so the young woman had been forced to integrate the limited knowledge she had learned directly from her aunt with what she'd been able to pick up by observing local customs. And that hadn't been a simple matter, because she was wary by nature and really not well disposed toward change, especially when that meant varying the traditions of which she considered herself an intransigent guardian.

She took one last look at the apartment, sternly gauging its cleanliness and tidiness, which could only be described as absolute; then she picked up her shopping bag and keys.

On her way out of the apartment, she passed by the mirror near the front door, but she didn't deign to give her reflected image so much as a glance. And in fact, there was nothing to admire: Nelide was ugly. She had a stout, muscular body, her shoulders were powerful and her pelvis was broad, her hands were large, rough, and strong, her face was square. The perennially furrowed brow was crossed from one side to the other by a single eyebrow, dense and thick, beneath which darted small, mistrustful eyes; her nose was large and her lips were narrow. Her hair was coarse, kinky, and bristly, of a vague and unidentifiable color, pulled back with considerable effort beneath the lashings of an immaculately clean bonnet. Her figure attracted the curiosity and derision of the neighborhood women, but she was supremely indifferent to the fact, and her pride was by no means offended thereby.

She shut and locked the door behind her, double-checking more than once to ensure that it was tightly closed. She didn't trust the building's doorman and she feared that some evildoer might venture downstairs from the upper stories and slip into the apartment while she was out; she considered herself to be in charge of security.

Nelide knew the mission with which she'd been entrusted: see to the well-being and safety of the young master, the Baron of Malomonte. That was the task for which she'd been raised by her family, chosen from amongst all her sisters and female cousinage, and trained by Zi' Rosa. And she had dedicated herself to that task, and that task alone.

This was by no means a minor responsibility for a young woman who had just turned eighteen, in silence and without any celebration. Aside from her household tasks, it was her responsibility to tend to the care and safety of a man who would otherwise neglect the well-being of his person. Aside from these daily matters, there was a more complicated aspect: it was up to her to keep a watchful eye lest sharecroppers, tenant farmers, and assorted peasants take advantage of the Ricciardi family's vast fortune and estates, since this immense wealth was a concern to which the young master devoted interest and attention roughly comparable to the zeal he lavished on his own self-care, that is to say, practically zero.

Rosa had devoted her entire life to these duties, and when she had sensed the end drawing near, she had summoned her niece to her side to begin to impart the necessary instruction and training. It hadn't taken all that long, the only topic not yet covered had been city life: all the rest was material Nelide had studied practically from the day of her birth, and her aunt, so similar to Nelide that they easily could have been taken for mother and daughter, knew it very well because she'd been monitoring her growth all through the years.

But assimilating the customs of that irrational metropolis had proved to be far more complex than she'd imagined. The young woman simply couldn't make heads nor tails of the place. Everyone was constantly laughing or singing or crying or dancing or screaming. You'd hear all manners of noise, even at night. No one ever seemed to shut up. No one ever minded their own business. No one ever stopped eavesdropping, gossiping, and chattering away about other people. The diametric opposite of her country home, where no one confided a thing, not even with parents or siblings, and it was common practice to go for days on end without uttering a word. Where she came from, they were hard workers.

But the Baron of Malomonte's housekeeper needed to know how to adapt. And also how to understand what might not be obvious to the untrained eye. That meant poking her nose into her fellow human beings' business, and to an even greater extent, the private affairs of the man she was caring for. First of all, of course, to anticipate his needs; but also, when warranted, to give fate a gentle, indispensable shove forward, steering it toward the Good and the Better.

Rosa had told her in great detail about the haberdasher's daughter, a young woman who lived in the building across the street; as well as the danger posed by the Other Woman, the Roman interloper too beautiful to inspire trust and to be a wife and mother. Rosa had expressed her decided preference for that young woman, perhaps not notably comely but certainly trustworthy, endowed with broad hips and a gracious bosom beneath her modest garments; most important of all, she was deeply and sincerely in love with the baron.

She had also told Nelide that Ricciardi returned the young

woman's sentiment but that, due to who knows what benighted enchantment, he couldn't seem to bring himself to take the proper steps: the propagation of the Ricciardi di Malomonte family line was at risk, and that threat must be neutralized. Rosa had tried to establish an acquaintance with Enrica and had almost turned it into a friendship. But then, too soon, she had died.

The new development of recent days was that the two of them had begun to see each other again. Nelide, who missed not a single detail, had noticed it, discreetly spying on the messages and gestures that they exchanged through the windows, convinced that she hadn't noticed a thing. Everything's fine, then, Zi' Ro': we need only wait for matters to take their course.

But now she had to solve the problem of New Year's Eve. Nelide didn't want Ricciardi to feel different among the other denizens of the city, but she also cared deeply about ensuring that the traditions of Cilento were observed. Her aunt had been clear and peremptory on this point.

In Cilento, New Year's wasn't a time of great festivities: the countryside allowed for no break in work, no frivolous distractions, because everyone knew they'd be going back to work the next day. There were a few customs, however, that distinguished the day. Children would venture out in a group, armed with the *piroccola*, a heather-wood cane, and knock at the doors of the village. They would dutifully be given white figs to eat that evening around the fire; there were doggerel rhymes equally dutifully memorized and recited in recognition of the gift; the Holy Mass and the *fòcara*, a dance in the piazza around a bonfire kindled with *ciòppari*, large logs harvested in the woods during the week before Christmas.

Then, on the first day of the new year, they would pay calls on the old people, deferentially kissing their hands, and receiving as a reward for that show of respect a dollop of sheep's milk ricotta or perhaps a sweet, hard biscotto or two.

In short, Nelide recalled only the customs that affected youngsters.

Concerning adults, on the other hand, there wasn't much to say: the good tablecloth, the aged olive oil, the driest firewood for the fried foods: the kind of things simple people knew about. There was no special ceremony to usher in the new year.

But there were a few items that no self-respecting Cilento table could lack. Alongside the broccoli, the *cinguli cu' l'alici* (anchovy fritters), the *baccalà fritto* (fried salt cod filets), the *zeppulelle salate* (savory zeppole), and the *nocche dolci* (sugary bow tie cookies) which Nelide had already prepared for the young master, there was no getting around the New Year's Eve mainstay, the nine fruits and nuts to hit the right note for the meal, a must in terms of ensuring good fortune in the coming year.

After replying to the concierge's hostile nod with a murderous glare, the young woman found herself walking down the main street. The fog, which bewildered the other pedestrians, only comforted her: she was used to fog, she didn't find it to be an unusual phenomenon, and there was no danger that she might get lost. She walked past the line of shops, without bothering to reply to the calls of the shopkeepers from their front doors trying to attract customers, terrified as they were of being left with too much merchandise in their shops at the end of the holidays, and then having to sell everything at a sharp discount in order to make back their initial investment, at least. She reached the small neighborhood street market, with the stands all arranged in a circle in the little piazza. She slowed down, narrowing her eyes to identify the fruit and vegetable stand.

She spotted one stand surrounded by a sizable crowd of women laughing and elbowing each other in the ribs. That stand belonged to Tanino, known as *'o Sarracino*—the Saracen—for his amber complexion. Tanino seemed to have stepped right out of the silver screen: curly black locks framed a perfect face, his eyes so dark they seemed carved from sparkling onyx, and his broad smile displayed two rows of teeth as white as an angel's wings. Cheerful and witty, endowed with a wonderful voice, he warbled love songs to satisfy his female customers' requests: he inhabited their dreams, whether married or unwed. He was the idol of that city quarter.

As usual, Nelide steered clear. She thought it pointless to stand in line to purchase products that she could find, identical, at the stand of Peppeniello, the elderly vendor who'd had the bad luck to find himself working side by side with this fearsome competitor. What's more, who knows why, every time she'd purchased her grocery needs from the handsome vegetable vendor, he'd immediately ignored all his other customers and devoted himself solely to her with such adoration that he triggered the laughter of all the women present, convinced that this must be a refined mode of mockery, aimed at making Nelide an object of fun. This behavior didn't offend or bother Nelide in and of itself. After all, to her mind both Tanino and the women shoppers of the market were as dust beneath her feet, or even less than that. The real point was that it was a waste of her time: and that was something she wasn't willing to accept. She had work to do.

And so, taking advantage of the fog and her own diminutive stature, she ventured over to Peppeniello's stand, while Tanino entertained his audience by declaiming the usefulness of the unaccustomed atmospheric phenomenon thanks to which he would be able to slip, unseen, into the secret boudoirs of his grateful female lovers.

Without deigning to offer the elderly street vendor a greeting and after evaluating the fruit on display with a glance, the young woman decisively announced her order, partly in dialect: "Oranges, three. Tangerines, four. Walnuts and *nucelle*, almonds, *ficusecche*, chestnuts, pine nuts, and two *cachisse*."

Peppeniello began to lay out all the items requested on his scale, but suddenly he stopped, mortified.

"Signori', forgive me, I have no pine nuts. I ran out of them at Christmas."

This was no minor issue. There were nine types of fruit to propitiate the new year. Nine, not eight. And the pine nuts, which symbolized incense, the gift brought by Balthasar, one of the Three Kings, to Baby Jesus in his manger, were the last to be consumed.

The young woman furrowed her unibrow. In that useless little market that seemed to stock all sorts of nonsense, actual necessities were not to be had. A voice rang out, emanating its message, in a sweet but stentorian tone, through the dense fog: "Lovely Signorina, why do you always take your trade to my competition? Come shop at Tanino and you'll find everything you need. And when I say everything, I mean everything, you follow me?"

The women within earshot all laughed at the salty wise-crack, tilting their heads in Nelide's direction. And the young woman turned and retorted, flatly: "*Non te fa' caca' da i mosche.* So you have pine nuts, do you?"

The proverb in dialect meant, "Don't think you're such hot stuff," but the words—literally, "Don't let the flies shit on you"—sounded like a slap in the face, dampening the smile of the prince of street vendors.

"I . . . pine nuts? No, Signorina, I'm afraid I don't . . ."

The young woman shrugged her shoulders.

"*La votte raje lu vino ca tene,*" she murmured under her breath. This basically meant: the barrel can only give the wine it contains; and you have nothing.

Tanino blushed, and shot back, addressing the young woman's back as she turned to go: "Let it never be said,

Signorina, that 'o Sarracino has left a customer wanting for more! I know where you live! I'll bring them to your doorstep, the pine nuts you've asked for!"

An attractive brunette weighed in: "Oooh, Tani', bring some for me, too. I guarantee I'll give you a New Year's Eve with a bang, forget about the ordinary fireworks."

There was a general burst of laughter, but Tanino continued to stare seriously at the stout back that was just then vanishing into the fog.

Suddenly he had lost any desire to joke around.

XXIV

In view of the pressure being levied by Garzo, Ricciardi decided to wait no longer for Maione's arrival, but instead continue his investigation.

He wanted to go to Gelmi's home, to take a look at the place where the victim and her husband had spent their daily lives, even if he had no real hope of finding any significant clues there.

He searched for the address on the report that had been drawn up when the actor was arrested and calculated that it would take him roughly a twenty-minute walk to reach the place. He didn't mind the prospect, there was a shortage of fresh air in the office.

The fog shrouded him the minute he set foot outside the main entrance to police headquarters, and he found himself in a silent world, where voices and sounds arrived muffled, and people seemed to have suddenly disappeared. He proceeded down the street, surrounded by the phantoms of the dead and the spectral figures of the living as they appeared before him without warning. The smell of woodsmoke, car engines, horses, and rotting food left unsold now that the holidays were coming to an end had become heavy and redolent, permeating the air.

The commissario believed that once he got down to the water's edge, that uniform mantle of mist would thin and lift, but instead it persisted dense and unbroken. As a result he came close to overshooting his destination, a venerable old palazzo on the Riviera di Chiaia. He identified himself to the doorman, a stern man, garbed in livery, who also seemed to have been cast, to perfection, in a dramatic role. Ricciardi climbed the broad and majestic stone staircase, built for the use of dignitaries of the Spanish court, and once he reached the third floor he stopped before a tall and ornately carved wooden door. On the brass plaque, elaborate letters spelled the surname "Gelmi." He knocked and waited.

After a short wait, a skinny and nearly bald male servant answered the door. The man's thin, wrinkled neck protruded from the collar of an oversized shirt.

The policeman introduced himself and stated his rank. The servant showed no sign of surprise, made a bow, and ushered him indoors.

The waiting room was large and luxuriously furnished and decorated, but the result was chilly and impersonal. The commissario had the distinct impression that he was in a place used for official functions and receptions far more than a lived-in home. That initial impression was further confirmed by the drawing room where sofas and armchairs, mirrors, items made of brass and gilded wood were displayed as if in a museum or a shop. The only features that conveyed even a bit of warmth were the photographs of Michelangelo, scattered all over the room, and portraying him and him alone, onstage and elsewhere, looking serious or posing next to fellow theater people and celebrities. In all those photographs, there wasn't a trace of his wife.

The servant murmured: "If I may, I'll go and summon the lady of the house."

With another bow, the man withdrew before Ricciardi had a chance to ask who the lady of the house might be.

A few moments went by before a middle-aged woman, tall, austere, and dressed in black, made her entrance into the room. Ricciardi had the impression that he'd met her before, and recently. It was an intense and vivid recollection, but the commissario couldn't seem to recall when or where.

The woman stepped forward, staring him in the eye, and extended her hand.

"*Buongiorno*," she said. "I'm Marianna Gelmi."

Ricciardi realized at that instant that he'd been deceived: the face before him was an incredible feminine version of the features of Michelangelo. She seemed to guess his thoughts, and a faint, sad smile danced over her lips.

"I know, we resemble each other closely; we're twins and our parents even gave us names with the same initials."

She invited Ricciardi to come in and make himself comfortable, and then sat down facing him. Then she spoke to her servant: "Achille, bring us some coffee, if you please. And two glasses of water. This fog is making me thirsty, though who knows why."

The commissario cleared his throat.

"I apologize, I had no idea that anyone else lived here, otherwise I would have phoned ahead. I'm investigating the events at the Teatro Splendor and I meant this as nothing more than a walk around the premises."

Marianna smiled again.

"Why, is there still anything to clear up, Commissa'? Michelangelo shot that woman. Period."

Her tone of voice wasn't lost on Ricciardi, who looked around.

"Do you live here, Signora?"

"No, I live upstairs. Once this was a single home, and it was owned by my family; but then we split it up. I was married before my brother; I've been a widow for five years now. Michelangelo and his wife lived here when they weren't away performing elsewhere."

This was the second time that Gelmi's sister had chosen not to use her sister-in-law's name. Ricciardi went back to studying the shelves and dressers covered with photographs of the actor and noticed several unmistakable empty spaces. Marianna once again guessed at the policeman's thoughts.

"Yes, I removed them, I couldn't stand to look at them. That woman, damn her even now that she's dead, was his ruin."

The commissario took the demitasse of espresso handed him by the servant and asked: "Why do you say that?"

The woman stood up, took a few steps toward the large window, and stood there, staring at the wall of fog.

"As you can see for yourself, Commissario, we were born into prosperity. And my father, had he not died too soon, would never have allowed Michelangelo to become an actor. That's not a world befitting our station. Oh, don't misunderstand me, my brother has a laudable talent, and he's earned handsomely by it: but to be the subject of vulgar chatter, the talk of the town without privacy or respect, is an affront to our honor. I've told him so a thousand times, but he's deaf to my words. He's had this passion since he was a child, and he's refused to desist."

Ricciardi ventured: "But instead his wife . . ."

Marianna's head snapped around.

"She's always been a good-for nothing trollop; she was a servant to start with and a servant is what she remains. I've never understood why Michelangelo, who is a genuine aristocrat, would ever have wanted to marry her."

"So you weren't on speaking terms with Marra?"

"No, Commissario, that's not the case. I tried to stay on speaking terms with her, because if I hadn't I would have been forced to give up all ties with my brother, as well. Moreover, I have to admit that, strictly speaking in formal terms, Fedora's behavior has always been impeccable. She was an actress, she knew how to perform a role, and with me she played the part of an affectionate sister-in-law."

"If that's the case, then why do you talk about her in these terms?"

Marianna sat down again.

"What happened makes everything clear, Commissario. Starting with the very reason that Michelangelo started drinking, something he'd never done in the past. And it explains why, in spite of the fact that she had offers of work coming in from all directions, she'd insisted on keeping the revue operating and staying here in this city for so long, in a medium-sized theater."

"What do you mean?"

In the eyes of Marianna Gelmi, an ironic gleam flashed, and Ricciardi felt as if he was looking at Michelangelo Gelmi himself, acting in women's clothing.

"She was cheating on him, I'm quite certain of it; I had talked to him about it, and he knew it, too. But he never wanted to delve too deep, he didn't seem interested in finding out the truth. He was just willing to settle for having her at his side, accepting her help in that damned line of work that utterly ruined him."

The policeman set down the demitasse and leaned forward.

"Did your brother have any suspicions as to who the other man might have been?"

She shook her head decisively.

"No, if he had, he would have been unable to go on pretending he knew nothing. He would have been forced to send her away. There are limits, you know. Our family name has already been bandied about to a fare-thee-well on account of that profession, the refuge of rogues and prostitutes. Michelangelo had no idea with whom Fedora was cheating on him; he was just afraid she might leave him."

The commissario half shut his eyes, pensively.

"But this doesn't fit with the murder. If he was afraid he might lose her, then why would he have killed her? It makes no sense."

Marianna shrugged her shoulders.

"Perhaps he just couldn't take it anymore. Or maybe she had made up her mind to leave him. Or else liquor might finally have fogged his mind. There are a thousand possible explanations."

Ricciardi nodded, thinking deeply.

"When is the last time you saw them?"

"Three days ago, when I came back from the town in the province of Benevento where my poor late husband is buried. Michelangelo was sad, but calm. I can't imagine how the situation could have deteriorated so sharply as to drive him to that act."

The commissario pondered whether or not to tell her about her brother's version of events, and specifically his claim that someone must have slipped the bullet into the pistol without his knowledge. In the end, he decided to keep that detail to himself. He was afraid he might sow seeds of hope that were altogether likely to prove unfounded.

He stood up and asked his host to accompany him on a rapid tour of the apartment. The woman nodded, stiffly, and led the way.

Like the front hall and the drawing room, the other rooms were impersonal and felt as if they'd never actually been lived in. The only two exceptions were the bedrooms, where husband and wife slept separately. Marianna Gelmi smirked, as if to emphasize what she had said previously concerning relations between the husband and wife.

In Fedora's bedroom, there reigned the same cheerful disorder that he'd seen in her dressing room. Garishly hued shoes and outfits were piled up everywhere; articles of toiletry crowded shelves, tables, dressers, and even the floor. There was such a vivid impression of vitality that once again Ricciardi could easily imagine that the actress was on the verge of returning at any minute.

Marianna hissed: "I must remind Achille to get rid of all these possessions of that hussy. I don't want the slightest trace of her to remain in the home where my mother once lived."

Michelangelo's room was very different. The single mattress indicated that he was the one who had moved out. The furnishings were spartan: a writing desk, a chair, a lamp, and a few books. No articles of clothing scattered around the room; the bed, too, was neatly made.

With a hint of pride, Marianna said: "You see, Commissario? Tidiness, cleanliness. My brother was a soldier to the bottom of his soul. You know that he was a captain in the Italian army and a war hero, right? He fought on the Piave in 1918. He was decorated, just look."

She pointed at a picture frame that contained a medal, complete with ribbon. Next to it stood several other framed photographs; one portrayed a group of soldiers, at the center of which Gelmi enjoyed pride of place, young and proud, his face serious, his fingers in his belt, his helmet on his head. At his side, a skinny man held two rifles and gazed at him devotedly.

The woman continued: "The Gelmi family has a long military tradition. My father was a colonel, and he would have liked to see Michelangelo follow in his footsteps. But my brother refused and chose his own road to ruin. My God, the shame of it. The shame."

Ricciardi studied the picture hanging on the wall. He thought about Marianna, so similar to her twin brother and so very different from him. And about Michelangelo as a young officer, so much the same as he was now, and so very different.

The commissario pondered the resemblances.

XXV

M aione arrived out of breath at police headquarters, a few minutes late, and stuck his head in the door of Ricciardi's office.

"Apologies, Commissa'. But have you seen the fog?"

His superior officer gestured for him to have a seat.

"Yes, but let's not let it get to our heads. Garzo told us that we either find some evidence by tomorrow, when the old year ends, or he won't be able to authorize us to continue with the investigation. And I still have my doubts, after having visited Gelmi's home."

Maione removed his hat and mopped his brow with his handkerchief.

"Really? And why is that?"

Ricciardi told Maione, with a rich assortment of details, about his visit to the home of the two actors and his meeting with Michelangelo's twin sister.

When he was done, the brigadier asked him: "So his sister, too, is convinced she was cheating on him. For that matter, we have the love letter. The important thing now is to figure out whether her husband knew who it was she was cheating on him with. That's the important thing, isn't it?"

"Exactly. Because, if he's the guilty party, and everything certainly points to that conclusion, he also wanted to send a message to someone. But if he's innocent, then the real killer had an interest in making sure that Fedora died and that Gelmi was accused of her murder. There are no other explanations."

Maione threw both arms wide.

"So what are we going to do, Commissa'?"

"Phone ahead and tell them to have the prisoner available for an interview. Let's go talk to him again."

Immersed in the fog, the prison of Poggioreale was even more frightful than usual.

Grim and gray, with watchtowers lost in the mist, it looked like nothing so much as a castle concealing obscure and lurking forces. And the sensation was only amplified by the shouts from the cells.

The guards led Ricciardi and Maione into a room where there were two wooden benches, facing each other. After a few minutes' wait, the prisoner appeared, accompanied by a pair of gendarmes. His wrists were shackled and he could barely stand upright. Looking weary and disordered, his eyes gazing into the middle distance, he seemed even older than the day before. The minute he recognized the policemen, he started weeping, heaving long, silent sobs.

The commissario asked: "Gelmi, have you changed your mind, or do you confirm your version of events?"

"It wasn't me, Commissario. And I'm increasingly convinced that it wasn't a tragic twist of fate, because, as I told you, I own only blank shells, no live ammunition. I haven't fired a gun to kill since the years of the Great War."

Ricciardi stared at him intensely.

"Listen carefully, we don't have much time. I have to know whether you were aware of your wife having an affair with anyone else."

The man said nothing and instinctively turned to look at the guards standing at either side of him.

Maione piled on: "This isn't the time to be ashamed about what other people might think, Gelmi."

The actor stammered: "I . . . but what does that have to do

with anything? Why aren't you trying to find whoever managed to sneak into my dressing room and . . ."

Ricciardi broke in: "I asked you a question. Please answer it."

The other man said nothing for a long time. Then he said: "There was something in her . . . I knew her well. I loved her, and when you love a person, you learn how to sense their mood, their emotional state, even from as little as a single glance or their tone of voice. And then if you work together . . . she was happy, full of a thirst for life. I'm sure that she was in love, but I don't know if she was having an affair, though I think she was."

The commissario persisted: "And did the fact that the members of the troupe or your sister might find out about it bother you?"

The man dropped his eyes, continuing to weep.

"No, Commissario, I didn't care, I only feared losing her; that it was only a matter of time, that from one moment to the next I might find her letter of farewell, never again to see her in this life. That is what drove me to desperation." He dried his eyes, and his shackles emitted a sinister clang. Then he went on: "You mention Marianna, so you've been to my home. You must have noticed that we . . . that Fedora and I were no longer sleeping together. As long as I could keep her with me, I'd told her that she could have a life of her own, that she wasn't obligated to . . . But she always respected me. She never fed so much as a tidbit to the gossips and backstabbers, those who maintained that sooner or later our differences in age, her renown, her success and my decline would add up to a final reckoning. I had no motive for killing her."

Ricciardi ran a hand over his forehead, as if warding away an evil thought.

"Listen to me, Gelmi. You went to war, am I right? Are you still in contact with any of your old fellow veterans?"

The actor blinked his eyes rapidly, stunned by that sudden change of topic. Maione, too, stared at his superior officer, looking surprised. He had no idea what Ricciardi was driving at.

"Yes, Commissario. That's an experience you never forget. Once you've shared life in the trenches with someone, it's a bond you never break. I'd started my military career, but precisely because of the war I realized it wasn't the path for me . . . I wasn't born to kill people. They were terrible months and years. We have a veterans association; we exchange letters, and every once in a while, we get together."

Ricciardi asked: "And if some former comrade needs help, can he reach out to an old brother in arms?"

Gelmi's gaze shifted from Ricciardi to Maione, as if asking for clarification about the strange twist that the questioning was taking.

"Well, I myself have helped many of my soldiers and their children to find work. And I've helped them out economically, as well, in cases of dire need. I haven't shirked that duty. Forgive me, Commissario, but I confess that I don't understand why . . ."

Ricciardi ignored him.

"No, instead, listen. Tell me: Did you leave the Beretta you fired there in the theater, or did you take it home? I don't know, to clean it, or else to . . ."

Gelmi replied without hesitation: "I would take it home with me, along with my dirty clothing to wash; I never let it out of my possession. I'm not so naïve as to leave a firearm behind in a dressing room."

Maione asked, in a low voice: "So, when you're not at the theater and you're away from home, then the pistol remains in your bedroom, doesn't it? Available to anyone."

The other man reacted, decisively: "No one enters my bedroom, Brigadier. I take care of keeping it clean and tidy myself, it's a custom that I've kept ever since my time in the military. And let me repeat that I load my pistol in the theater, before the performance: five shots plus one in the chamber. If there had already been a bullet in the clip, I would have noticed."

The commissario stood up.

"Gelmi, I can't state that I believe you, at least not yet. But certain probatory elements in our possession do tend to fit with different dynamics than those that would appear to be more obvious, namely that you shot her out of simple, human jealousy. And so I intend to continue investigating in that direction."

The actor got to his feet, with some effort.

"Commissario, I realize clearly that all appearances are against me. And I appreciate what you're saying. It would be so much easier to just decide that an older husband, an actor at the sunset of his career, a Pygmalion who has lost control of his own creation and who envies her success, had decided to put an end to their relationship in this manner. And I even have to admit that if I never did it, it's only because I would never be capable of killing someone in cold blood, not even if I'd been insulted in some unacceptable manner. And Fedora never insulted me, nor could she ever have insulted or offended me in that way."

Maione coughed and looked up at the ceiling. Gelmi took it as an expression of mockery and upbraided the policeman.

"Yes, Brigadie'. She wouldn't have done it. She no longer loved me, that's true; and perhaps there wasn't love even at the beginning. But she respected me, and she was grateful to me. Fedora was well aware that without me, she would have remained one of the many women willing to do anything for success, that she wouldn't have gotten anywhere if she hadn't met someone who could see the talent as well as the beauty."

He went back to staring at Ricciardi.

"I help, I don't kill. Ask around: the world we work in is a terrible place, full of vicious gossip, but no one has anything bad to say about me. Everyone's loyal to me, because I do only good."

Before the guards took him away, he murmured: "If I'd shot Fedora, Commissario, it wouldn't have been the only fatal gunshot. There would have been a second bullet, and it would have been for me."

XXVI

L ivia sat waiting in her living room, staring out at the fog. She had her hat in her gloved hands and was ready to go out.

Her posture betrayed nervousness; her back was rigid, her feet were neatly aligned, her fingers were tormenting the hem of her hat. In contrast to her usual attire, she wore a gray skirt suit with a simple cut, trimmed in black fur, that did nothing to enhance her natural allure. The appointment for which she was about to leave was devoid of charm or gallantry.

She had been contacted in the usual way: the evening before, as she was returning home, she'd found an envelope awaiting her. Inside was a sheet of paper on which was written only the number 14. That represented a time: 1400 hours, or two in the afternoon, when she would be expected to begin walking toward Monteoliveto, remaining on the opposite sidewalk from the direction of traffic along Via Toledo.

At the first strike of the chime from the wall clock, she stood up and walked toward the door. Her housekeeper glanced at her with a look of bafflement and murmured a farewell, to which Livia made no response. In the courtyard, the chauffeur, Arturo, leaned against the car, smoking a cigarette. He stood straight the instant he saw her, ready to open the passenger door for her. She shook her head and pointed toward the main street door. The look of surprise on the man's face followed her until she vanished out onto the street.

Cautiously, the woman crossed the street. She headed off,

wondering as she walked how he would be able to spot her in the heavy fog. After less than a minute a medium-sized black automobile pulled over and a hand opened the rear door from within. She slid onto the seat and the car pulled away.

In the front seat sat two men with hats and a nondescript appearance; the man at the wheel struck her as perhaps slightly younger than the other one. She didn't know them, and in fact they changed each time, and in any case no one had ever uttered a word to her on these occasions, not even to say a simple hello. Even though it did convey a degree of disquiet, that behavior, when all was said and done, also came as a relief. It was wiser by far not to engage people like that in casual conversation.

Like always, the drive was lengthy and the route made no sense. Livia often wondered why the trip had to last so long, only to come to an end in a location that, in some other circumstance, she might easily have reached on foot with an enjoyable stroll. She presumed that her chaperones must have some reason known to them, but it didn't concern her: so she never asked, and she certainly wasn't about to start today.

The driver proceeded slowly, focusing intently on staying in his lane; it seemed evident that he wasn't accustomed to such limited visibility. Suddenly an obstacle appeared in front of the vehicle and he was forced to brake suddenly; a curse in dialect escaped him. When it happened again, the older man turned ever so slightly and apologized for the inconvenience. Livia thought she detected a Roman accent, but chose not to inquire further, limiting herself to a small, tight smile of gratitude.

The city streamed past outside the windows, from time to time producing a scenic view, without color, like so many black-and-white photographs. Livia noticed that they were leaving the city proper, and that the sea was on their left. Posillipo, perhaps, or possibly Pozzuoli. She was not curious to know where the umpteenth meeting was going to take place. She just wanted it to be over soon.

She went back to pondering why and how she had landed herself in that situation. Perhaps it was due to her friendship with highly placed figures in the Fascist regime, or her tendency to comply with government measures and instructions, or even her love of the fatherland. Perhaps it was the gratitude she felt toward people who had helped and protected her in the past. Or else the fear she felt of the terrible violence that lurked beneath the surface, and which she certainly did not wish to encounter, even in passing.

Or else, more likely, love was to blame.

Her desperate love for someone who had made it perfectly clear that he was rejecting her, yet who still populated her dreams and her thoughts, like some incurable disease, like that fog, which insinuated itself into her soul through the pores in her skin.

Whatever the original reason might have been, Livia was now at the ball and she would be expected to dance. She had been transformed into a character in one of those pulp novels that were now so popular, or the protagonist of an operetta or a cheap, second-run movie. She was now some sort of spy.

She didn't like this role. It didn't amuse her, it imparted no shiver of excitement. She couldn't understand the dark underlying motivation or the secret ends. She didn't know how to operate. She felt false and insecure. And a recurring doubt tormented her: what would happen if she failed? Any error she committed could put many people at risk, or even someone she loved.

Someone she loved . . .

She felt as if she could glimpse two green eyes in the gray mantle of fog, precisely as the automobile lurched to a halt. Two green eyes that at the very thought transmitted to her a languid thrill even more intense than what she had experienced in the nights of passion she could remember. Two green eyes that had been hers once and once only, burning with fever and dreams. Two green eyes.

The older man stepped out to open the door for her, without uttering a word, his head bowed, displaying to her view only a section of chin beneath the brim of his hat. A precaution to ensure she wouldn't recognize him if, by some chance, they happened to cross paths in the future, in some other context. As if Livia weren't the first to hope she'd be forgotten once and for all by these individuals.

She found herself standing outside a low gate that led into a terrace where a number of small tables stood in array, all of them empty but one. She walked toward that one occupied table, and the sole occupant stood up, solicitously, offering her a chair.

"Good afternoon, Falco," she said.

The man executed a dutiful bow and sat down once again. The air, steeped in mist, seemed to shroud them both, isolating them from the world. It was damp, but not chilly. Being outdoors suited the nature of the conversation she was about to have: in and of itself, that wasn't unpleasant, but it could be dangerous in terms of final consequences.

Falco smiled. He appeared neither old nor young, neither tall nor short, neither fat nor skinny. He had facial features that appeared to have been designed at a drawing board to go unnoticed; his short gray hair was parted down the middle. Freshly shaved and scrupulously attired, he emanated a vague scent of lavender. Nothing about him stood out as exceptional, with the exception of his eyes, sharp and intelligent, ironic and chilly, and they impressed themselves in your mind, impossible to forget.

"Hello, Livia. You don't mind if we remain out here, do you? I'd chosen this place because out front, theoretically, you can glimpse the sea. I certainly didn't expect this weather, and by then it was too late to make any changes; you know the procedures." He broke off and gestured as if they understood each other, as if the woman was well acquainted with the mechanisms involved in designating the locations for that sort of meeting. Then he went on: "But the atmosphere is interesting, there's something symbolic about it. It makes me think of our conversations: we could compare them to a whisper in the fog. A lovely image, don't you agree?"

Livia felt uneasy.

"I have nothing for you, Falco. Manfred is very reserved and . . ."

The man interrupted her: "No names, I beg of you. Call him the German. What's come over you?"

He snapped his fingers and out of the nothingness there emerged, as if by enchantment, a waiter. He must have been acquainted with the secret nature of this meeting, because he kept his eyes downcast.

"An espresso, thanks."

Falco lifted forefinger and middle finger together, and the man vanished without a sound.

"I wasn't expecting any special news. Our friends in Berlin would surely have never entrusted a mission like this to the kind of naïve fool who'd reveal his intentions to the first woman who smiled at him, even if she were as dazzlingly splendid as you, madame. But progress, yes, that's I was expecting. And I continue to expect it. Instead, I notice difficulties."

Livia grew agitated and shifted on her chair.

"He's going through a difficult period. He tends to overdo it with the drinking, and he can be aggressive at times. I don't know how to . . ."

The waiter arrived with his tray, started to say something, and stopped abruptly. Falco nodded, as if confirming that the man had made the right decision. He waited until they were alone again and began to speak again: "Ah, yes, young Signorina Colombo. Her rejection of his proposal of marriage. I confess that it took us all a bit by surprise. And yet, sitting face to face with a woman like you, a man ought to see the bright side: the opening of a path toward a new opportunity."

Livia couldn't quite detect whether those words were meant ironically, and she replied harshly: "There is more than just beauty, Falco. Perhaps Manfr . . . Well, anyway, he might to sensitive to other considerations."

The man leaned forward and his voice suddenly cut like a very sharp knife: "Or else you're not putting in enough enthusiasm."

The words were unleashed like a straight-armed slap, so much so that Livia recoiled.

"Why, how dare you? Have you taken me for a . . . for an easy woman? I'm not going to reel men in at your command. I can make friends, I can wheedle information out of them, but I'm certainly not about to . . ."

Falco smiled at her, pretending that that exchange had never begun.

"I remember seeing you sing in *Un ballo in maschera*, in Parma; it must have been back in 1924. You, of course, played Ulrica. *'Re dell'abisso, affrettati, precipita per l'etra, senza librar la folgore il tetto mio penetra.'* Fantastic, just fantastic."

He'd lightly sung the beginning of the aria, directing the melody with his right hand. Livia noticed that he was in tune. Absurdly enough, she felt flattered.

"That was a lifetime ago."

Falco's eyes opened wide.

"Oh, no! You're still the most alluring woman I know. And believe me, I know plenty."

Livia shook her head.

"Perhaps not alluring enough. He's got his heart set on that young woman, and I . . ."

He replied coldly: "Listen to me carefully, Livia. The German has an assignment and he's carrying it out without any particular haste because his superiors haven't told him to hurry. But he's moving forward. His reports are being sent on a regular basis and they are subject to our examination; we have tracked down their route, shall we say."

Livia failed to see the meaning of that line of thought: "Then why should I . . ."

Falco ignored her.

"He's not a first-line agent in their intelligence service. But through him, the organization I work for has an interest in arranging for Berlin to receive a series of . . . let's just call them misdirections. It's therefore of vital importance that he be kept here in the city and that he continue his assignment: monitoring the operations of the Italian Royal Navy here in the port. Have I made myself clear?"

Livia nodded, and Falco adopted a gentler tone.

"Very good. Now, let's suppose that this gentleman should happen to be overwhelmed by an emotional crisis, personal sorrows, or even just a bad case of homesickness. He's not a full-fledged member of the forces that work in . . . in this field, which means that his superiors would have no difficulty replacing him with another, comparable individual. Do you follow me so far?"

She nodded her head.

Unexpectedly, Falco took her hand and squeezed it; Livia started at the gesture.

"Do you understand what that would mean to us? We'd have to start over from scratch: identify the new agent, gather intelligence on him and reconstruct his habits, interactions, and friendships; intercept his reports, which most assuredly would travel by different channels. It would take a great deal of time, and other information would filter back instead, causing enormous damage—and let me underscore the word 'enormous'—to our national military strategies."

Livia tried to wriggle free of that grip, which was hurting her, but Falco wouldn't loosen his hold on her, as he stared at her with his ice-cold eyes.

At last, and quite suddenly, he released her, and she yanked her hand back to her chest, in fright.

"What can I do about it? If he doesn't . . . If he isn't *interested*?"

Falco moved the empty demitasse in front of him and replied, amiably as if he were chatting about the weather: "There's more. Since we are determined to keep him at any and all costs, we're willing to remove the obstacles that might persuade him to return north to Bavaria or wherever the devil his little village full of barbarians is located."

Livia blinked her eyes even as she continued massaging her hand.

"What do you mean by that?"

Falco turned to gaze out at the unseen sea. Then he started to spin the demitasse around on the small tabletop, stopping it every time it came into contact with the sugar bowl.

"Let's imagine that the presence of our mutual friend in this land, usually so sunny and bright, depends upon the favors of a certain young woman. And let's further imagine that she, for who knows what incomprehensible reasons, happens instead to be in love with another man . . ."

Livia felt her heart pounding in her ears.

"Falco, you can't . . ."

The man went on, in a monotone, continuing to toy with the demitasse: "It's clear that the real stumbling block is that other man, don't you agree? If we got rid of him, perhaps the young woman would give more serious consideration to a lasting relationship with the German. If so, he'd remain here, continuing to pass information to us, without even knowing it, even before it reached his handlers back in Germany."

With a single sudden blow, he knocked the sugar bowl off the table; it landed on the pavement and shattered, scattering a fine snow across the floor of the terrace. Livia lurched in startlement.

Sweetly and persuasively, Falco ended his little talk: "It's not just for your own sake, for the sake of the fatherland, or for whatever reason you might think of, that you must succeed in this little mission. It's also in order to preserve the life of another shared acquaintance, who by the way happens to do a rather dangerous job and might very easily fall victim to some disagreeable mishap."

Livia felt tears well up in her eyes. Frustration, sorrow, and fear: who could say which of these emotions would be the first to emerge.

"Could you sink so low, Falco? To this level of cruelty, of infamy? What does he have to do with any of this? It's not his fault."

The man threw his head back and burst into a hearty laugh as if he'd just listened to the most amusing joke imaginable.

"Do you seriously imagine that we care one iota about the life of a small, useless policeman? Every day that man has dealings with unscrupulous criminals, individuals who are accustomed to handling knives and pistols. Who could accuse us of being at fault, if he were to have an accident? You? But *you're* one of *us*."

He stopped laughing and his face returned to its usual impassivity.

"Do as you think best, Livia. Take him to bed, push him to continue courting the young woman, find him another lover, but it is indispensable that he remain here to do what he does. At any and all costs."

Now Livia was frantic.

"He's been invited by the Colombo family to come celebrate New Year's Eve, tomorrow night: I'm sure things will fall into place. I'll find the way. Just give me time."

Falco stood up.

"You have the time, Livia. As long as everything remains as it is, you have the time. Perhaps."

With a courtly nod of the head, he vanished into the fog.

XXVII

Ricciardi laid out his theory to Maione, couching it in veiled language and hedging it with the proper caution, because it was a somewhat precarious hypothesis, based on vague sensations and lacking solid foundations. A theory born in the fog, a theory which still seemed to be enveloped in fog.

But time was short, far too short to allow them to wait for solid evidence or for others to make false steps.

The brigadier pulled out his pocket watch and held it far away from his face to check the time.

"Damned old age; I'm afraid that I'm going to have to wear reading glasses soon . . . Anyway, from what I've gathered, we're going to have to go to San Giovanni now, am I right?"

His superior officer nodded.

"Yes. The key element in this situation is the dresser, Erminia. We need to figure out exactly what happened, whether it's true that the pistol arrived in the theater unloaded, or not."

Maione's face split into a broad smile.

"In that case, Commissa', we're absolutely going to have to take the car; if we try to get there on public transportation, we'll arrive at midnight. We're in luck, I talked to the garage and they're holding it for us."

Ricciardi grimaced.

"We're in such good luck . . ."

His comment had been entirely ironic, because Brigadier

Raffaele Maione, a man abounding in fine human qualities, was nevertheless the worst driver you could possibly imagine. The weird thing about it was that Maione thought the exact opposite of his skills as a driver. For that matter, however, there were no alternatives: the urgency was absolute, Erminia's address—identified with a phone call to the theater's box office—was quite distant, and Ricciardi had no driver's license of his own.

What's more, the fog was showing no sign of lessening.

The commissario ventured a timid suggestion: "Listen, Raffaele, since I'd like to continue discussing this idea I had during the trip, why don't you see if there's someone free who could serve as our driver. I don't know, say Camarda, Cesarano, or some other officer."

Maione's only response was to slip on a pair of driving gloves.

"So what's the problem with that, Commissa'? I drive so well, as you know, that we can chat freely. There's no way to take men off their assignments during the holidays, there's too few on duty. Don't worry, we'll talk."

Police headquarters possessed two automobiles, one of which—the newer and more intact—served purposes of official prestige and ceremony; in other words, it was for the sole use of the police chief and his family. The other car, a 1919 Fiat 501, was a service vehicle for the officers and detectives, and was almost always in the workshop. Maione was personally responsible for most of the damage and breakdowns, but since he was greatly feared, no one dared to file an official request with the higher-ups to bar him from driving it.

Customarily, Ricciardi wasn't made privy to the gossip that circulated at police headquarters, but he did know that the brigadier's limited skill as a driver was the subject of jokes and secret wisecracks among the staff.

With a sudden lurch, the 501 bounded into the fog. Two

men on foot dove headfirst for the sidewalks. Maione didn't even notice them.

"Well, Commissa', what sort of impression did Gelmi make on you? It's true that prison can soften you up, but a single day behind bars might not have been enough to convince him to withdraw his original version of events."

In front of them, a pushcart managed to get out of the way just in the nick of time; otherwise it would have been smashed to bits, scattering its merchandise across the cobblestones. The commissario glimpsed the vendor waving his fist at them before being swallowed up by the mist, and he thought sadly about the cruelty of fate: to die just now that he'd finally made contact with Enrica.

Defensively hunched in the back seat, holding tight to the door handle, he replied to his underling's observation in the hopes that engaging him in a conversation might at least induce him to slow down a bit.

"Gelmi strikes me as sincere. What baffles me is that he doesn't seem to have any particular interest in getting back out. His sister was angrier about it than he was."

Maione turned around to respond, without lifting his foot off the accelerator in the slightest. Ricciardi stiffened in anticipation of impact and swore inwardly that, if he survived, he would not utter another word until their safe arrival.

"Commissa', what is this sister like? From what you've told me, this woman considered her sister-in-law, Fedora Marra, to be her sworn enemy. It strikes me that this is a factor worth bearing in mind: women can be something awful."

Ricciardi pointed at the windshield, eyes wide in alarm, and Maione gave a sharp yank to the steering wheel, thereby missing a mother and a little girl by an eyelash: the two pedestrians had seen the car bearing down on them and had frozen in place in the middle of the street, resigned to being crushed under the onrushing wheels. Overcorrecting, his fender slammed into a fireworks stand ready for the coming New Year's Eve, knocking it sideways.

The brigadier chirped, cheerfully: "Well, no doubt about it, in this fog only a talented driver would know how to maneuver successfully. And if I do say so myself, Commissa', you can rely on yours truly. Our colleague Cozzolino, for instance, drives so slowly that if you ask me, it might be faster to walk."

Ricciardi found himself suddenly revaluating Cozzolino, who might very well be an idiot but at least couldn't be branded a public menace.

Incredibly, they managed to reach their destination without killing anyone. They limited the damage to a few automobiles run off the road, a second pushcart overturned, and four little old men, playing a game of cards around a folding table in front of a social club, forced to beat a hasty exodus in as many different directions. Ricciardi regretted that he had no particular facility when it came to praying and made a mental note, the next time he found himself obliged to drive somewhere with Maione, to invite Don Pierino along as a form of ecclesiastical life insurance.

The real irony was that the whole way there, the brigadier had never once stopped inveighing against those who dared to be driving in his oncoming path or even in the opposite direction, albeit in the appropriate lane on the far side of the street—these *other* drivers, in Maione's estimation were in clear violation of the legal code governing motor vehicles and traffic. Once they'd reached their destination, Maione ventured to ask: "Commissa', let me take this opportunity to ask you for a favor. Since we have the car, I need to go somewhere afterwards, of course on a matter of police business, let me make that clear. Perhaps I could take you partway home first, and . . ."

Ricciardi didn't even give him time to finish his sentence.

"No, no, you go on ahead, by all means. I can get home on my own. A nice stroll will help me clear my head."

He got out of the car while it was still rolling and staggered uncertainly.

Maione scolded him sternly: "Careful how you cross the street, Commissa'. In this fog, it can be dangerous."

The area was very poor and the general atmosphere made the houses look even more drab and poverty-stricken. A small group of children playing soccer with a ragball turned to stare at them from afar. Ricciardi noticed several young men high-tailing it away and slipping through an entrance door into an apartment building, like surprised rats burrowing into a pile of garbage.

The two policemen entered the front door of a tumbledown apartment house in their turn, in pursuit of what might turn out to be nothing more than an idea.

XXVIII

As they climbed the steps, they ascended through an oppressive stench of garlic. Ricciardi was trying to master the shakes that the car trip had triggered in him, while behind him Maione sang softly: "*Ma staje durmenno, nun te si' scetata, 'sti ffenestelle nun se vonno aprí . . .*" (But you're fast asleep, / You haven't awakened, / These windows refuse to open.)

The commissario turned around in surprise and the brigadier put on an apologetic expression.

"Forgive me, but this morning I saw Bambinella. You won't believe it, but she sings. And very nicely, with a fine tenor voice. This tune stuck in my head. You know it, don't you? *Scetate, bella mia . . .*"

Ricciardi shook his head.

"You're all full up on resources in this city. The *femminielli* are noted tenors and the brigadiers are racecar drivers. Versatile folks that you are."

"What else can you expect, Commissa'? We have to be able to get by, heaven forbid we might need a new job someday. Around here, one of these days, that idiot Garzo is bound to fire us. It's only a matter of time."

They'd arrived at a tiny landing with an apartment door. Maione knocked. From inside came a strange scratching sound. The door swung slightly open and an eye peered out, hostile and mistrustful.

"Who are you looking for? There's no one here."

The policemen exchanged a baffled glance. Then the brigadier asked: "Then who are you?"

The man said nothing for a few seconds, evidently confused.

"I meant to say, there's no one here but me."

A smile spread across Maione's face.

"Then it's you we want to talk to. You see this, the uniform I'm wearing? I'm Brigadier Maione from police headquarters, and here beside me is Commissario Ricciardi. Open up, if you please."

In response, the man simply slammed the door. Maione was disconcerted; but a moment later came the sound of a chain sliding and the door reopened.

"Please, come right in."

The front hall was shrouded in shadow, and the two policemen had a difficult time making out the details of the figure before them. The man, who appeared to be in his early forties, had assumed a strange stance, turned to one side: he displayed only his left side. With a gesture, he invited Maione and Ricciardi to precede him into the adjoining room.

The place was unadorned but neat and orderly. The furnishings consisted of a table upon which rested a yellowed doily and four chairs pulled up to it, a blackened hearth, and a low, beat-up credenza. The only light that filtered through the window was a somewhat diseased, milky glow.

The man followed them in, taking care to keep the right half of his body turned toward the wall. In the light, Ricciardi noticed that his posture was bowed and bent.

He told him, courteously: "We're investigating the murder of Fedora Marra, which took place at the Teatro Splendor on the evening of December 28th last. And you would be Signor . . ."

The man shot him a rapid glance without venturing the least movement. The commissario noticed that he had stopped in a dimly lit corner. There was something familiar about him; Ricciardi thought he might have met him before, but that came as no surprise.

"Yes, I heard about it. But I was right here, at home. I don't have much occasion to go to the theater; or anywhere else, come to think of it."

His voice was hoarse, as if his throat were scratchy from labored respiration. The man took a handkerchief out of his pocket and dabbed at the corner of his mouth on his unseen side.

"I'm Pacelli. Cesare Pacelli. Perhaps you're here to see my wife, but at this time of the day she's at work."

Maione nodded.

"Signora Erminia, yes, we've already talked with her."

Ricciardi added: "But we wanted to ask you something as well, Pacelli. We understand that you know Michelangelo Gelmi, the actor, and that you're friends. Is that right?"

The man furrowed his brow.

"Of course I know him. But we aren't friends. We fought in the war together; he was my captain and I was his attendant. I was with him when . . ."

Maione leaned forward to get a better look at him.

"Pace', do me a favor, come a little closer so I can see you better."

The man didn't move, as if he hadn't hear him. Then, with a long sigh, he dragged himself toward the table and took a seat.

The brigadier could hardly help but start in alarm. One half of Pacelli's face, on the right side, was horribly damaged. His shiny scalp, devoid of hair; the flesh of his face patched together in an endless succession of old scars, an empty eye socket, the teeth left bare with a no longer extant lip from which dripped a perennial trickle of drool, which the man dabbed at with sharp gestures of his sole remaining hand. His trousers covered a stiff leg.

To relieve Maione of any doubt on the matter, the man rapped his knuckles sharply on the limb, making a dull noise.

"That's right, it's wooden. I also lost the leg."

Maione coughed, his throat suddenly dry.

"But how did . . ."

Pacelli turned in his seat, offering his better profile to view.

"A grenade, Brigadie'. A grenade. According to the doctors, at that distance survival was impossible. They were wrong about that, don't you think? Otherwise, I wouldn't be here chatting with you today."

Ricciardi noted the bitter, angry, sarcastic tone so typical of mutilated veterans of the war. But Pacelli wasn't bemoaning his fate: his stance was quite dignified, even if it did make it more complicated to obtain information.

The commissario said: "We know that Gelmi recommended your wife for her job at the Teatro Splendor. Did you ask him to do that?"

The man's profile smiled: "I never even leave this apartment, Commissa'. Like I told you. He came to see me a couple of times, after the war ended, when I was recuperating. But he hasn't been around here since 1924. Perhaps he didn't enjoy the sight of my face. Odd, don't you think? He ought to be relieved, because it would have been easy for him to be wearing it now instead of me. And in that case, he could have kissed his acting career goodbye."

Maione probed further: "What do you mean, he could be wearing it now?"

That conversation, with a man who somehow managed to change his interlocutor without moving so much as a millimeter, limiting himself to rotating just one eye, was truly bizarre.

"At the moment of the explosion he was standing beside me," Pacelli explained. "But he was on the safe side of me. It took him a while to wipe off all the shreds of my flesh. But when all was said and done, he didn't have a scratch on him. A matter of luck, wouldn't you say, Brigadie'? A matter of luck."

And misfortune, Ricciardi thought to himself. That voice throbbed with bitterness, sorrow, and regret. The commissario searched for traces of hatred.

"Did he take shelter behind you?"

The sudden question threw Maione off balance, and he turned to glance at his superior officer.

The veteran, in contrast, hardly seemed surprised. Who could say how many times he'd asked himself that question in his years of solitude and suffering.

"No, Commissa'. The captain isn't a coward. It just turned out well for him, as it did for me. Otherwise we'd have both been killed. Instead we survived. Even though now he's in prison, and in a certain sense, so am I."

Maione nodded his head.

"Certainly, so many men never came back home. But if you haven't seen him in all these years, why did he help your wife?"

"She went to him. She took him my regards, told him I paid my respects, as people say. He was performing at the Teatro Splendor, in fact; a couple of years ago, I don't remember exactly."

Ricciardi weighed in: "Whose idea was it? Yours or your wife's?"

The man fell silent, staring into the empty air. His off-kilter position, however understandable it might be, made Maione feel ill at ease. He felt as if he were talking to a chicken.

Pacelli replied: "I'd have preferred not to, truth be told. But Erminia . . . We have a daughter who's been a theater nut ever since she was a little girl; she's always had that dream. We were getting by, but it isn't easy, Commissa'. I'm the way you see me, and I certainly can't work. One time I applied for a job as a watchman, but . . ."

Maione looked him up and down.

"As a watchman?"

The other man straightened his back proudly.

"I know what I'm doing when it comes to weapons, Brigadie'. I still have my old sidearm from when I was a soldier, my daughter helps me to keep it clean and oiled, ready for use. As a watchman, I'd be better with half an ass-cheek than some good-for-nothing dragged in off the street."

Maione raised both his hands.

"Oh, I have no doubt. Still, you didn't manage to find a position, did you?"

Pacelli shook his head.

"No. And I remained here, in this confinement. When Erminia learned that the captain was here in the city, she told me: since he's always cared for you, he'll help us. Maybe he at least he can give a few dance lessons to our daughter, which we could never afford on our own."

The commissario broke in: "And what did Gelmi do?"

"He was deeply touched and embraced her. He's a man with a big heart, even if he has an array of commitments and can't spare the time to come pay a visit upon me. And so he said to her: Signo', let me talk to the proprietor of the theater, who is a friend of mine. And the next day, by the grace of Our Lord Almighty, she started her job at the Teatro Splendor."

Ricciardi touched his forehead.

"So are you both grateful to Gelmi?"

Pacelli nodded.

"I'll say, Commissa'. He's a saint. He saved our lives, and even now he occasionally sends us money."

The brigadier asked: "And what about your daughter?"

The man smiled, and that must have had an effect on the other portion of his face, because his hand moved rapidly to dry his mouth.

"She's found a fine young man of her own, and maybe soon

she'll settle down. So, you see, everything works out for the best if you're honest folk."

Ricciardi said: "Did Signora Erminia tell you anything about the evening that Gelmi shot Fedora Marra?"

"Of course she did. She tells me everything. The captain went to the dressing room to talk to that slut and came out sobbing. What could she have said to him to make him lose his mind? He must have been on the verge of despair."

Outside, it was evening already. Maione looked around, discomfited.

"The fog isn't dispelling, Commissa'. Listen, let me drive you home, then I can take care of the service I mentioned to you; you'll catch your death, walking in this damp chill."

Ricciardi rejected the offer in no uncertain terms: "No, no, Raffaele, don't worry about me. I need to stop by somewhere on my way home. We'll see each other tomorrow, but you listen to my advice: be careful. It's hard to drive in this weather."

Maione proudly climbed into the car.

"Don't worry, Commissario, if a driver is gifted and cautious, then there's nothing to fear. I'll drop by and see the doctor and give him your regards."

He started the car and began singing in a tenor voice: "'*Sti ffenestelle nun se vonno apri'* . . . *è 'nu ricamo, 'sta manduli-nata* . . . *scetate bella mia, nun cchiú durmi'!* (These windows refuse to open . . . this mandolin piece is an embroidery . . . Wake up, my lovely, sleep no more!) It's no good, I can't get it out of my head, this song. Damn you, Bambinella, damn you! *Buona sera*, Commissa'!"

Ricciardi wondered if he'd ever see him again.

XXIX

In the hospital, it had been a tough day. As long as he could remember, Bruno Modo had been aware that holidays tended to awaken in people their worst emotions and most damaging feelings.

Time took care of the rest. When people had to work hard and survival was the daily objective, there was little time left for anything else. And the work itself sapped what energy might be left over for arguing, quibbling, confronting the phantoms of the thousand torments that life produced in such vast quantities, and which were tucked away under the carpet in the hopes they might simply disappear. But it was during the holidays that those same phantoms returned to the surface, like something filthy and foul-smelling tossed into the murky harbor waters.

A candle had set fire to the clothing of two little girls who'd been playing tag around a table. To be exact, the younger sister, Teresa, had slipped and grabbed the tablecloth in her fall, dragging the lighted candle with it. The elder sister, Maria, terrified of a scolding from her mother—who was locked in a drag-out argument with their father in the next room—had thrown herself on her sister's burning body in an attempt to douse the flames; the only thing she achieved thereby was to transform herself and the other girl into a single, brightly glowing bonfire. The parents' shouts drowned out their daughters' screams, and therefore help came too late.

Burns far too serious to recover from. The very best prognosis, and Modo was by no means sure that it really would be the best outcome, was that the little ones would live on, but remain disfigured. As things stood now, however, the chances that they'd both survive were flickering like a dying flame. The flame of a candle, to be exact.

Four patients had been admitted for injuries associated with fireworks; these were the vanguard of the army of injured patients expected after the night separating New Year's Eve and New Year's Day: so, have a happy end and a happy beginning. For the moment, in that small, advance scouting party, the casualties involved the loss of a hand, an eye, and three fingers, as well as extensive burns on one arm. Modo would willingly have kicked them from one ward to the next, if that hadn't meant simply increasing his own workload.

Three other patients were the aftermath of a brawl between small-time hoods, or *guappi*, in the city quarter: a substantial number of stab wounds, but no one in grave danger of their lives; only many, many stitches to be sutured. The true stars of the evening's entertainment thus far, however, were two women from the Spanish Quarter. They'd decided to duke it out because allegedly one of them had courted the other's husband. That would have been at least a relatively unremarkable occurrence had the two rival women not been more or less eighty years of age, and the object of their jealousy eighty-five. The man in question sat in the waiting room, eyes downcast, awaiting news: though no one could say whether it was news of his wife or his lover that he was awaiting. The two women continued to scream fanciful and elaborately framed insults from one room to the other, to the utmost amusement of patients and nurses who practically seemed to be jotting down notes for future memory.

Whenever he could, Modo went to see Lina.

Sister Luisa, who continued to blame herself for having underestimated the severity of her condition, had devoted herself to Lina's care to the virtual exclusion of all other patients, reporting dutifully to the doctor. Lina's respiration remained labored, and the rough expansion of an area of her chest confirmed that there must be, at the very least, a double rib fracture. At least one piece of good news: the hard cast on her arm was holding up well.

With a view to monitoring the consequences of the various traumas, especially to the head, Modo had refrained from administering morphine: the result had been a steady, lugubrious moan of discomfort.

Unfortunately, heartbeat and blood pressure, which Sister Luisa measured on an hourly basis, left little room for optimism: the heartbeat never dropped below a hundred beats a minute, and the blood pressure never rose above 90. And those suspicious numbers pointed to an endocranial problem.

Modo was tormented by the memory of his last meeting with his sweet friend. As was their custom, he had talked about the situation in the city, how oppressive it was to live under a regime that was decidedly anti-democratic, the fact that the populace was growing increasingly poor and discontented, to the absolute indifference of the public institutions and the aristocracy. Chatter, to think back on it now. Idle, pointless chatter.

More taciturn than usual, Lina had listened to him without the gentle, ironic smile she generally wore during his chaotic monologues. At a certain point, he had asked her whether she had something else on her mind. He'd made an extremely disagreeable wisecrack, which he'd regretted instantly and which now echoed through his mind like the aftermath of a grave and grievous misdeed. He'd said to her: After all, I am paying you, am I not? If nothing else, I'd ask you to pay attention.

A stricken expression had appeared on the woman's face, as if she'd received an undeserved insult, but she'd apologized and explained that her mind was elsewhere, focusing on a family problem. Modo had asked her to talk to him about it; Lina, however, had preferred not to discuss the details and urged him to continue his political sermon, kissing him sweetly on the cheek.

The doctor realized that he was now caressing the same spot on his face, bristly with whiskers he hadn't had a chance shave. Then he felt it turn wet and salty.

At the end of the convulsive morning's work, he'd had a brief conversation with Maione. The brigadier had told him he'd managed to pick up a few nuggets of information, and he now knew where Lina had been beaten and how she had made her way to the hospital. Modo had been overwhelmed by a bottomless sense of anguish when he learned it had been Lina herself who'd begged to be brought there specifically. Maione thought it was important to go to the address he'd been given by Mamma Clara, in order to understand the connection between that place and the assault. The doctor told him about Lina's mention of a family problem, and the brigadier had nodded as if that fact confirmed a theory of his.

Maione had offered to go there, alone, at the end of his shift. But Modo, tired though he was and in need of a rest, insisted on accompanying Maione to the Masseria del Campiglione so he could be there too.

By now it was nearly time. Modo made sure his patients were all stable and under control, and gave instructions for the coming night to Sister Luisa and the sleepy colleague who would be standing in for him. Modo expected to return to work after his expedition with Maione.

Before leaving, he went one last time to take a look at Lina. The ward room was shrouded in dim light; nuns and nurses moved between the beds like beneficent nocturnal birds. Every so often a moan filled the air, but otherwise silence reigned supreme; even the two octogenarian rivals in love had resigned themselves to a sleep inhabited by difficult dreams.

Modo bent over the bed and touched her forehead to see if she had a fever. He felt he could at least rule out that further complication. Suddenly, the young woman's unfractured hand emerged from under the sheets and grabbed his wrist, making him start. One eye, red and bloodshot, stared at him.

The doctor leaned down toward the poor thing's face, seeing that the split lips were trying to articulate sounds. His heart pounded violently in his ears: he had despaired of her ever regaining consciousness.

At first he couldn't make out what she was trying to say. She was mumbling and he could guess how much pain that effort was costing her. Modo understood, or thought he understood: "Bruno, don't do a thing. Don't do a thing."

He hastened to reply: "Lina, don't worry, I'll care for you and you'll get better, but help me now. How is your head? Can you see?"

The woman tightened her grip, as if she were irritated.

"It doesn't matter to me, it doesn't matter to me. Don't you do a thing, you understand? Leave him alone."

"What do you mean, don't do anything? I have to care for you, Lina. But tell me what happened. Who did this?"

The woman moaned without releasing his wrist.

"If you can, save me. But leave him alone. Swear it to me."

The doctor felt a sense of helplessness fill him.

"Damn it, Lina: who am I supposed to leave alone? What are you . . ."

Then he realized that her eyesight was failing, and that a tear was rolling down her cheek.

She muttered again in a frantic tone: "Swear it, Bruno. Swear it or I won't fight anymore."

"No, no, for heaven's sake, don't give up. I'll swear, I'll swear on whatever you want. I don't understand, but I'll swear. And you stay here with me. Do we have a deal, Linare'? Do we have a deal?"

She slowly moved her chin in an imperceptible gesture of consent, while her breathing again grew heavy. Her grip loosened and Modo tucked her arm back underneath the sheets.

He stood there, watching over her for a while. Then he signaled to Sister Luisa, who came trotting in response.

"Sister Lui', I'm going to . . . to run an errand. I'll be back as soon as possible. You, if you would, just check her pressure and heartbeat in an hour and write them down in her chart."

The nun nodded, gazing at Lina's silhouette.

"Who could it have been? Who can hate so much that . . . that they'd do this?"

Modo shrugged and turned to go.

In the hospital courtyard, Maione was waiting for him, leaning against the automobile.

"Oh, *Dotto'*, *buonasera*. I checked out the car from police headquarters, so we'll get there quickly. It's not exactly around the corner."

The doctor looked him up and down. The fact that Maione was the closest thing that Ricciardi had to a friend had earned the brigadier Modo's esteem.

"But you have to do me a favor," he said. "Let me drive. Otherwise I'll get carsick and vomit on the driver."

Maione's eyes bugged out.

"If that's the way things are, I'll give you directions. For that matter, I'll confess to you that I'm a little tired of driving in this fog: people just jump out in front of you, and even if you're an accomplished driver like me, things could go wrong. I just rammed a market stall out front and sent it flying. Good thing it was closed."

XXX

The trolley that ran from San Giovanni to Piazza Dante was number 54. It emerged from the fog, iron wheels screeching, like the dragon in a fairy tale. The bored driver was more snugly bundled up than seemed to be required given the fact that the temperature remained well above the average for the season. Aboard his trolley, thirty or so passengers, for the most part port workers, were hanging from straps and poles and snoozing on their feet.

Ricciardi considered that he'd arrive at *Caminito* a few minutes late, and hoped that Enrica would wait for him. She usually had to foist off a little white lie to justify her absence: the drawn-out completion of a private lesson for the three children of a needy couple in Capodimonte. She'd told him about it once, with a smile, and added that she didn't like to lie, especially not to her father.

The young woman's bonds of affection with her parents were a mystery to Ricciardi, who had only had a family for a few years and could hardly remember the warmth of the experience. His father, that previous Baron of Malomonte so very different from him—according to the accounts of those who had known him—died when Luigi Alfredo was just a small boy; his mother, whom he so closely resembled, had died when he was a teenager, but only after spending the last years of her life in the hospital. The comfort of the household hearth had been provided by Rosa, the kindhearted housekeeper who had raised him and had only died the previous summer. Now there was Nelide to look after his needs with absolute devotion, but it couldn't be anything like the same thing.

Enrica, in contrast, never talked about anything but her mother, the suspicious Signora Colombo, disarming in her numerous prejudices and intent on shaping her daughter in her own semblance; her married sister and her brother-in-law, their passion-filled marriage, and her little nephew, whom she adored as if he were a child of her own; and her other sister and brother, both of whom had distinctive traits. And then there was Giulio, her Papà, with whom she had a deep and abiding affinity and a boundless complicity.

Ricciardi listened to her speak holding both her hands in his, allowing himself to be lulled by the sound of that voice he'd so long only dreamed of, and which he could now finally enjoy up close. In the meantime, he was trying to allay the pang of suffering he felt in his heart that, in all likelihood, he'd never be able to offer her the joys of a family.

As the 54 trolley ran along the seaside heading toward the city center, his mind turned to the investigation he was working on. The deeper he delved, the more the various elements available to him seemed to jibe with the first hypothesis: namely, that Gelmi had murdered his wife with premeditation out of jealousy. Still, though, there were various characters in the couple's milieu who could prompt intense sentiments and unusual emotions, and Ricciardi had long since learned the fundamental role played by passions in the genesis of a murder.

Marianna, for example, detested her sister-in-law and was Michelangelo's sister: a particularly close sibling relationship, the kind between twins, which frequently engendered attitudes that defied easy comprehension.

Another individual who left Ricciardi uneasy was Cesare Pacelli, the badly mutilated veteran whose war injuries had so scarred him that the man still wished he'd been killed by the explosion of that grenade. The words he'd lavished on his former captain certainly expressed gratitude, perhaps even affection, but at the same time there was no mistaking a lingering resentment: the envy of a man who'd suffered horrible mutilations with respect to someone else who, though guiltless, had avoided injury and, as fate would have it, had built a spectacular career on his own physical appearance. The man's rancor might also have infected Erminia and her daughter, but they owed a great deal to Gelmi's benevolence, and what's more, had nothing to gain by his arrest.

Then there were the various members of the troupe, probably silent and complicit witnesses to Fedora's relationship with one of their own, willing to hush up the truth in order to preserve a fragile equilibrium that served the personal interests of them all.

Even Renzullo, proprietor of the Teatro Splendor, had spoken in somewhat ambiguous terms about Marra, as if trying to establish a certain distance from her. Ricciardi stepped off the trolley at the Piazza Dante stop. The fog persisted, in fact, it seemed to have grown even heavier. The monument to Italy's greatest poet was invisible, except for the statue's base. The street, generally crowded, was empty even of the poor beggars who would have been unable to attract the attention of passing donors in this dense mist; it was likewise deserted of the strolling vendors, who had no doubt grown tired of shouting their wares and singing their praises to an empty, fog-shrouded square.

And the sound of his own footsteps on the cobblestones seemed muffled. Fog, Ricciardi mused, was different in the city than in the countryside. As was everything else. For no good reason, he remembered the rose laid upon the stage next to the curtain: red next to red. A flower cut and somewhat fading, lying upon the same boards where actors feigned hatred, love, and good cheer. Poor Fedora. He'd never seen her act, though she was famous. But he'd heard her speak, yes, that he'd heard.

Love of my life. Love of my life. Love of my life, she had repeated to him, blood gushing from the bulle thole as well as from her mouth and nostrils. And the note he'd found in the pocket of her robe? "Again, tonight, I'll wear your embroidery before falling asleep, and in my heart it will be the last thing I hear." Who were you angry at? Who were you talking to? What life, what love killed you?

An illogical association of ideas, the origin of which he'd be unable to identify, led him to wonder about Maione's behavior. The brigadier had seemed strange to him. He hadn't arrived on time at the beginning of the shift and he'd chosen to keep the automobile, which he would surely drive so recklessly as to run over some innocent soul. And why? What was he planning to do? What further bizarre events might there be, in the last gasp of that year, as it disappeared into the calendar of the past?

Not even the thick blanket of fog that covered everything was enough to conceal the dead of the Sanità Bridge. Their despairing chorus once again plunged him, as always, into a state of uncertainty concerning Enrica. The expectation of see-ing her, his heart in his mouth, the happiness that issued from skin and eyes—it was all quenched by his sense of inadequacy to construct a simple, normal, human relationship. He needed to see her before him, radiant in the intimacy of their secret rendezvous. That alone could restore his courage.

That evening, however, Enrica wasn't smiling.

If anything, in fact, it seemed that she'd been crying. Her eyes were reddened behind the lenses of her spectacles and in her hand she was clutching a handkerchief. When she offered him her lips in greeting, he detected a faint quaver.

He asked her, with concern in his voice: "Forgive me for being late, I was in San Giovanni for work. What's going on?"

The young woman opened her mouth, but she didn't know how to begin. She dried a tear, irritated at herself for her weakness: but she'd spent a sleepless night, and she had to open her heart to someone. And he, the man she loved, was the only thinkable recipient of her anguish.

"My mother is such a stubborn woman . . . There are times when I really can't stand her. I thought I'd made myself clear, that I'd made my intentions unmistakable to her."

Ricciardi tried to stem that chaotic flood of words.

"Calm down, I beg of you. And start over from the beginning."

Enrica took a deep breath, in what was clearly an attempt to regain control. Ricciardi put his arm around her shoulders and led her to the bench, where they sat down. The gray shroud of fog enveloped them in the faint light of the streetlamp.

"She's invited Manfred to our home tomorrow evening, to the last dinner of the old year. I'll be forced to dine with him after rejecting his proposal of marriage. What will he say? And what can I reply?"

Ricciardi felt as if the world were collapsing in on him. Again, that German, and again, the promise of an untroubled life. He heard in his mind's ear Fedora's mute cry, as if it were a personal curse: *Love of my life. Love of my life. Love of my life.* The litanies of the people of the bridge also echoed in his mind, as if they had crept closer to spy on him, taking advantage of the dense curtain of mist.

"I'm sorry, but hadn't you already . . . Why did she invite him? What does she have in mind?"

Enrica blew her nose.

"She doesn't believe in my decision, she thinks that I just don't want to move to Germany. She's fooling herself that she can persuade me to go back on my decision out of a fear of living alone for the rest of my life."

Ricciardi hardly knew what to say. The part of the universe that included the worries of a mother for the loneliness of a marriageable daughter was utterly mysterious to him.

"Can't you simply tell her that . . . you're not interested?"

The young woman stared at him in surprise.

"Me? How would I do that? Should I confess to her that I love another man, that I have no thoughts for anyone but him, that the mere idea of standing next to any man other than the one I love makes me feel nauseous?"

The beauty of that statement, the emotional transport wrapped up in it comforted him. He'd have kissed her now and never stopped.

Instead he asked: "And can't you just tell her that?"

Enrica shook her head.

"No, I cannot. She'd say that this man fails to return my devotion. Otherwise he'd shout it out to the world at large that he desires me. He wouldn't ask me to meet him in a deserted and isolated alley."

Ricciardi fell silent. He couldn't yet decide: because of those visions, his own madness, and the thought of the woman who had given birth to him and had died a raving lunatic, which was the same fate that awaited him, whereupon he'd leave Enrica alone and much less attractive as a widow than she was now, young and beautiful as she appeared to him. He still couldn't bring himself to rescue her from her mother's cunning maneuvers, which might yet represent the best thing for Enrica.

And yet he knew he wouldn't be able to withstand the pain and grief of glimpsing her once again locked in the arms of that fair-haired officer, as he had the previous summer on the island, when he'd watched them kiss in the sweet, perfumed evening. He realized that the agony of seeing the object of one's love torn away, the pain of betrayal, was enough to make you die. And, perhaps, even enough to make you kill.

Suddenly, the veil fell away, and every tile in the mosaic snapped into place.

And as that happened, the commissario continued to say

nothing. That silence communicated to the young woman the very clear message that no assistance could be expected from him.

Enrica and Ricciardi felt like the only living beings on the planet. If only that were the case, they each thought. But neither of them said a word.

XXXI

The automobile driven by Dr. Modo arrived at the small outlying village called Masseria del Campiglione.

It was a miserable agglomeration of farmhouses, not more than a dozen or so, which had originally belonged to a family of farmers and shepherds. Then a steel mill, thermal springs, and a renewed interest in the archaeological digs had created new job opportunities in the area, and gradually the countryside had been abandoned.

The roadway ran right through the heart of the village.

Out front of the only trattoria and bar, a number of teenagers were busy playing cards and smoking cigarettes; at the entirely exceptional sight of a car bouncing and jerking down the dirt road, they all looked up. Maione locked eyes with the vacuous, hostile gazes of a couple of those youngsters, who had glimpsed his uniform through the passenger window. It was a reaction he was all too familiar with, but one that never failed to fill him with sadness: that fear of the police, the perception of the authorities as an enemy army, told a more eloquent story of these places than any newspaper could.

Modo had read with churning emotions the note that the brigadier had received from Mamma Clara, penned in a large, uncertain, looping hand. Once, many years before, Lina had confided in him that, if she'd only had the good luck to be born to a prosperous family, like most of her customers, what she would have liked to do was study, even more than find a situation of economic comfort. Instead, who knows how much effort it had cost her to write those few words: an address where her belongings could be sent in case of misfortune.

The unusual pair of investigators reached the home that matched the address indicated. They stepped out of the vehicle and knocked at the door. Somewhere, in the fog, dogs began to bark. The damp air was redolent of smoke and manure.

The door was opened by an old man who dragged his feet as he walked. His expression betrayed not the slightest surprise at the uniform that filled his doorway: instead, he seemed overwrought, as if bracing for bad news. Without asking his visitors who they were and what they were doing there, he turned and walked back inside, leaving the door ajar behind him. After a moment's hesitation, the doctor and the brigadier stepped in and found him sitting next to the hearth. On a table there stood two dirty plates and two glasses each with a remaining half-inch of wine, clear evidence that the man hadn't dined alone.

The policeman exchanged a glance with the doctor and spoke.

"*Buonasera*. I'm Brigadier Maione, and this is the Commissario. You would be . . . ?"

During the drive there, they had agreed on that small lie concerning Modo's identity. Potential witnesses might be reluctant to tell the truth if questioned by a powerless private citizen.

Instead of introducing himself, the old man, turning his back, pushed at the flames with a fire poker and asked: "Is she still alive or already dead?"

The voice, deep and husky, sent chills down the doctor's spine. The room was poor but clean and tidy. Maione replied, harshly: "First, tell us your name."

The man turned and stared at the brigadier defiantly.

"The fact that you're here means that you already know it."

But the policeman had chewed and spat out much tougher bones than this one.

"You can tell it to us anyway. Or perhaps you'd rather take a little ride with us back to police headquarters?"

The man hesitated briefly, then replied: "Scuotto. Beniamino Scuotto. I'm the father."

"Whose father?"

The other man stood up with some effort and then went over to a corner and bent over a crate. Maione lowered his hand to his holster and unfastened the leather strap, freeing the pistol for a quick draw. Modo took a step back.

Slowly, Scuotto stood up; in his arms he was holding more firewood.

"Well? Is she alive or dead?"

The doctor decided to take a stab in the dark.

"Your daughter is still alive," he said. "Though I'd say that's practically a miracle, considering what she's been through. She's strong. Very strong."

The old man added couple of quarter logs to the flames and murmured: "Yes, she's strong."

Then he regained his confidence.

"What do you want from me? Why are you here?"

Maione maintained his composure.

"We'll ask the questions around here. If you're aware that your daughter is in the hospital and in serious condition, why aren't you at her bedside? I ask you that as a father. I feel sure I'd be on the verge of losing my mind."

Scuotto shot back with a chilling retort: "Why, is your daughter a whore, just like mine?"

The doctor seized the brigadier's arm, just in time to restrain him from lunging at the old man, and said: "She'd come to you, Lina had, isn't that right? She'd come to see you, perhaps to give you money. She'd taken the day off. Was it you who beat her like that? Who reduced her to a pulp like that?"

The old man remained impassive.

"No. I wasn't here. My daughter came here every month, and yes, you're right, she brought me money. All the money she earned practicing that trade of hers. She's been doing it since she was sixteen, she's never once failed to come by. We live on it. She'd just left when I returned. Do you think I'd have killed the one person who gives us money to live on?"

Maione let loose with something approaching a roar; he was furious.

"Then tell us who was responsible for that beating. You understand that, if two kind souls hadn't come by aboard a van, she'd have just died at a street corner like a stray dog? Don't you feel even a hint of rage?"

Scuotto heaved a sigh.

"Brigadie', each of us lives the life they choose. And a whore needs to take into account that she can come to this kind of an end. I'm sorry about it, that's certainly true. But I know nothing."

The policeman was speechless. But for that matter, it was clear that the feeble old man could never have massacred a woman like Lina with his bare hands.

Modo shook his head.

"I don't believe you. You're lying. Lina is a kind and wonderful person. Who could have harbored such hatred for her? Because it wasn't a robbery, if she'd already given you the money."

The old man studied him; a flicker of curiosity appeared in his eyes, which were surrounded by a dense spiderweb of wrinkles.

"You know her, don't you?"

Maione leveled his finger at the old man.

"I'm going to tell you one more time, it's the police's job to ask the questions. If you know the name of the guilty party, talk. Otherwise, we'll be glad to take you to prison."

The man turned to look at him.

"Take me wherever you please, Brigadie'. I'm not going to tell you who it was. I won't tell you now, and I won't tell you ever."

His tone was one of resignation. There was no bold defiance. Maione was well aware that there were no crimes he could charge the man with; if he arrested him, he'd be out on the streets again in a matter of hours. He shot Modo a helpless glance.

The doctor pointed at the two settings on the table and asked: "Who lives with you, Scuotto?"

The old man turned toward the fire and resumed his poking at the logs. Then, speaking to the flames, he replied: "My grandson. His name is Camillo. When you leave, please shut the door behind you."

XXXII

Welcome, ladies and gentlemen, welcome to the show of shows, the most spectacular performance human beings know how to present on any stage anywhere. Please, be our guests, take a seat. Take any seat you please, it makes absolutely no difference; whatever your angle of sight, you'll enjoy the exhibition to the fullest, without missing so much as a shred of entertainment. You'll witness an extraordinary undertaking, the battle supreme, the one challenge whose outcome can never be taken for granted: the long journey through the night.

Because it is the dream, none other than the dream, that constitutes the highest mountain we can scale, the deepest abyss we can explore. The dream, where you will have no means of defense, where mere reason can be of no assistance. The dream, where everything is both possible and impossible; where you'll fly high through the sky, but you can also be wounded by the petal of a flower. The dream, where you will walk, staggering under the burden of a love affair, where you will not have a future to rely upon in your attempts to escape from your past.

Tonight, moreover, we are pleased to bring you a very special effect: fog. You will spend the last night of the year in fog, and not just any fog: the swampiest and most impenetrable fog; fog outside and fog inside, the better to let your monsters nest deep in darkness, with nothing to hinder them.

You'll have the opportunity to become invisible to yourselves, tonight. And you will become actors in the most grandiose and intriguing performance of all time.

Step right up, ladies and gentlemen: come one, come all. We're about to begin.

In the two hours of sleep available to him, the doctor dreams of Lina in another life. He pays a call on her at home; not at the brothel, but at the farmhouse. He's never seen her there, but it's well known, in dreams this and more can happen.

It's Sunday in the dream, and the sun is shining. The countryside is verdant; he's gathered flowers: an enormous bouquet, colorful and sweet-smelling.

Lina opens the door when he knocks, and she's like the first time he saw her: a cream-colored robe, a white undergarment; cheerful and without a sign of suffering on her face. She welcomes him in; the room is the same as the lobby at Mamma Clara's, the only difference being that, behind the counter with the cash register, he now sees her father instead of the old maîtresse. The old man is not harsh, he's not sad in this dream. Lina's father smiles at Modo and then he tears off a "marchetta," the official brothel "ticket," though in this case, the time isn't written on it. The doctor notices that it's the only ticket on the pad.

Modo and Lina go up to the room. Lina holds his hand and plays with his finger; it's something she's always done. Lina, Lina, the doctor says in the dream, and in real life his restless lips utter that name as he sleeps. She accompanies him to the washbasin and rinses him with her gentle hands, gazing at him sweetly. Lina, Lina, the doctor says again, his voice breaking into a sob, but there are no tears in his eyes.

Lina lays him down on the bed and takes off her clothes. Her body, her poor, poor ravaged body, displays all the wounds it's received and still others, too. All the wounds of the world: the wounds of soldiers at war and the wounds of the storm-tossed poor whom the doctor takes in from the city streets every single day.

Lina, Lina, I beg of you, let me care for you, let me save you, *he tries to tell her. But his voice, the way it happens in dreams, sticks in his throat. So then she looks at him, without joy and without sorrow, and whispers: Let him be, Bruno. Let him be, like you promised me.*

Afterwards, she leaves, and he stays there, drowning in the tears that finally arrive, filling the universe with a damp fog.

You must understand, ladies and gentleman, that this is a music hall variety show. And the wonderful thing about music hall theater is that it's unpredictable. Every number is astonishing, every number is different from the one that precedes it and the one that follows. You'll experience sorrow, certainly, but also giddy joy. Regret and hope. Love and death. We'll do whatever we can think of to keep your eyes and your hearts glued to the stage. The spectacle of dreams will surprise you so thoroughly, on this last, fog-shrouded night of the year, that you'll no longer be able to distinguish the boundary with reality.

The brigadier drops off to sleep the instant his head hits the pillow, with Lucia still grumbling about his prolonged absence. As soon as he shuts his eyes, he finds himself driving through the fog, which is as dense as ever, if not more so. Obstacles suddenly pop out of nowhere, and it's only thanks to his extraordinary skill at the wheel that he's able to prevent a massacre. But he doesn't mind the burden of being behind the wheel under those terribly difficult conditions, because someone inside the vehicle is singing a song in a splendid tenor voice. "Si duorme o si nun duorme, bella mia, siente pe' 'nu mumento 'sta canzone." Meaning: "Whether you sleep or don't sleep, my lovely, listen to this song for a moment!" The brigadier is tempted to turn around to see who it is, but he can't, otherwise he might easily slam into a pushcart.

So he asks: Who are you, that you sing so well? And why this song? Then he can't resist any longer and he turns to look. In the back seat is Fedora Marra, with blood gushing out of her nose and mouth. The brigadier sighs: And now what am I going to tell the officer manning the garage, when I bring this car back, all smeared and stained with blood and gore?

Fedora, however, is not alone.

Romano, the young actor, the one who wet his trousers, asks the brigadier to change him; he speaks just like his son Luca did when he was small. Papà, Papà, hurry, I peed in my pants, if Mamma sees me . . .

Luca, don't be afraid, I'll take care of it, says the brigadier in his sleep.

A woman with a slightly horselike face laughs coquettishly in a masculine timbre, holding her hand in front of her mouth, and replies: Brigadie', what on earth are you saying? Don't you remember that your son is dead, that he was murdered? Maione replies, harshly: Bambine', don't you dare. Didn't you hear him? He's peed in his pants and I have to change him.

Bambinella starts to sing: "È 'nu ricamo, 'sta mandulinata! Scetate bella mia, nun cchiú durmi'." *Meaning: "This mandolin piece is an embroidery! Wake up, my lovely, sleep no more."*

Bambine', says the brigadier, where did you get this beautiful voice of yours? Meanwhile, the car rolls on through the fog, utterly without a driver but also without hitting a soul, because this is a dream, and in dreams cars drive themselves.

Lina, whom the brigadier has never heard speak, with her bruised, swollen face and her ravaged body, smiles at him and says: Brigadie', you understand what happened to me, don't you? You understand. And he replies: I understand, Signori'. It was Luca, wasn't it? Yes, Brigadie', yes. But he's innocent. How can he be innocent, if it was him? Fedora raises her head and, continuing to spew blood from her mouth, says: Don't you know, Brigadie', that it's possible? You pretend to shoot, but instead it's real. It's possible. And she points her finger at Gelmi, sitting beside her, his hands in shackles.

The man asks whether by any chance Rondinella—Swallow, by name—has come back, because every night he leaves his door open, in hopes of seeing her again.

Wait, how many of you are back there? asks the brigadier. And they all call out in chorus that this is a dream, and in a dream anything can happen.

"È 'nu ricamo, 'sta mandulinata! Scetate, bella mia. Nun cchiú durmi'." *Again: "This mandolin piece is an embroidery! Wake up, my lovely, sleep no more."*

The brigadier squints but continues sleeping.

Don't be deceived, ladies and gentlemen. Don't think to your-selves: these are just dreams. Nothing could be more important than dreams, especially dreams that come on the last night of the year. Dreams, on this last night, are all so much more powerful because they spring out of hopes and illusions. They're magical, the dreams of the last night of the year. They're always magical, so just imagine how much more so when there's fog.

The green-eyed man dreams of the bespectacled young woman, and the bespectacled young woman dreams of the green-eyed man.

He sees her through the window as she welcomes the German major to her home once again, and she welcomes the German major as she sees the green-eyed man through the window.

He has his mother sitting on his bed, behind him, telling him: Let her go, you know that you can't hope for this, just let her go. She has her mother at her side, telling her: Kiss him, hold him tight, this is the man for you.

He asks his mother: Why? You did it, you followed love and you had me. Why shouldn't I? She asks her mother: But how can I hold him and kiss him, if I love another? I love him! And so saying, she turns to look at the apartment building across the street.

His mother replies to him: Yes, I did it, and how many times have you cursed my memory? Her mother replies to her: Why, don't you understand that he's nothing but a silhouette behind a pane of glass? Don't you understand that he'll just go on standing there and he'll never move and you've only ever imagined him?

He says to his mother: No, I never cursed your memory, except for having abandoned me and for having kept the knowledge from me that you were suffering from the same disease that afflicted me. She tells her mother: No, that's not true, he is real. I know the taste of his lips, I know the feel of his hand trembling on the back of my neck. He's real, I know the color of his eyes.

His mother tells him that there is no way to confess to a son that you've infected him with a cursed life, that you've condemned him to live in a world populated by death, filled with bleeding wounds, broken necks, stabbed hearts, and that if he goes on with this relationship he'll discover it for himself. Her mother tells her that what happens in the fog, in an isolated alley and by the light of a streetlamp isn't the truth. The truth takes place before the eyes of one and all, in broad daylight.

He says to his mother that no, that's not necessarily so, that green eyes can vanish, that maybe his son will see the day and not the night, and he'll only suffer the sorrows and horrors that belong to him, not those of other souls. He tells her that curses are not infinite. She tells her mother that what happens in the alley, in Caminito, is so wonderful, so magnificent that unless she can have it, nothing of all the rest has any meaning or makes any sense, well, then, that's where she wants to live, in Caminito, and she wants no part of all the rest.

His mother tells him: Enough is enough, let her at least live a happy life. If you truly care for her, now that you've tasted the flavor of her lips, let her go. Her mother tells her: This is your destiny. And she points at the German major as he stands there, stock-still, smiling, as if frozen in time, like a photograph in an illustrated newspaper. Your destiny is him, embrace it.

He tells his mother: Go away, I beg of you, let me live. Just this once, let me live my life. Then he turns to look at her and she is Fedora. She lifts her dead head, blood spews from her mouth and nose, and she stares at him with her green eyes. Then she starts saying over and over: Love of my life, love of my life, come to me. He nods, defeated, and says: Yes, Mamma. I will come to you.

She tells her mother: You're wrong, Mamma, and you're right. I know that life is outside of Caminito, and that I need to leave my happiness there. Maybe I never found it, Mamma. Maybe I only dreamed it.

He says: You know, I had a dream, Mamma. I dreamed that I, too, could be happy. What a strange dream, Mamma. It must be the fog.

Yes, his mother says to him, spewing blood from her mouth. Yes, love of my life. Sleep, now. Sleep.

So you see, ladies and gentlemen? Nothing is impossible in dreams. No fear, no silent terror that may have taken root in you, albeit for as little as a thousandth of a second, will ever go away. It lurks there, hunkered down in the fog, ready to lunge at you when you least expect it, when you're asleep, that is, helpless and incapable of fighting back.

But before ringing down the curtain on the last night of the year and ringing it up on the dawn that will kill that night, we would offer you, in closing glory, a choral number. A winged journey through the dreams of other souls and other hearts, to unveil for you just a few more monsters.

The beautiful woman walks naked in the fog. But she doesn't feel beautiful, she feels poor. Lonely. Desperate. In the fog, she searches for a pair of green eyes to which she can display her body, nostalgically, not seductively. The other man, gray and ambiguous, emerges from the fog and fails to see her. He goes past quickly, with a pistol in his hand. So quickly that the woman wonders whether she ever really crossed paths with him. So she starts to run: She has to find those green eyes before the other man can. But with all this fog, she can't tell where she's going and she runs in a circle, finding herself in the same spot over and over again. Through the impenetrable mantle of fog comes a gunshot. The woman awakens in a lake of tears and sweat.

The contessa dreams that she's riding a horse on the beach. She's with the duke, but now he's well and he laughs and rides with her. The contessa tells him to ride faster, but he slows down and his face turns sad. The duke is left behind. She can't even hear his voice anymore, and when she looks ahead to discover what she's galloping toward, she spots someone waiting for her. She recognizes him. And in her sleep she smiles.

The young housekeeper doesn't hide, in the dream. She doesn't battle against emotions. In her dream she arrives at the market and all the other women stand aside to let her through, murmuring words of envy at her attractiveness. In the dream, there is an Arab horseman at the fruit stand, a dark-eyed Saracen wearing a turban, and he sings. In the dream she approaches him as haughty as princess, and he bows before her obsequiously. The young housekeeper stares at him and tells him: You have your thumb on the scales when you sell pears. Then she turns disdainfully and leaves. In her sleep, she furrows her brow.

The little girl dreams of confused flashes of light. She dreams of the moment when she threw herself onto her sister, whose brand-new outfit was in flames; who knows how angry Mamma will be when she notices, after she's done arguing with Papà. The little girl says: Tere', Tere', but her younger sister doesn't reply. Then she feels the fire clamping down on her flesh, and in her dream, she remembers it clearly, the smell of burning skin, like a steak left on the coals to cook for too long: Mamma mia, how it smells. The little girl feels no pain; it's her body that feels the pain. She dreams of a large door with the light behind it, like *when they go out on a Sunday and she brushes her hair back, tying it in a couple of ponytails: How lovely you are, Papà's little princess, how lovely you are, little one. The little girl recognizes her sister calling to her from the doorway; she understands that it's her, even though the dress is gone, even though her flesh is hanging in shreds and the bones of her cranium are protruding, black. Tere', Tere', she says. The other girl smiles back.*

The little girl runs to her and shuts the door on her last dream of the year and of her short, very sweet life.

Lower the curtain, now. Lower the curtain.

SECOND INTERLUDE

After the second verse, having completed the refrain, the old man starts talking again with his usual subdued and scratchy voice, so different from his voice when he sings. In the meantime, his twisted, talon-like fingers have never ceased playing. The young man watches him, captivated, because when the old man plays, he doesn't limit himself to replicating ad infinitum the melodic theme, but instead works variations on it, turning it into something new and yet consistent; as if he'd written it himself and knew something that the countless musicians who have performed their own versions over the years didn't know, still don't know, and never will know.

He's a genius, the young man thinks for the umpteenth time since the day he first set foot in the room with the window overlooking the sea, outside which the swallows sing their high-pitched song. How can it be that this man isn't world famous? How can he be a legend only among us musicians? Why isn't his name on the lips of one and all? Why hasn't he given concerts before oceanic audiences? Why isn't he staggeringly wealthy, why doesn't he live in a house glittering with silver, surrounded by household servants?

Lost in those thoughts, and in the melody, both age-old and brand new, he pays no attention to the old man's question. While they're traveling, you understand? the old man had said to him. And he had replied: Forgive me, Maestro, I missed what you said. The old man shakes his head. He seems saddened more than annoyed. Again, he repeats: A theatrical troupe is like a sort of family in constant movement. And it's precisely during their travel, their stays at run-down little hotels where up-and-coming young actors and old over-the-hill artists are sent to sleep, in the smoky, crowded trattorias where they eat their meals, that those cursed dreams begin to intertwine. It happens during their journeys that the hellish loneliness, the thwarted pursuit of perfection, the envy and the home all get mingled together and muddled up, as if they were separate and distinct ingredients set to simmer in an enormous cauldron.

The young man struggles to understand what this sidetrack has to do with the story. He waits to discover what else will happen around the diva's corpse. The old man prolongs in a sublime fashion the notes between the refrain and the final verse. The young man knows every single syllable of the song, and yet nonetheless he waits on tenterhooks for the next verse to arrive, as if it were some unexpected plot twist or some horrifying revelation.

The old man says: Their dreams mingled early. They were good looking and in the flower of their youth. And they were talented. Only the ballast of the present weighed down the future in which they'd surely take flight and conquer the world. Their opportunities, however, were not identical. It's one thing to be a line dancer, one more actor among many, a starlet in the presence of established giants, but the art we practice is quite another. When we take our instrument in hand, there is no appeal for us. Those who are talented really are, those who are merely competent are well aware of the fact. The opinions of others count for nothing.

What changes is our self-confidence. We cherish the belief that we can improve, become increasingly good at what we do. But in fact a radiant smile, an enchanting face, a perfect body will wither with time. No different than a rose, red and proud and magnificent, which will lose its petals and its leaves as it dies, if dropped on the wooden floorboards.

The young man grasps the concept, even though the flower metaphor escapes him. So he asks: How important is this difference, Maestro? And how did their dreams intertwine?

The old man says nothing for a while, but the music, which has never stopped, fills the silence along with the cries of the swallows as they come and go, come and go from the rain gutter, reiterating their destiny: the eternal return.

Then he speaks. An attractive woman is always afraid, and that fear grows by the second. Fedora was afraid, too. In her husband, she glimpsed an omen of what would happen to her soon enough: wrinkles on her face, bleary eyes, the weariness that sleep is no longer enough to erase. It's not even a matter of beauty: beauty changes, it doesn't vanish, at the outside, it is transformed; at forty you can be more captivating than you were at twenty. Terror sinks its roots in the ambition to stop the passing minutes. It has nothing to do with sensuality, admirers, or backstage bouquets and candies: what is desired is simply for time to stop. And if you have power, as she does, then you believe that you can make that happen. But hers were not the only dreams hovering in the air between the stage and the dressing rooms. Other people had dreams, as well.

With his eyes focused on the old man's left hand, as he says a silent prayer to God above to let him remember at least one of the series of chords, the young man murmurs: Maestro, whose dreams clashed with Fedora's?

The old man stares up at the visible shred of blue sky, crisscrossed by the wild flight paths of the birds.

First and foremost, her husband's dreams. He hoped to keep her at his side because he had invented her. The dreams of those who feared they'd lose their livelihoods, if the two of them broke up. The dreams of those who had other plans and a different future, with her or without her. The dreams of the man who desired her but had been spurned. The dreams of the man whom she desired. Who could even say how many other dreams pirouetted and plunged through the sky overhead?

Look at the swallows: there are so many of them, and each of them seems to hover and swoop at random. And yet they never crash in midair.

But dreams do.

The old man plays on and on: a melody that has neither beginning nor end.

Then he says: the curtain. We all pay too little attention to the curtain, and yet that curtain means that the show has ended. It can be pushed to one side for curtain calls, for standing ovations, but still, the show is over. And yet we never talk about it, we focus on the stage, the various movements, or the repertory, onstage entrances and exits, the marks we are meant to hit and occupy.

And we refer to the audience as if it were a single person. What will the audience say? What will the audience do? Will the audience be satisfied, or will it be disappointed? We ponder and scheme, we lose our wits, we spend hours and hours as if it were the tyrant of our existence, and we forget about that hanging strip of cloth which, let it be clear, is the single most important thing. It opens every time, true enough, but then, inevitably, it closes, too, once again separating dream from reality.

The swallow, you see, can remain behind the curtain. It can die. What will happen to all the other dreams once the swallow stops flying and the rose has lost all its petals? What will become of them?

The young man realizes that there is no answer to that question, but that it is the real reason why those wonderful fingers have failed to give joy to generations of delirious crowds.

He suddenly understands that the Maestro, the possessor of that unrivaled talent, is confiding in him the reason he drew that curtain and will never open it again.

In that instant, as if reading the young man's mind, the old man begins to sing again.

Torna. Ll'amice mieje sanno ca tuorne.
Tutte se so' 'nfurmate e a tutte dico:
"Dint'a 'sti juorne."
Uno sultanto, era 'o cchiú buono amico,
nun ll'aggio visto e nun c'è cchiú venuto, fosse partuto?
E torna rundinella,
torna a stu nido mo' ch'è primmavera.
I' lasso 'a porta aperta quanno è 'a sera
speranno 'e te truva'
vicino a me.

(Come back. All my friends have heard that you're coming back.
They've all asked, and I tell them all:
"Soon, one of these days."
There's just one, my best friend,
but I haven't seen him and he hasn't come by,
could he be away?

So come home, little swallow,
come back to this nest, now that it's springtime.
I leave the door open when evening falls,
hoping to find you again,
by my side.)

And with a sudden stab of pain to his heart, the young man understands.

XXXIII

The dawn of December 31st killed both the last full night of the year and the fog. Just as everyone had begun to grow accustomed to the muffled sounds and the mist that hides ugliness and misery, when it seemed almost natural to see no further than a few yards past the tip of your nose, almost natural to be utterly alone with yourself, the air suddenly turned clear and pitiless, delivering to each the world as it had always been, and the city found itself once again floating between an end and a new beginning.

Aside from sweeping away the fog, of which only the faintest of memories remained, as if that fog had never descended over the city to shadow its people's thoughts, the wind had also carried off the chill and pushed away the unnatural heat. Much like a beautiful woman who is incurably late for any appointment, the strange metropolis now put on the right attire for such a solemn moment, because—just to make this point perfectly clear—without the chill of winter, that holiday didn't seem very special.

The few citizens free of care, the few who had no need to plot and scheme in order to feed children who stubbornly insisted on eating regularly, indifferent to the cost and inconvenience, sniffed at the sharp snap of chill in the air and went to retrieve their overcoats, long forgotten in their armoires. Paradoxically, they came outdoors in droves, and traded idle comments about this sudden drop in temperature, the disappearance of the horrible white blanket of mist, and the fact that the word winter had suddenly regained meaning.

In the streets preferred by strollers, the ladies and gentlemen of polite society showed off for the first time their cunning little hats and handsome ties, gifts given at Christmas, and the new outfits stitched by seamstresses for a season that was making itself known so starkly late. Red noses, hands covered with gloves or plunged deep into the warmth of pockets, ears shielded by raised lapels or fur collars, as well as by head coverings of various shape and style, the discomfort of the cutting wind that sliced down to the bone through layers of thick cloth—none of this did anything to quench the smiles or undercut the diffuse sense of satisfaction. It was as if, after a lengthy wait, every actor on the stage of that holiday had finally embodied their role to perfection and the performance could truly begin.

Ricciardi had gone to the office very early. He had slept badly, with a weight on his heart too heavy to be pushed aside. He continued to brood over Enrica's anguish, her anxiety at the now imminent evening's entertainment, something she had no choice but to participate in; and he felt crushed by his own inability to reassure her, his own inadequacy. What a coward I am, he thought. Be sincere, at least with yourself. She wanted you to say: All right, let's give this love the importance that it deserves, let's bring it out into the light of day. Tomorrow, he ought to have told her with utter conviction, I'll be the one to come to your home, and well before the German officer: I'll introduce myself to your parents, I'll tell them a little bit about myself, my family, and my profession, and perhaps I'll even hint at the wealth that can assure any theoretical future wife of mine comfort and security. Then I'll ask them for permission to see you regularly, because I'm in love, more than I'd ever have believed possible, because I can't imagine a life without you. And then we'll see what they have to say.

That's what he ought to have said, but instead he had remained silent, as he embraced a young woman who was disappointed and terrified at the future, denying her the comfort she so badly needed even as he knew that he alone could come to her rescue.

Is this love, what I'm experiencing? he wondered. Wouldn't it have been better if I'd never even approached her? Perhaps her mother was right, he reflected. Perhaps, forced to accept the courtship of this man, Enrica would surrender and discover happiness, instead of weeping in an isolated alley on the shoulder of a man who lacked the mere courage required to live.

He focused on his work, which had always helped him to forget, which had always been a useful distraction. The quest for the solution to a mystery, the unveiling of a deception— these were the things that gave him the strength to lie to himself.

Maione appeared in the doorway, carrying the little espresso tray.

"*Buongiorno*, Commissa'. Have you seen? The fog has moved on and the winter chill is here. At least now New Year's seems like New Year's and not Easter."

Ricciardi asked, vaguely concerned: "How did it go yesterday, Raffaele? Did you manage to avoid any accidents?"

The brigadier replied promptly, as he served him his espresso: "Why, certainly, Commissa'. I'm an ace driver, isn't that obvious? Anyone else would have had serious problems driving with that limited visibility. You couldn't see a thing. In any case, no damage and the car is in the garage."

Ricciardi scrutinized Maione attentively. The brigadier's expression left him in doubt; it seemed to contain an undercurrent of melancholy. But he decided not to insist; if the brigadier had needed something, he wouldn't have hesitated to confide in him.

"I've been thinking about Marra's murder," he said, changing the subject. "I may have figured out the meaning of the note that we found in her robe; and it's all thanks to you."

"Me? But why?"

Ricciardi set down his demitasse.

"You know that melody you were singing, the one you couldn't get out of your head?"

Maione heaved a weary sigh.

"Don't talk to me about it, Commissa'. I even dreamed it last night. My father was obsessed with that song, and that idiot Bambinella stuck it back in my mind, and now I can't get rid of it."

Ricciardi raised his forefinger.

"I was referring to a specific verse. The message says: 'Again, tonight, I'll wear your embroidery before falling asleep, and in my heart it will be the last thing I hear.' Do you remember?"

The brigadier nodded.

"Certainly, and . . . Ohhhh, *madonna mia* . . ."

"Exactly, Raffaele. *È 'nu ricamo, 'sta mandulinata* . . . 'This mandolin piece is an embroidery . . .' What Fedora was going to wear that night was the sound of a mandolin. The last thing she'd hear in her heart."

Maione stood openmouthed.

"In fact, that's how it went: she died while the mandolin was still playing. It's as if she had a premonition."

Maione's superior officer confirmed with a nod of his head.

"In and of itself, it doesn't mean much. By now, it's clear that Marra was having an affair, and learning the lover's identity doesn't help greatly to solve the case. It would however help us to discover something more about the fight with Gelmi that Signora Erminia told us about."

"Do you think that he might have guessed? And that . . ."

"These are mere conjectures, if we assume that the clue

concerning the embroidery is correct, though we can't say for sure. Let's summon the young man to come in, but let's let him think that this is just a normal second step in the investigation. Let's bring him in and question him here, and see if that softens him up."

Before Maione had a chance to reply, there came a discreet knock at the door. The brigadier opened the door and his face brightened in a broad smile.

"Oh, *buongiorno*, Contessa. How are you?"

Bianca entered the room, radiant. Raffaele had never concealed his admiration for the woman who had been so melancholy when he'd first met her, proud and obsessively attached to a long-lost dignity, but who had now become fierce, cheerful, and kind. What's more, he had become convinced that her frequent visits to Ricciardi at police headquarters and the occasions that, he knew, the two of them had gone out together weren't entirely unrelated to the change of mood that he had perceived in the commissario. Therefore, alongside his appreciation there was a further form of paternal gratitude.

Bianca returned the greeting.

"*Buongiorno* to you, Brigadier. We early risers always seem to see each other, don't we? While all the others are on holiday . . ."

Maione let out a theatrical sigh.

"My dear Contessa, I'd gladly be one of those who are fast asleep, but work calls."

She gave Ricciardi an ironic glance.

"What about you, Commissario? Would you have gladly stayed in bed this morning, or are you glad to be here, in your favorite place on earth?"

Maione noticed that a faint blush had appeared on Ricciardi's face. He found that understandable: Bianca was enchanting in her gray-and-black outfit, with a short, dark fur cape over her shoulders and a cloche hat over her copper-hued hair. The commissario, however, was feeling quite awkward, because after frankly and openly confessing to the woman that it was not a good idea for them to socialize, he had supposed that Bianca felt toward him, if not full-blown resentment, then at the very least some annoyance. Coming face to face with her so soon, on the one hand, gave him a sense of relief but, on the other hand, made him suspect he might not have been sufficiently frank in that conversation.

"My favorite place on earth? You've misjudged me badly. We have some matters to iron out before the day ends, before midnight on New Year's Eve, and nothing more."

The contessa studied him intensely, violet eyes locked with green eyes.

"Seriously? Well, I wanted to ask you something specifically about this evening."

Maione started to step discreetly out of the office, but she stopped him, waving her gloved hand.

"No, no, Brigadier, please stay. Let me just ask a quick favor of Ricciardi and then I'll let you return to your official duties. Listen, Commissario. An old family friend, Princess Vaccaro di Ferrandina, has asked me to spend the evening at her home. She lives on the Corso and from her balconies there's a spectacular view of the whole city; from up there, the fireworks are simply magnificent. I'd very much like to go but, unaccompanied, as you can imagine, it's out of the question. Would you be so kind as to be my companion for the evening?"

Her tone of voice was lighthearted, but her eyes and hands betrayed her tension. Maione felt a surge of tenderness. Ricciardi replied: "Bianca, I'm very busy and tomorrow I'll be on duty. Also, I hardly think that we ought to . . ."

The contessa gave a nervous laugh.

"Come, come now, what would it cost you? Do you seriously want to stay at home in the concluding hours of a year that's been so difficult for me? Be my squire. Unless, of course, you're already otherwise engaged."

Maione coughed softly.

"Commissa', I would have invited you later this evening, but if you wish to grace our table, Lucia would be overjoyed. Contessa, to you I don't even dare to make the offer, but it goes without saying that if you wished . . ."

Ricciardi hesitated. To go out with Bianca after having clarified the nature of their connection would be a gross contradiction in terms. And yet he deeply dreaded the prospect of witnessing, aghast, what would surely take place that evening in the building across the way. After all, what could be the harm in a little distraction, watching a fireworks display in the middle of a crowd of strangers?

Maione added: "Commissa', we'd all be happy to know that you're somewhere nice, and in cheerful company. Make the contessa happy, go on."

Ricciardi threw both arms wide.

"It's a general conspiracy, best I can tell. All right, then, but I'll come by and pick you up latish. I'll probably have to swing past the Teatro Splendor to complete an investigation."

XXXIV

They sent an officer to bring in Aurelio Pittella, the mandolin player who, along with his colleague, the guitarist Elia Meloni, had witnessed Fedora Marra's murder from a privileged point of view. All that would have been necessary was an urgent request to come to the office, but the brigadier thought that the sight of a uniformed officer might help to communicate the gravity of the moment; the time for reluctance and partial answers was over.

Pittella therefore showed up at Ricciardi's office escorted by Camarda, who had spoken not a word to him the entire way. The musician was looking around in bewilderment, continuously licking his lips. There was something awkward about him: his tall, bony physique made him look like a child who'd grown up too fast.

The commissario invited him to take a seat, scrutinizing his physiognomy in search of the secret allure that would have won over the resistance of a woman like Fedora, the constant target of a bevy of admirers and suitors. Perhaps it was the large, dark eyes, which were given a faintly feminine touch by the long eyelashes, or else it was the intense and emotional expression; maybe the hands, with their long, sensitive fingers; maybe the shy and frightened demeanor, as if of some wild and untamed animal finding itself in a bewildering, strange setting. Or else it could be the simple naïveté of youth.

As usual, Maione took up his position, standing next to his superior officer's desk, motionless and wearing the typical sleepy-eyed expression that came over him when he was engaged in the utmost concentration. He was well aware that his imposing bulk unfailingly put their interviewees in a state of unease, reminding them that it might be best to stick to the whole and unvarnished truth. Perhaps in this case the extra encouragement might not prove necessary, but it could certainly do no harm.

Ricciardi said: "Pittella, let's get down to brass tacks. According to the evidence in our possession, we have sound reason to believe that Fedora Marra was carrying on an affair with a member of the troupe. Even though we have no solid confirmation concerning the identity, we presume that the person in question is you."

Aurelio said nothing, focusing his eyes on the policeman's face as if Ricciardi were expressing himself in some incomprehensible foreign language.

Ricciardi went on: "That fact is not in and of itself definite in terms of the criminal responsibility for the murder; we have no doubts about who pulled the trigger. But this would allow us to establish a motive, and proving premeditation is a fundamental step to prevent the hypothesis of misadventure from being put forth during the trial . . ."

Pittella murmured: "How can you talk about misadventure. That miserable bastard shot her down like a dog, in cold blood."

Maione cleared his throat, letting it be understood that he did not care for interruptions when his superior officer was speaking. Ricciardi nodded.

"We ourselves suppose that to be the case, but in order to be certain about it and, far more importantly, in order to persuade the judge, we need proof. And you can help us."

The other man still seemed unwilling to cooperate.

"How do you know that I was Fedora's lover? No one ever suspected."

That was an aspect which needed to be cleared up immediately, otherwise they were likely to get nowhere. Maione stepped in: "We found a note that Marra had written for you. Now talk, please. We don't have all day."

The threatening tone of voice startled the mandolinist who, after a momentary indecision, spoke again: "I didn't deny anything . . . I just wanted to understand how you'd figured it out, that's all."

Ricciardi asked: "Tell us how it began, how long it had been going on, and whether anyone else knew about it."

Aurelio was twisting his hands, clutching them together in his lap as if they were endowed of a will of their own and he was struggling to hold them still.

"It had been less than a month, Commissa'. I . . . well, you can imagine that I could never dream of hoping that a woman like her . . . I mean, she was Fedora Marra, no? *The* Fedora Marra, the celebrity, the international star, and she was looking at me, an ordinary *posteggiatore* . . . It just so happened that there was a table full of people sitting outside the trattoria, and Elia and I were performing; usually, those people don't even bother to turn around, they just toss us a tip and . . ."

In certain situations, it was important to let the flood of memories flow without restraint. Maione and Ricciardi had experienced it on more than one occasion, and so neither of them interrupted Pittella, neither one thought of telling him not to wander off topic. They just waited to hear what would come next.

"But that time," Aurelio went on, "they stopped talking to listen to us. I hadn't even recognized them, but Elia had, and he elbowed me to make it clear we ought to give it our all; as I told you before, Gelmi even started singing along with us. Then they made two or three requests, and toward the end I struck up *Scetate*. I couldn't seem to take my eyes off her: she was gorgeous. And later, she told me, when . . . Later, in other words, she said that it had all been on account of that song, that I had truly *awakened her* with my mandolin, as the lyrics of the song put it, from a slumber she had no idea she'd fallen into alongside her husband."

Ricciardi asked: "Was she the one who suggested you be hired?"

"No, Commissa'. It was Gelmi. He was enthusiastic about us, he wanted to cast us in at least two numbers. He liked us because we were commoners but also virtuosos; he used those exact words. Me, in particular. That put me in a slightly awkward position with Elia, who is a maestro, an accomplished musician. But Elia was happy about it, too; this was a great opportunity and we had no intention of letting it slip through our fingers."

The commissario persisted: "Then what happened?"

Pittella looked down at the desktop.

"At the end of the auditions, Fedora asked me to stay on a while longer. She said that she wanted to sing *Scetate* with my accompaniment and no one else present. That struck me as odd, because it's a song sung by a man, but I suspected nothing, Commissa', you must believe me. Her husband let her have her way, though he never included the song in the lineup. She didn't object, but she wanted to rehearse it anyway. Afterward, I understood the reason why."

Maione broke in, roughly: "When?"

Pittella blushed; he looked like a little boy forced to confess a misdeed to his father.

"About a month ago. One evening we were alone at the theater. She pretended she was lightheaded, and she asked me to bring her some water; and she insisted that I accompany her to her dressing room. Brigadie', I felt . . . I was afraid, but . . . Fedora was irresistible."

And you're a young man in a world very different from the one you were born into, Ricciardi mused. A world where it's inconceivable to say no or turn to leave when the lead actress, the star, wishes to bestow her favors upon you.

"And it had been going on since then, hadn't it? Had any-one noticed anything?"

Pittella's eyes opened wide.

"No one, Commissa', are you joking? I was risking my job and my future! If Gelmi had had even the slightest suspicion, I'd have been out on my ear, and everyone in the world of theater and music would have known why. It would have been a black mark against my name that I never could have erased: the end of any chance of ever getting work on a stage again as long as I lived! I could just as well resign myself to going back to playing in the street. I would never have let word leak out!"

Maione persisted: "What about Marra? Could she have confided in a girlfriend or anyone else?"

Aurelio shook his head, decisively.

"No, no, Brigadie', she would never have done that either. Even less likely. She cared very much about sparing her hus-band any public ridicule, she told me that over and over. She respected him, she cared for him. If you ask me, she wasn't planning anything different in the future. It's just that she liked me, that's all. Maybe because I was . . . or, that is, because I *am* young. Maybe it helped her to believe that she, too, was still young. Sure, she could have had anyone she pleased, but some-one outside of the theater staff would have been harder to con-ceal."

What the young man had to say matched up nicely with the idea that Ricciardi had developed of the situation. *Love of my life* had been the woman's thought. Who knows whether, as she lay dying, her gaze really had been turned to her husband.

"All right, Pittella, you've kept your secret. And you believe that Fedora did the same thing. But is there anyone, among those who were closest to you, who might have picked up on anything?"

Once again the musician shook his head.

"No, Commissa', I'd rule that out. We were very careful. Only two people could even have imagined, but neither of them ever hinted at it. So . . ."

Maione demanded, brusquely: "Who, Pitte'? Who could have imagined? Come on, don't make us force those words out of your mouth."

The other coughed once.

"Well, one would have been Elia. We always played together, except for *Scetate*. He never said anything to me, but I could tell he was worried, because his professional future was bound up with mine. Ten days ago or so, he asked me whether he had any reason to worry. I reassured him, and that was the end of that."

Maione prodded him to continue.

"And the other person?"

Pittella shrugged his shoulders.

"The only person who stayed late at the Teatro Splendor was Signora Erminia. Fedora had to make her leave if she wanted to take me to her dressing room. She might have guessed, but she never said a word about it."

The brigadier tried to obtain the piece of information for which they'd summoned Pittella to the office.

"But either one of them could have informed Gelmi or anyone else."

The man promptly denied that possibility.

"No, I'm sure they didn't. Elia was terrified of Gelmi in particular; if Gelmi had been sure of the affair, he would have had us both fired."

"What about Erminia?"

"No, not her either, Brigadie'. She knows that Fedora would have fired her if she'd breathed a word. Marra was the most prestigious name in the troupe, even if the lead actor was officially Gelmi. Reporting such a wild piece of gossip, for Erminia, Elia, or anyone else, would have spelled the end of their careers. It was in no one's best interest."

That was true. But it was every bit as true that people don't always act in accordance with their own best interests.

Ricciardi ran a hand over his forehead.

"How many times were you together, and where?"

The mandolinist stared at his hands, clamping his lips. Maione expected him to say nothing; instead, after a while, he looked up and murmured: "A dozen times, more or less, and always in her dressing room."

Ricciardi nodded his head in Maione's direction, and the brigadier, having received the message, dismissed the young man: "All right, Pitte'. You can go. Make sure you say absolutely nothing about this conversation. Are we clear?"

The young man stood up; he was visibly relieved. He was about to leave when Ricciardi, who hadn't budged from his seat, stopped him: "One last thing. You also have a relationship with another member of the troupe, isn't that so?"

The phrase exploded like a bomb. Maione turned to look at the commissario with a stunned expression. Pittella first turned pale and then bright red.

"What does that matter? It's my own business, don't you think?"

Ricciardi was cutting.

"No, not if we're talking about a murder. It might prove to be unimportant, but we need to consider every possible lead."

After a lengthy hesitation, the young man replied: "There's a . . . there's a woman. I want to marry her; I'd never have betrayed her, if it hadn't been for . . . I can't lose this job, Commissario. I'm ashamed of myself, it's true, but I can't afford to lose this job. And I don't want to lose her, either."

Ricciardi's lips curled into a sad smile, filled with melancholy.

"I understand you, Pittella, I understand. But nonetheless I'm going to have to ask you who this person is."

Pittella, in a rush, uttered the name.

XXXV

When they were alone again, Maione took off his cap and ran his hand over his bald head.

"Commissa', the kind of plot twists you come up with, they can only dream about in real theaters! You made me jump! How on earth did you come up with this idea?"

Ricciardi threw both arms wide.

"I thought that if betrayal can make someone crazy, that doesn't mean that the actions taken as a result need necessarily be deranged. Even a person driven mad by jealousy can assemble a complex plan."

Maione was impressed.

"Certainly, if this turns out to be true . . . Now how can we find out, Commissa'? How do we close the circle?"

Ricciardi drummed his fingers on the desk.

"We need to move quickly and with total discretion. It's fundamental that we assure they have no contact between them. Did you tell Camarda to keep Pittella's home under surveillance?"

"Yes, exactly as you instructed. And I've already checked to make sure that the young man has no telephone; he lives in a furnished room in the Spanish Quarter, not far from here. Once he returns home, we can rest assured that he won't be in touch with anyone else."

"Very good. So we have a few hours. I want to talk to Erminia before she goes into the theater, around four in the afternoon, then the other person before the artists start getting ready for the show. Today there's just one performance, is that right?"

The brigadier pulled his watch out of his pocket.

"Yes, Commissa', the evening show, at 8:30. We'll meet there and we can conclude this case, which will give you time to attend the party with the contessa."

Ricciardi heaved a frustrated sigh: "I'd be so glad to skip it, I'm really not in the mood for it. But I've made the promise and I don't imagine there's any way to go back on my word. What about you, where are you going to be until four o'clock? Back home?"

"No, Commissa'. I have a personal matter to take care of."

His superior officer stared at him, with a hint of anxiety.

"Do you want to tell me about it, Raffaele? The other day you arrived late, and you kept the automobile, and now you have a mid-morning appointment. Are you sure you don't need anything?"

Maione smiled, touched by Ricciardi's concern: "Oh, no, Commissa'. Dr. Modo asked me to look into something on his behalf, and I'd like to take care of it by this evening so I don't have any lingering worries on New Year's Eve."

"Dr. Modo, eh? Let's hope he doesn't get himself into trouble and drag you into it with him. Do I need to worry?"

Maione snapped a very military salute.

"Don't worry at all, Commissa'. We'll see you at four o'clock in front of the Teatro Splendor. We'll exchange a few words with Signora Erminia and we'll ask about her family."

Having taken care of the outstanding matters of the year's end, Ricciardi discovered that he was suddenly quite hungry; so he ventured out in search of a vendor who sold fried pizzas.

Once he was out on the street, he heard a subdued voice calling from the entrance of a building a short distance from police headquarters. He turned and glimpsed a figure in the shadows.

He looked more carefully and recognized Livia's chauffeur. The man wasn't wearing his usual uniform, but a rather dented hat and a tiny, tight jacket. He stopped closer and asked: "Arturo? Is that you?"

The man looked around furtively. His behavior worried Ricciardi.

"Has something happened? Is Livia . . ."

The man lifted a finger to his lips.

"Please, Commissa', no names. The lady asked . . . I was told to inquire whether you could come with me for a moment. It'll only take half an hour."

He was whispering, and seemed uneasy. Which only further alarmed Ricciardi.

Arturo added: "I'll go ahead of you. You follow me to the corner of Piliero, past Mercadante. The car is parked there. Walk on the side of the street toward the sea, and then when I walk past you, you can get in. All right?"

Ricciardi furrowed his brow.

"Listen, Arturo, either you tell me what this is about, or else . . ."

The chauffeur begged him: "Please, Commissa'. Please."

His tone was so desperate that Ricciardi finally gave in.

Ten minutes later he was in the car; Arturo drove for a few miles in silence before stopping in front of a nondescript out-of-the-way café. Ricciardi walked in and studied the room, and finally spotted Livia in a secluded corner, sitting at a small table.

He stepped closer. Even if she was dressed in dark clothing, as was customary for her, with a petite hat trimmed with a dark veil that covered her face, long gloves covering her forearms, and a fur stole over her shoulders, the woman still emanated an aura of elegance and sensuality. She was smoking nervously; in front of her sat an untasted demitasse of espresso, now cold.

The commissario took a seat. It had been quite some time since they'd last seen each other alone, and a great many disagreeable events had taken place over that span of time. The commissario greeted her with a nod of the head, studying her through her veil.

"Ciao, Livia. Would you care to explain the reason for this charade? I'd have listened to you even if you'd come directly to me."

She crushed out her cigarette in the ashtray and pulled the veil away from her face. She'd lost weight and her features had sharpened a little, though they had lost none of their refined beauty. Her eyes, filled with a liquid melancholy, were now devoid of the old cheerful gleam that used to animate them whenever they lit on Ricciardi; but there was something else, now, too.

Fear.

"A charade, quite true. But discretion has nothing to do with it. It's not to avoid the idle chatter of a gossipy city, or to keep people from spreading ugly rumors. The situation is serious, deadly serious."

The commissario kept his gaze steady. Livia's voice betrayed extreme anguish. He said to her: "Are you alright? If you need help, you know, I'm here and I always will be, for you."

These words of reassurance and concern had the effect of touching her deeply. Her nostrils quivered and her lips compressed as she struggled to choke back tears.

"No, my dear man. I don't need help, any more than I've ever needed it in my whole life, on account of . . . of the way I was born. You're the one running a great risk, and that's why I've chosen to see you, and in this unusual manner. To warn you."

Ricciardi was bewildered: "Me? Rest assured, I'm very careful, don't be afraid for me. The work I do is far less dangerous than you might suppose, and . . ."

Livia angrily slammed her fist down on the café table, over-turning the demitasse. The viscous liquid filled the saucer and spattered the tablecloth. The waiter, from a distance, furrowed his brow but didn't move.

"You don't understand," she hissed. "You don't have the slightest idea of what I'm trying to tell you. You're so pre-sumptuous that you think you have everything under control, but the one who's under control is *you*. They may already have us under surveillance, though more likely we still have a few— a very few—minutes."

Ricciardi took a look around. Aside from the waiter, who had gone back to focusing on the sea, beyond the low wall on the other side of the street, and Arturo, who was standing by the door, there was no one in sight.

"Livia, you summon me here, after all this time and after what happened between us, just to tell me to be careful? Careful of what?"

The woman regained her composure, but her hands were trembling. Her state of agitation was unmistakable. She took a deep breath and murmured: "I can't explain why, nor can I tell you about the circumstances, but I have to put you on the alert. There's someone very powerful who might have an inter-est in getting rid of you. This Enrica . . ."

Ricciardi interrupted her, sadly: "Livia, I don't believe that my relations with Signorina Colombo are any of your business."

She grew so vehemently exercised that her cap tilted rak-ishly to one side. She straightened it with a brusque gesture.

"I'm not interested in what you do or with whom. It's noth-ing to do with affairs of the heart, love, or marriage. It's a mat-ter of life and death. These people will stop at nothing. Establish your distance from the young woman and leave her to her fate. Otherwise they'll . . ."

Ricciardi scrutinized her. She seemed to mean what she was saying, but the meaning of those words might trace back to the feelings she had nurtured for him and that, to all appearances, she still did.

"Listen to me, Livia, unless you're clear with me, I can't take what you're telling me seriously."

The woman's face was an expressionless mask.

"I'm terrified of these people. You have no idea what they're capable of. People disappear from dusk to dawn, as if by some horrible form of magic. Their families never hear from them again, and no one investigates. In Rome and Milan, it's becoming increasingly frequent, and now it's happening here, as well."

Ricciardi thought he understood.

"I'm not involved or interested in politics, and I can't see how this concerns Enrica."

Livia lowered her voice even more, leaning forward as she did.

"There are important, high-level maneuvers. They don't concern you, her, or me, but certain conditions in higher spheres of endeavor are affected by our actions. We are mere pawns on a chessboard: we're not playing the game, we're pieces in a larger game that *they* are playing. Does that make it any clearer?"

Ricciardi grimaced.

"No, and I have no intention of delving any deeper. Plots disgust me, and even in the most favorable circumstances, I take no interest in them. You must be more explicit or else . . ."

Livia stood up. Her fists were clenched. She smiled cheerlessly at Ricciardi.

"Convince her not to refuse the German's courtship, and not to let him leave. If he were to leave, your life would be in danger. Just remember that."

She lowered her veil and started to head away. Ricciardi put a hand on her arm; that contact released an electric spark that they both sensed, a spark that was still filled with profound significance.

He asked her: "Why did you warn me, Livia?"
She stared at him intensely, behind the thin layer of tulle.
"You know why, Ricciardi. You know perfectly well."
And she left without looking back.

XXXVI

Standing motionless in the narrow passageway between two buildings in utter ruin, Brigadier Raffaele Maione scrutinized several young men sitting outside the Osteria del Campiglione. To keep from being noticed, he'd left the automobile some distance away and had moved stealthily to that observation point.

His mind went back to the brief conversation he'd had with the doctor before setting out. Modo had joined him in the hospital courtyard, and they'd stood talking, battered by the chilly wind that was already sweeping away the old year and which would soon, just a few hours from now, usher in the new year. Modo's lab coat was spattered with blood and his face was marked by unspeakable weariness; his snowy white hair was tousled and messy. His eyes, ravaged by grief, were empty of the wit and spirit that distinguished them; this was yet another crime that whoever had beaten poor Lina so mercilessly would have to answer for.

The doctor had spoken in no uncertain terms. He had come to the same conclusions as the policeman, but absolutely insisted that no arrest be forthcoming. He had mentioned the unfortunate woman's unshakable determination, expressed clearly before she lost consciousness; now the reason for her words had become eminently understandable. As he sadly took a drag on his cigarette, Modo had told Maione that he of all people could grasp the reason for that request. He had then explained that he was every bit as reluctant as Maione to let that beating go unpunished, but it was unfortunately not up to them to make that decision.

Maione had objected vehemently: he was still a public official and, having become aware of a crime, he could hardly turn a blind eye. A violent act of assault and battery, moreover, demanded punishment as the law prescribed.

The doctor had replied firmly and grimly, reminding Maione of the terms they'd established when he'd asked for his help and had shared important and confidential information with him. Therefore, if Maione recognized the bonds of friendship that linked them, he was honor-bound to respect his wishes, which in fact happened to be Lina's wishes: a mother who, via the person of someone dear to her, was asking a favor of a father. No request could be more sacred than this.

In spite of his instincts, Maione had been forced to agree. As he left the hospital, however, he'd felt a seething pool of rage bubbling up inside him, so much so that, instead of returning home to enjoy a nice, hot slice of the onion pizza that Lucia had made to snack on while awaiting dinner, he'd instead headed straight to the garage at police headquarters, where a pair of mechanics were busy repairing the damage to the bodywork of the Fiat 501, accompanied by a string of furious curses. The two mechanics had detected something distinctly discouraging lurking in the brigadier's eyes, and had preferred to make no objections when Maione had demanded the use of the vehicle.

And so now Raffaele was at the Masseria del Campiglione, sheltered from the breeze that was kicking up clouds of dust all along the wide road, staring at those young thugs, brutal beaters of women, as they laughed wildly, in all likelihood already tipsy even though it was still many hours until midnight. Every time he wondered what he was doing there, he gave himself the same, irrefutable answer, quite suitable when it came to allaying any doubts he might feel.

He crossed the street, heading straight for the little group.

The thugs elbowed each other and darted looks in Maione's direction to alert the others. There were four of them, they were young, and they thought they were stronger and meaner than anyone else they were likely to encounter; they were about to encounter a bastard cop from the city police, the sort of person they despised above anyone else on earth; what's more, this reviled denizen of the halls of justice had been so reckless as to show up, unaccompanied, on their own home territory. Two of them furtively caressed the knives that lurked, unseen, in their pockets. And they exchanged smiles.

When he arrived at their little table, Maione said: "Good afternoon, *guagliu'*. Which one of you is Camillo?"

The four young men slowly rose to their feet. The youngest of the group, a handsome fellow with a light complexion and fair hair, asked: "Why? Who wants to know?"

The policeman pretended to take no notice of the bold response.

"I'm Brigadier Maione from Royal Police Headquarters."

To his left, one of the other three let out a faint raspberry. Keeping his eyes on the fair-haired young man, Maione let fly with an open-handed smack and caught the one who'd made the rude noise full in the face, knocking a couple of incisors out of his mouth and laying him out flat on the ground, blood oozing from his face.

The remaining two pulled their knives, ready for a brawl, but Raffaele was too fast for them. He grabbed them both by the collars and slammed their heads together, making a sound like cracking walnuts. Their bodies slumped to the ground, stunned.

It had all unfolded in the space of a handful of seconds, during which time Maione's calm and seemingly sleepy eyes never wavered from the eyes of the young man, whose expression rapidly shifted from insolence to astonishment and then to pure terror.

The young man looked down at his companions, now rolling on the ground and moaning in pain. The one who'd been hit first held his hand over his bloody mouth. He tried to get to his feet but fell back to the ground; then he got up and vanished at a dead run.

Maione spoke calmly: "I'm going to ask you for the last time: Are you Camillo?"

The other man nodded, taking a step back. The brigadier lifted his fist and the man froze in place, as if obeying a direct order.

Raffaele went on, softly: "Again, I'm not going to ask you twice. Tell me what happened, calmly but without stopping. And don't try to lie to me: I give you my word I wouldn't hurt you, but I'm still making up my mind if I feel like keeping that promise."

Camillo gulped. When he finally spoke, his voice came out in a falsetto: "Matteo, my friend, the one who ran awa . . . who left, was in the city fifteen days ago. He helps his uncle, and sometimes he goes to construction sites to unload building material. A bricklayer took him to a . . ."

Midway through that sentence, thinking he could take Maione by surprise, he whirled around and tried to take to his heels. The brigadier's arm, as if endowed with a mind of its own independent of the motionless body to which it was attached, shot out at lightning speed, snatched the would-be fugitive up by the collar of his jacket, hoisted him into the air without apparent effort, forcing him to pirouette on his toes, and then returned him to the exact spot he had just attempted to flee.

"*Guaglio'*, let me give you some advice. Finish what you were telling me, and maybe you'll come out of this in one piece. Maybe. If you try that again, things will not go well for you. Nod your head if you understand."

The young man confirmed with a vigorous nod of the head, as he massaged his neck.

"They went to the brothel, and he saw my . . . She comes here when she can, but my grandfather sends me away, he doesn't want me to meet her. I'd never understood why, but Matteo explained to me. Can you imagine, Brigadie'? My mother is a whore! The others said that . . ."

One of the two young men still lying on the ground, not yet fully conscious, tried to reach out for the knife that had skidded close to him. Again, without losing his composure, Maione lifted one boot and slammed it down hard on the young man's hand. There was the sound of dry sticks breaking, and the young criminal screamed.

The brigadier went on as if nothing had happened: "Go on, if you please."

Staring in horror at his friend who was desperately clutching his fractured fingers, Camillo hastened to reply: "They wanted to punish her, Brigadie', and I was ashamed of being the son of a brothel whore. How could I take that? If they hadn't found out . . . But now that everyone knew, what could I do?"

The brigadier replied in a tone that almost sounded empathetic: "Your mamma is always your mamma, *guaglio'*. Still, just maybe, the doctor is right: to go on living with the knowledge of what you've done to the only person in the world who cares for you is a sufficient punishment, for someone like you."

And with that, Maione turned and headed toward his car. Then he had a second thought and turned on his heel. With a wide wheeling motion of his arm, he described a semicircle in the air: this terrible backhanded smack split Camillo's lip open and knocked him back a yard through the air.

"I just thought you might need a little reminder. Happy ending, and happy beginning."

XXXVII

At four PM on the dot, Maione joined Ricciardi out front of the entrance to the Teatro Splendor.

The commissario gazed quizzically at the brigadier's dusty boots, and Maione immediately tried to clean them by rubbing them against the back of his trousers, justifying himself: "Forgive me, Commissa', I took a little trip out in the country. What about you? Have you had anything to eat?"

In a flash, Ricciardi's mind turned to Livia. The woman's concern, fear, and references to a looming threat, devoid of any precise details. The thought that she might be in trouble fed his anxiety; but he also was forced to admit to an obscure surge of emotion that he'd felt when he squeezed her arm, a body memory that he thought he'd deleted without a trace.

"I just had an espresso," he replied, forcing himself to push those memories out of his mind. "Maybe we'll be done quickly here and we can head home for a bite of dinner."

They didn't have to wait long. Before five minutes were up, they saw Erminia Pacelli arrive, the dresser who had been guarding the lead actors' dressing rooms; the only witness to the lead actors' last quarrel.

Maione emerged from the shadow of an apartment building, his lapels raised tight to his throat to ward off the cold.

"Signo', *buonasera*. May I have a word?"

The woman stopped, alarmed. Her stout physique looked even more robust in her too-long overcoat, with a masculine cut. Rebellious tufts of red hair poked out from under the cap pulled down over her ears.

After a moment's hesitation, she replied: "Actually, Brigadie', I'm about to start work: I wouldn't want to be late. Can we speak the day after tomorrow, when we reopen?"

Maione shook his head and pointed to the entrance of a small café.

"I'm afraid not, Signo'. But it won't take long, trust me."

Making no secret of her unwillingness, Erminia followed him into the café. As soon as she spotted Ricciardi sitting at a table, a pained grimace flashed across her face.

"Please, I need to get to work on time. Signor Renzullo is keeping a very sharp eye on things ever since the tragedy."

The policemen caught the subtext: the woman felt less protected without her guardian angel.

The commissario said: "Signora, we're on the verge of concluding our investigation. You've told us about Gelmi's brief visit to his wife just before the beginning of the second performance."

Erminia sniffed.

"Yes, that's right."

"Do you confirm that you never left your post the whole time?"

The woman tried to hedge her position, retreating behind her usual laconic wall.

"No. I never left my post."

"And are you sure that no one entered Gelmi's dressing room while he was away? Think carefully."

There was a moment of silence, and then the woman replied, brusquely: "Forgive me, Commissa', but you've already asked these questions and I've already answered them, I believe. So why are you detaining me here?"

Before Maione had a chance to upbraid the witness for her disrespectful tone of voice, Ricciardi dug in at her: "Because we're trying to give you another opportunity to tell the truth. We're convinced that someone managed to get into the lead actor's dressing room and managed to insert the fatal bullet into the Beretta's magazine. Now we're just trying to establish exactly what you're lying about: whether it was that you saw no one or that you never left your post. That's the reason we're having this conversation."

Erminia clamped her mouth shut: her small, mistrustful eyes darted from one interlocutor to the other. She kept both fists clenched and her stance was reminiscent of a boxer ready to weigh in.

"I didn't . . . I never budged . . . it seems to me."

Maione prompted her like a schoolteacher trying to help a recalcitrant pupil: "What do you mean by 'it seems to me'? You were so positive about it until just a second ago."

"It seems to me, it seems to me!" the woman blurted out. "I can't remember every detail, you know. I certainly never saw anyone, that much I can assure you. As to whether I might have stepped away for a moment and someone . . ."

The commissario nodded; this was the answer he'd been expecting.

"All right, let's talk about other things. As you must know, we've talked to your husband."

"Yes, so he told me. He's a little . . . You've seen him, right? He lives in a world all his own. And I have to take care of the family."

"It was a very interesting conversation. We learned what Michelangelo Gelmi has done for you and the gratitude that you feel toward him."

The woman ran her tongue over her dry lips.

"He's helped us enormously, but now he's gone and he may not be coming back, am I right? So now we're going to have to take care of ourselves. I tried to explain that to Cesare. He believes that even now, even without the captain, we're untouchable, but that's not the case. We're barely hanging on by a thread."

Ricciardi studied her impassively, practically without blinking.

"That's right, it's 'we' that are hanging on by a thread, isn't it? You're not the only member of the family that works in the theater, are you? There's your daughter, too."

The woman's head retracted ever so slightly, sinking between her shoulders a bit. Maione was focused on every movement she made, and from time to time he turned his gaze to the Teatro Splendor entrance.

"Yes, my daughter works there, too. But she's so good at her work, she doesn't need any help."

The brigadier broke in: "And what does she do in the show, Signo'? Seamstress, costumes, backdrops?"

Erminia turned, her cheeks flame red as if she'd just been slapped in the face.

"How dare you? She's not a dresser. She's a dancer, and the best of them all, not one of those little amateurs who . . ."

Ricciardi stopped her.

"She's the redhead, isn't she? She resembles her father, even if she has your hair color."

A tear rolled down Erminia's right cheek, and she quickly dried her eye.

"She takes after him more than looks. My husband was a good dancer. He was capable of doing a great many things, before . . . before the war. Italia was born in 1913. We named her that because he is a patriot and cares about the fatherland. But afterward, we saw just how much the fatherland cares about him."

The bitterness of that statement was palpable. Ricciardi decided that he could hardly blame her: Cesare Pacelli had experienced a fate that was, in some ways, worse than death.

He asked: "We know that your daughter is engaged; to a fine young man, we've been told. Is that right?"

She shot him a defiant glance.

"Why, is there some law against that? She's pretty and talented, doesn't she have the right to a sweetheart of her own?"

"Indubitably. But I'd like to ask you who he is. Because, with the workload involved in the revue, it must be difficult to find the time to see anyone outside of work."

Erminia puffed up her chest.

"For your information, he is a serious and impressive young man. He's an artist himself, here at the Teatro Splendor. For now, they're just dating, but soon he's going to come to have a talk with us at home."

Ricciardi felt a lurch in his stomach. The idea of someone meeting his beloved's parents to talk about marriage brought his mind back to what was about to happen in the Colombo household that very same evening.

He let out a brief cough.

"So they've been together for just a short while?"

"For a month and a half. But they love each other dearly, she's very happy, and . . ."

Maione interrupted her, decisively.

"Who is the future husband, Signo'?"

The woman turned to look at him and replied proudly: "Aurelio Pittella, the mandolinist. I'm told he's the most talented musician in the city, even if he's still just young. He'll become a maestro. A real maestro."

XXXVIII

The hospital had begun to empty out, starting in the early afternoon, as if triggered by the increasingly intense sound of fireworks in the alleys.

It was the same thing every year. Holidays and suffering weren't good friends. In order to enjoy themselves and cultivate the hope that the new year might be better than the one now ending, people tended to push away the thought of someone fighting sickness in a bed, surrounded by the unpleasant harsh odors of disinfectants and urine, amidst nuns—walking, talking emblems of ill omen—moving busily from one ward to another, and with old people for company who often shut their eyes, never to open them again. The dead were covered with a sheet and wheeled down to the horrible room on the bottom floor, where they were arrayed in rows as if in a warehouse.

Visitors hurried through, to offer uncomfortable greetings to their relatives forced into a hospital stay. They might bring a slice of cake or pizza: Here you are, Mammà, you rejoice in the New Year, too, have a happy end and a happy beginning. And they'd stop doctors and nurses: Happy new year, *dotto'*, nothing's going to happen today, anyway, is it? Can we leave without worries? As if anyone could predict the exact moment when the Lady in Black decided to celebrate after her fashion: with cowl and scythe. As if life and death paid any attention to human conventions: What the devil, does the great misfortune have to strike tonight of all nights, *dotto'*?

Modo always left unanswered those senseless questions, as if he simply hadn't heard them. The alternative would have been to reply harshly, telling them to go off and raise a toast but with full consciousness of what they were doing, showing complete disregard for whomever they were leaving behind in the hospital. Those who die lie flat, those who live get fat. At least some self-awareness, and the courage of their actions.

He checked in on the conditions of the most gravely ill. One of the little burn victims hadn't pulled through, and this death of a little girl had scattered a further sprinkling of sadness. The departure of a young soul was no rarity, unfortunately, but that disaster was, in many ways, worse than the usual run of misfortunates, creating an ironic, horrifying link between the symbol of recurrence, the candle burning on a tabletop, and that blinding death in a blazing fire. The other little girl, however, had regained consciousness and, whining at the painful burns that would leave her disfigured for life, was now asking insistently after her sister. No one dared to tell her the truth.

Once he'd finished his rounds to establish the cycle of treatments that the nurses would be carrying out on this first day of the new year, Modo went back to the uncomfortable stool by Lina's bedside, upon which he had spent the last two days, almost without interruption.

Since ordering him to take absolutely no measures against her son for the acts he had committed, the woman had not yet regained consciousness. The doctor had been forced to speak with unaccustomed firmness to Maione who fully intended, as was perhaps right, to punish the perpetrators. Even Bruno was struggling against a dull rage engendered by the suffering that the poor woman was experiencing, and for which there was no remedy except for heavy sedation, and that, in and of itself, constituted a risk. But Modo was familiar with Lina's tenacity and given the fact that he couldn't argue with her in an attempt to change her mind, he'd decided to respect her wishes.

He sat down and uncovered her in order to evaluate the situation; sheets and mattress were drenched with sweat. Not far away, Sister Luisa was staring at him with unmistakable disquiet: she was every bit as experienced as he was, and she had no difficulty identifying a stark clinical situation. Through the closed window came the muffled fracas of a series of firecrackers and cherry bombs, accompanied by reflected flashes from the detonations. The festivities were underway and growing. The contrast with the interior of the hospital was sharp and heartbreaking.

Modo noticed that the woman's skin was reddened and, when he touched it, he found it scalding hot. With a lurch of horror, he noticed that small black dots, like so many freckles, had appeared on her skin. He summoned Sister Luisa.

In her dream, Lina was holding her baby in her arms. She was outside the farmhouse, her mother was alive and was bringing her a cup of milk so that she in turn could produce milk for her son. What a lovely day, she thought, as she looked up at the sun. What a lovely day.

Sister Luisa could see the anguish in the doctor's eyes and she hurried to get some wet bandages to alleviate at least some small measure of the young woman's torment.

In her dream, Lina lifted the cup to her lips and drank the milk. It was fresh and delicious: it infused her with a subtle pleasure. She could feel the baby's sweet weight. She looked down at him.

The doctor delicately lifted her head to dab a little water on her lips. In her current state, it would be too risky to let her actually drink. If she were to regurgitate, the effects could prove lethal. He thought he could hear Lina heave a sigh of relief.

In the dream, her baby smiled up at her, extending a pudgy little hand. She counted his fingers, just as she had when he was first born, after the raging pain of labor. It had been a piercing, violent, unprecedented pain. And yet she'd been happy, no less so than she was now, holding him in her arms.

While the doctor continued to hydrate her, Sister Luisa applied fresh damp compresses. The symptoms left no room for doubt: her internal organs were collapsing. The woman was losing her fight.

In her dream, Lina wondered what would become of that beautiful baby boy. She knew that certain questions about the future simply shouldn't be asked under a bright blue sky, when problems seem far away and, to all appearances, nothing bad can possibly happen; but she wished for a magnificent destiny for her boy. She glimpsed her father returning from the countryside, hoe on his shoulder, and she waved joyfully to him. Come see how beautiful your grandson is, Papà.

Modo followed Sister Luisa's line of sight and came up with the same interpretation of the symptoms. In his mind, he pictured the young woman's big heart, which had dispensed so much love and had received so little in return, blackened and swollen with the effort of pumping in spite of the occlusions that were beginning to form in the coronary arteries. He imagined himself later, opening up her cold body, with immense melancholy, extracting the inert cardiac muscle, and turning it over in his hands, trying to gauge a thousand questions why, without being able to come up with a single answer.

In the dream, Lina was filled with a strange somnolence. All around her, evening had fallen, a hot summer evening. The lights were blinking on one by one in the farmhouse: oil lamps and candles. The air was sweet-smelling. She slowly began to rock the baby, as he struggled uneasily. Then she sang a lullaby in a low voice. A song that spoke of swallows and springtime returns.

Before realizing it with his rational mind, the doctor's soul sensed with a premonition that Lina was on the verge of leaving this life. He understood it despite the fact that there came a moan from her throat that resembled a song; on her face she had—not an expression of pain, but one of nostalgia—like when you remember a long-ago moment of tenderness. In the throes of anxiety, Modo rummaged through his pockets in search of something to support the heartbeat that was weakening like that of a dying bird. He found some drops and squeezed them into her open mouth, mixing them with that faintly uttered melody that was Lina's unconscious farewell to the world.

Sister Luisa took a few steps away, her hand on her face, her eyes open wide, in sorrow and affliction. She looked at the doctor and saw his cheeks streaked with tears, his hair untidy, pasted to his forehead; she heard his despairing words: Lina, Lina, I beg of you. I could have loved you, if only you'd given me the time. I beg of you.

In the dream, the baby dropped off to sleep as the mother whispered to him: Sleep, my little love, sleep. Mamma will be here beside you forever, as long as she's alive, as long as her heart is beating.

Lina's heart had a small infarction, followed by another, and then it simply broke. For a few more seconds, a dribble of blood reached her brain, allowing her to formulate one last thought:

And even afterwards. Mamma will be with you even after her heart stops beating.

Sister Luisa burst into tears.

Dr. Modo let out a shout, but no one heard it. The sound of firecrackers drowned it out.

XXXIX

There was one final step remaining.

Maione and Ricciardi had tried to reconstruct events, developing a number of hypotheses. Pittella, the young mandolinist, could have gone into Gelmi's or Marra's dressing room to talk about the situation. Or else the young woman, Italia, could have discovered the affair between her own sweetheart and Fedora, and gone to inform the lead actor to get him to put an end to it. Or else, Erminia herself, in virtue of her close personal ties to her husband's onetime captain, might have asked him to weigh in once again to help her daughter.

What they now needed to figure out was whether one of them—finding Gelmi's dressing room empty because the actor had gone to argue with his wife—had taken advantage of that chance situation to reload the prop pistol. Certainly, whoever did it would have had to be quite familiar with firearms, considering how little time there would have been. What's more, why did Gelmi never tell them that he had gone to Fedora's dressing room? The brigadier ventured that, perhaps, he had preferred not to admit that he'd been aware of his wife's betrayal; but it struck Ricciardi as odd that a man would be willing to go to prison for a crime he hadn't committed just to keep a thing like that from getting out.

The one thing that they could state was that the murder and its consequences constituted a very serious blow to the crews and artists at the Teatro Splendor, who were now facing the loss of their livelihoods. The only ones who actually benefited in any way were none other than the two young lovers; that is, if we admit, and it's by no means a certain thing, that Aurelio, the mandolin genius, really did intend to stop seeing the lovely celebrity, as opposed to having simply pulled the wool over the young dancer's eyes.

Anyway, all that the two policemen could hope to do was talk to Italia Pacelli. They had no evidence, there had been no confessions, no glaring contradictions, and the investigation needed to be completed by midnight that day: Garzo had given an order and he'd been categorical.

They headed toward the artists' entrance. With a little luck, they'd be able to solve this case in a matter of minutes.

Bianca looked at herself in the mirror one last time. Carlo Marangolo had made the enormous sacrifice of leaving his bed and getting dressed, in order to accompany her to buy the entire array of finery for that evening's outing.

The choice had immediately fallen on a gown with a richly ruffled skirt, shorter in front and longer in back, in a chiffon velvet spangled with rhinestones; not only did it show off to good advantage the contessa's elegant figure, the fabric happened to be the same color as her eyes: a rich and shimmering purple.

She had objected to the cost of the garment, exaggeratedly expensive in any case and out of all proportion given the occasion, but Carlo had insisted: "Vaccaro di Ferrandina is an old harpy, and she'd be so delighted to detect even the slightest shortcoming in your attire that to me, the pleasure of imagining her with her jaw hanging open in admiration strikes me as cheap at the price. Yes, we'll take this one, thanks."

Along with the gown, they had also bought a hat the same color, a satin astrakhan vest, and a broad belt in soft leather that emphasized the woman's narrow waist and long, long legs. Also, a woolen overcoat with a wide fur collar and a small black clutch bag made of antelope hide, with tiny embroideries.

"I can't do anything about it," she had told the duke with a smile, "at my age I feel like going back to playing with dolls."

Bianca had gone along in order to make him happy, and also out of vanity. Now, though, she felt just a little uneasy: that opulence was alien to her, at least it was now. She went to show it off to the duke, who was waiting for her, exhausted, in the drawing room in her home in Palazzo Roccaspina, a magnificent building that had been neglected and run down due to Bianca's husband's bad gambling habit but which now, thanks to Marangolo, was slowly being restored to its former splendor.

As soon as he saw her, the duke opened his eyes wide in amazement. Then he coughed, dabbing at his mouth with his handkerchief, and said: "Never. I've never seen you look so lovely. Not even when I met you at age sixteen, in your parents' garden, red in the face after dismounting from a ride on your horse. You are enchanting. No man, however mad or masochistic he might be, could possibly resist you."

The contessa smiled at him, tilting her head to one side.

"All credit due to you, my friend. And your stubbornness. Do you realize that all this stuff costs more than an office worker earns in a year?"

He shrugged his shoulders and threw both arms wide.

"So what? I'm sorry for the office worker. I don't believe I've ever made a better investment. If I have the strength, the last thing I'll try to remember when I shuffle off this mortal coil will be the sight of you as you stand before me now."

Bianca raised her hand to her mouth.

"Please, oh please, don't talk like that. You'll live forever. Without you I can't even imagine facing life."

Carlo smiled, sadly: "If only God Almighty took His orders from you, sweetheart. If only. But, rather, can I give you a piece of advice? Your Ricciardi said that he had to go to the theater for work, didn't he? Go and meet him there in my car, after dropping me off at home. As soon as he sees you, he'll quickly forget any temptation he might feel to avoid coming to pick you up."

Bianca thought it over: "Maybe you're right, Carlo. Although I don't know him well, but what I do know does suggest that he's likely to work late on purpose, just to give himself that excuse. It might be better for me to go meet him."

From inside the café across from the Teatro Splendor, Ricciardi and Maione watched nearly all the artists go by, one by one.

Erminia had gone inside after their conversation, and she had not come back out; that meant they were reasonably certain that she would be unable to warn anyone about the conversation. Half an hour later, Aurelio Pittella appeared, followed at a safe distance by Officer Camarda. The mandolinist was pale and, even from a distance, seemed very nervous to Maione and Ricciardi. He loitered outside for a few minutes, in spite of the icy wind, smoking a cigarette. The two policemen exchanged a knowing glance: perhaps he was waiting for Italia in order to confer with her before the show began.

But the dancer didn't show up, and the young man, responding to the urging of Elia Meloni, was forced to desist and go in.

Time passed. Ricciardi and Maione wondered what had become of the young woman.

The imminence of the great celebration rendered the atmosphere increasingly charged and electric. The fireworks were intensifying and old pieces of junk began to rain down from the balconies, especially chipped or dented pots and pans set aside especially for the occasion. The noise of glass and pottery smashing to the pavement below was a steady counterpoint to the whistles, syncopated reports, and clacking of noisemakers;

the smell of gunpowder filled the air. Maione pulled his watch from his pocket and sighed as he thought of Lucia's savage reaction at his umpteenth late arrival.

He realized that he needed to pee, and asked the proprietor of the café if there was a restroom.

Bianca asked the chauffeur to drop her off a hundred yards or so from the Teatro Splendor. A horse drawing a cart and returning home late had reared up in panic at an exploding firecracker, and the drayman was trying to calm the animal down, to the mockery of the street urchins, the *scugnizzi*, who were clustering around; there was no way the limousine could get through there.

The contessa made arrangements with the chauffeur: they would meet back up at that exact location as soon as she managed to capture Ricciardi and spirit him off. As she walked along the sidewalk, she crossed paths with two young men; one pretended to faint and blew her an impertinent kiss. The little vignette put a smile on her lips.

The evening, thought Bianca, was looking promising.

At last Italia Pacelli appeared.

Spotting her from a distance, Ricciardi realized that she was really quite fetching. She'd taken the best of both her father's and her mother's sides, and the result was as noteworthy as it was unexpected. She was wearing a camelhair coat and a little black hat that was too small to contain her thick red mane of hair. She wasn't walking fast; she seemed indifferent to her late arrival, as if lost in other thoughts, distracted.

Ricciardi looked to one side for Maione, and then remembered that the brigadier had gone to the restroom. If the young woman had a chance to enter the theater, they'd be forced to question her in the presence of the other artists, with the risk of contamination of the testimony.

So he decided to go it alone. He left the café and walked toward her.

Bianca turned the corner.

That short walk had taken her to the rear of the Teatro Splendor, near the artists' entrance; so she was going to have to walk around the building.

She was just deciding which way to go when she saw Ricciardi walk toward a young woman and call out to her.

Italia Pacelli had a clutch bag in one hand and her eyes were downcast. She must be concentrating on who knows what.

She heard someone call her name and she looked up. About ten yards away from her was the very same specter that had haunted her last two sleepless nights: the green-eyed policeman who had questioned her and her mother, and had even visited their home.

The man who had understood everything.

Concealing her right hand with her overcoat, she opened the bag and clasped her father's pistol.

Bianca, who was in a favorable vantage point, realized that the young woman was pulling a pistol out of her bag.

She was five or six yards away from her. She wouldn't be in time to grab her arm or even just shove her aside. Nor could she lunge into the line of fire.

She understood that Ricciardi had not yet glimpsed the weapon.

On the other side of the street, Brigadier Maione had just stepped out of the café and was looking around, at a loss.

The red-haired young woman aimed the pistol.

Bianca did something that the strict nuns who had raised her had soundly imposed upon her, ever since she was a little girl, that she should never, *ever* do.

She screamed with every ounce of breath in her throat.

Ricciardi, over the noise of pots and pans crashing down off the balconies and the shrill whistles, the clacking of the noise-makers and the bangs of the firecrackers, over the laughter and other happy noises coming out the windows of the apartments, heard Bianca's voice and he turned to look.

Maione broke into a run.

Italia Pacelli took aim and fired.

The Gunshot

I'm so sorry, Brigadie'.

I'm especially sorry for those two days and those two nights spent with my eyes focused on the ceiling, trying to figure out what to do. How to get out of this situation.

You can't imagine what hell is. What it means to have a circle closing in on you a little at a time. In those green eyes I glimpsed the spark of understanding from the very outset. From the minute he assembled us all backstage to talk to us. And yet I thought it was all clear: Gelmi had killed the whore, because a whore is what she was, Brigadie', and the very worst kind. Some whores do the work just to survive, she did it to have everything and keep from feeling old, but old is what she was becoming.

In short, he'd fired the shot, with his own pistol, in front of artists and spectators; that idiot Romano had even wet his pants and no longer wanted to get up off the floor. It was hard to keep from busting out into open laughter, he truly was ridiculous. No one had any doubts, did they? Then why did the man with green eyes keep insisting on asking questions, Brigadie'? Because he didn't believe it. He'd never believed it.

I've always hated Gelmi. For years, long before I ever met him, before I first saw that fake face, made up like a woman, with his dyed hair and his tailored outfits. I've hated him from the stories my father told me.

It was his fault that my father became the way he is now, did you know that? No. Of course you didn't. All it took was the charitable act of giving us jobs, my mother and me, to erase those memories. My father has no longer even mentioned it, and neither have we. Thank you, Signor Gelmi. Thank you for giving us food to eat, thank you for rescuing us.

But no, Brigadie'. The way he tells it wasn't the way it worked at all. The captain had failed to order the retreat in time. He'd been too afraid of leaving the trench. He'd waited for the enemy to come because he was paralyzed with terror, it hadn't been an act of courage, at all. And when the grenade landed, he'd hidden behind the thing that was closest to hand: my father. That's who the hero really was. The officer decorated for military valor.

As soon as Papà was able to speak again and we understood that he would live, unfortunately, because the fate that awaited him was worse than death, he told me everything. And I began to hate Gelmi's face, the face that appeared on posters or on the silver screen. There he was, handsome and strong, smiling and rich, in the limelight and on magazine covers; while my father was ravaged, deformed, and poverty stricken; we were condemned to scrabble for a living amidst hardships.

Still, I managed to put up with it. When he hired me, making my dreams as a little girl come true, my dream of dancing in front of a packed house to the applause of the audience, I even considered forgiving him.

Then on the boards of the stage I met Aurelio.

There aren't many young men in the revue, have you noticed? There's Pio Romano, but he . . . well, he's not especially interested in women.

Aurelio is special, you hear him play and you're immediately enchanted. You can't understand, Brigadie', no disrespect but you're not an artist. His hands extract words from his instrument: he's a genius.

We took to each other almost from the very start. Who could be luckier than me? I was dancing, I was in love, and he loved me back. He was the first man in my life, and at this point, he'll also be the last. What a pity.

But my happiness didn't last long. Because one day that tremendous whore laid her eyes upon him.

If you ask me, she wasn't even interested in him, and you can trust me on that. But he was the youngest one in the troupe. And she was obsessed with age. She was constantly looking at herself in the mirror, applying makeup, massaging her face. And she'd ask each and every one of us: How do I look? Do you think I look pretty? I don't have any wrinkles, do I? Does this dress hold my breasts up?

Brigadie', Aurelio was nothing more to her than a cosmetic, a makeup kit. Like a jar of face powder or greasepaint. He was just a tool that helped her forget the passage of time. That said, even the whore's obsession, if you stopped to think, was Gelmi's fault: because as he drank and aged rapidly, he showed her day by day what was bound to happen to her, eventually. So what could be better, if she wanted to continue to feel young and desirable, than a young man, already betrothed, in the prime of his life, hungry for success, and blinded by the image of such fake beauty?

Aurelio told me: Forgive me, Ita'. I can't afford to lose my job. And neither can you, right? If we're not careful, they'll fire us both. And he was right, Brigadie'. I cared about my job, too.

That was then I started to cast about for a solution. Every day, three times a day, I witnessed the fiction of Gelmi killing the whore, shooting her down like a bitch, the cheating bitch that she was, while my Aurelio embroidered on the melody. With all the times that I'd watched her die, wishing with all my heart that it really could happen, I started to wonder how my wish could finally come true.

As you've seen, I'm quite familiar with handguns. To help my father feel he's still alive, I keep his uniform and pistol clean and in good order—that same pistol I used to shoot the commissario, the same model handgun as was used onstage. I practiced at home, I calculated the shots, I ran through the steps over and over again. It wasn't even necessary to make it complicated: I only needed to replace Gelmi's clip with the one from Papà's gun. It took me a minute, no more.

My mother stands guard on the dressing rooms. I involved her because her help was indispensable. She needed to alert me when Gelmi left his dressing room.

She didn't want to do it, Brigadie', even though she hated him, too. It was still a murder. I had to explain to her that I wouldn't be killing anyone. No, it would be that worthless, piti-ful man, that coward, who would actually shoot the whore. I would simply put him in the position to do justice, that's all, to do what he ought to have done if he hadn't been a miserable wretch. Because Gelmi knew, Brigadie', he knew perfectly well that his wife was cheating on him, and not just with Aurelio, but also with other friends of theirs, but by now the only reason he still had work was her, and he couldn't afford to lose her. Which is why he whined and sniveled, why he got drunk, and why he said nothing: out of self-interest. Like I told you, a coward.

I switched the clip before the 5:30 performance. Mamma let me know when he went out to get a bottle; he always drank at that time of day, sometimes he had trouble staying on his feet. After 8:30 he'd recover a little, and that's why I chose the second show: I was afraid that for the first show he'd be too tipsy and by the third show he'd be too tired. I put my money on the fourth bullet, hoping that his aim would be better. And so it was.

How I rejoiced as I watched her breathe her last, Brigadie'. She fell against the backdrop drooling blood: ugly, so horribly ugly. Do you remember? She looked like a broken doll. And if you ask me, it looked as if she'd aged. I took a close look and she had wrinkles around her eyes, once she was dead. She could no longer stretch and massage her skin.

I thought I'd gotten away with it. Then that damned green-eyed man started asking question after question, digging into the manure and the filth as if he knew what he was looking for.

When you two came to talk to my father, I realized that by now you had almost reached the truth.

But I fooled myself into thinking that it was an idea of his, of the commissario's, an idea that he still hadn't shared, because it was just too farfetched of a theory. A man murders his faithless wife in front of hundreds of spectators and there's actually someone who believes it wasn't him. How absurd.

I thought to myself that if he still hadn't talked about it with anyone else, then I only needed to get rid of him. Certainly, if he'd entered the Teatro Splendor and summoned me in front of my fellow cast members, I would have simply denied everything, I'd have pretended to be stunned and outraged; whereas if you and he, Brigadie', had detained me, I'd have known that he'd told you about it, or else that he'd probably put it all down in writing somewhere.

Instead he approached me all alone, in the street, and so I thought: now I'll kill him and that will be the end of it. I can still get away with it. There was all the noise of New Year's Eve, firecrackers and rockets, noisemakers, and showers of old plates and glasses tossed down, off of balconies. Veterans from the Great War shooting their guns out of windows in celebration. It could easily have been a stray bullet, or a criminal just settling an old score. I would shoot him, one bullet to the chest, and then be gone, I'd slip into the theater. I'd blend in with the others, commenting: Oooh, look at that, isn't that the commissario who questioned us all? Poor soul, I wonder who could have done it.

But that woman in an evening gown appeared out of nowhere. I should have known it would turn out badly, and you know why, Brigadie'? Because of the gown she was wearing.

It was purple: for theater people in Italy, purple is unlucky.

EPILOGUE

T he old man falls silent once again, and the young man
wonders, in disbelief, whether he really has stopped
telling the story. He follows his gaze as it points vaguely
up at the sky, resting on the swallows and the city filled with
light and shadows, alive with murmurings, so similar to that
same city sixty years ago.

Then he realizes that the other man is starting to sing a
song. But he can't figure out what song it is, because it's less
than a faint moaning, like when you think of something far, far
away. In space or in time.

The clawlike fingers hold that instrument, at once sorrowful and tragic, comical and surreal, that helps him make it
through the shadows and reach the new morning.

The young man clears his throat and asks in subdued voice:
Maestro, after that? What happened after that?

The old man turns around slowly, a little surprised, as if
he'd utterly forgotten the young man was even there. What do
you want to know?

The young man is breathless, it seems impossible to him
that this is how it ends. He points to the world outside the window, as if the presence of streets and people, automobiles and
airplanes somehow justified his curiosity. But after that, what
happened to them, Maestro? Did the young woman go to
prison? Did the commissario die? Was Gelmi released? And
the . . . The young man doesn't know how to finish that sentence, but there's no need after all.

The old man shrugs his shoulders: Ah, he says, I have no idea. That same night I boarded a freighter, and after that, another one, and another one after that. I was terrified, I was afraid they'd drag me into it, charge me with complicity or, even worse, say that I'd organized the whole thing in cahoots with that lunatic Italia. Far better to take to my heels.

The young man sits there openmouthed: You ran away? Where? For how long?

The old man smiles, while the darkness advances little by little. Yes, I ran away, with nothing but this. And he lifts the mandolin in the shadows. My only luggage. And it was a good thing I brought it, because where I stopped, in South America, there were no instruments like this one. Who knows what kind of garbage I'd have had to settle for.

South America, the young man whispers.

That's right, says the old man. I stayed there for forty years, with no further contacts with my past. I changed my name two or three times, and I had a thousand different jobs. But in the evening, I always found my way to a campfire, to play my mandolin. In front of hundreds of pairs of eyes welling over with tears. You know, *guaglio'*, so many people migrated from here. And they've had children who've had other children: but they all still have the desire to come back, even if, for one reason or another, that hasn't happened. These people, when they hear the sound of the mandolin, for a while they dream of their long-ago home. And I gave them that dream.

The young man listens in wonderment. Then he asks: but Italia . . . and Fedora? Who were you in love with, Maestro? Was it true what the dancer confessed to the brigadier? The old man shakes his head. I cared for Italia, she seemed like a fine young woman; I hadn't understood that she was completely insane. Fedora . . . Fedora was beautiful. A very special woman. She gave me the feeling that I'd . . . grown up. Become a strong, adult man. In a certain sense it was me who killed her, at least in part, don't you think? If she hadn't loved me, she would have lived to see other days.

The young man reflects and decides that the old man is right. Now he knows why that artist endowed with supreme talent has never left a mark on the musical landscape of the past decades. It's because he wasn't there. He was somewhere else.

Maestro, but what have you done in all these years? Did you give concerts, did you make records, maybe under some pseudonym, did you teach important students? And why have you come back?

The old man scrutinizes the mandolin, as if stunned to find it still in his hands. He struggles to his feet, with a creaking of bones; he places the instrument in its case, closing it gently. He runs his hands over its flaking black surface, the dulled buckle, the leather strap.

He steps over to the window and observes the swallows as they fly, following trajectories that are mysterious and perfect and useless.

He looks out at the lowering night, at the sea somewhere between sky blue and black, the mountain in its perennial wait, and he says: I am the swallow that, as winter ends, nurtures the dream of returning; and if it's alive, then sooner or later, it returns.

He turns to look at the young man: I don't know whether the kind policeman with the strange green eyes died that night. Or whether the big strong brigadier, who seized Italia and took her away, managed to figure out what had actually happened. Whether Gelmi remained in prison, with his diseased liver, or whether he found himself out from behinds bar and a free man again, though without the love of his life. Every swallow has its journey, *guaglio'*. I had to set out on my own. I returned to die where I was born. In the only place I've ever been happy.

He looks out the window again and says in a low voice: In the only place where it's possible to be happy.

Then he turns, slowly bends over, and takes the case in both hands. He takes a step toward the young man and hands it to him, as if it were a newborn fast asleep in its crib.

The young man feels his heart skip a beat in his chest. He feels a mixture of inadequacy, sorrow, and sheer terror.

Maestro, he says, no. Not to me; I'm not capable, I'm not ready. I'm not worthy.

The old man smiles and he already seems dead, while the night glitters behind him; a skull with hair: thinning, white, weirdly long hair. He's the tall, bony young man, the one who embroidered golden fabrics for Fedora's sleeping hours, murmuring in tune with the swallows: *Love of my life*.

The old man replies, softly: You're wrong. Before you weren't worthy, just as anyone who plays and sings and has no idea what story to tell is unworthy. But now you've learned. And you understand that you need to depart, because you're a swallow. A swallow needs a journey, to be happy.

The young man takes the case; never has any object felt so immensely heavy.

The old man drags his feet back to the armchair; he sits, with the blanket over his legs.

And he starts to dream. For the last time.

XL

Hands on her hips, brow furrowed, and jaw jutting in an unintentional but highly successful imitation of the head of Fascist Italy's government, Nelide reviewed the table for the umpteenth time. The young master had been laconic but precise: I'll be home for dinner, possibly latish, and then I may go out again.

I'll be home for dinner: therefore, dinner would be expected, and dinner would be ready. All strictly in the Cilento style, the way that Zi' Rosa had prescribed, to ensure that the roots weren't lost, that they were preserved. And so the young woman had procured well in advance the necessary ingredients to complement what she had in her pantry, conveyed by horse cart from the Malomonte farmlands.

The last meal of the year, being as it was a meal on the eve of a feast, a vigil, had to consist of lean food, by ecclesiastic rules. That did not mean, however, that it had to consist only of *humble* food. As a result, she had prepared several mainstays of the cuisine of her homeland, cleaving closely to the ancient recipes handed down from mother to daughter. *Cinguli cu' l'alici*, a long pasta cut to pieces, obtained by *cingulianno*, that is, rolling the flour and water mixture under one's hands, and then saucing it with anchovies preserved in old olive oil. Or *baccalà fritto*, fried salted cod, preserved at a constant temperature, in coarse salt, and then debrined with two daily baths of cold water for three days. *Zeppole salate*, fried zeppole with bits of anchovies and served hot. For now, they lay white and innocent, while the large frying pan stood ready to accommodate them.

The antipasto, obviously, would be the sautéed broccoli, with garlic, black olives, and anchovies; that's an absolute must.

The sequence of the nine fruits and nuts, which would culminate with the pine nuts, would put an end to the traditional ritual before the sweets, the *nocche 'i Natali* and the *pastoredde*: cinnamon, honey, sugar, and cloves for the first dish; chestnuts, chocolate, and grated lemon for the second. Actually, one dessert would have been enough, but Nelide had preferred not to be put in the position of choosing one over the other. After all, sooner or later, the young master would eat it all. When it came to eating, the young master could eat. But he always seemed distracted, as if his mouth and his stomach weren't communicating with his head.

The tablecloth was decorated with leaves, branches, and flowers. In Cilento, this was a tradition; young women gathered them in the wood early in the morning of the day, and then wove them together. Since she was in the city, Nelide had already resigned herself to the necessity of doing without; venturing into the nearby Capodimonte forest and defying the royal guards in order to procure the makings of that adornment struck her as excessive. Then something odd had happened. Tanino 'o Sarracino, the fruit and vegetable vendor, the odious fancy man who, instead of sticking to his profession, put on pointless shows in the neighborhood street market, had shown up at her door with the traditional fruits of the year's end, even including pine nuts. Unfurling his finest and most dazzling smile, the young man had begun singing a romantic serenade, pulling from behind his back an exquisitely assembled bouquet.

For a few seconds, Nelide had stared at him through the space in the door left open by the chain. Without warning, she'd reached out her hand, grabbed the exquisite little bouquet, and shut the door in the young man's face. A verse of the song had died out midway through, as if someone had rudely shoved a gramophone needle across the record.

The flowers had turned out to be perfect: Zi' Rosa would have been contented to see even that custom respected. Now she had only to await the young master's return so she could begin frying the *zeppole*. He would sit down, make himself comfortable: a happy ending, to ensure there would be a happy beginning.

She was drying her hands on her apron when she heard a knock at the door. Her jaw tightened at the thought that this might be Tanino again: she went to answer the door, ready to slam it shut again promptly.

There was a policeman at the door.

Enrica had been tempted to run away.

She'd thought about it all day long while helping to prepare dinner, without any desire to do so: silent, eyes downcast, indifferent to the atmosphere of expectation that always accompanied that special evening.

To run away. Considering that as a real possibility, something she could organize in secret, alone, under her own power—it helped her. To run away. That wasn't her style. It wasn't something Enrica would do—flee in the face of difficulty, refuse to take on a challenge, calmly and with determination, without any sudden moves or harsh words, without raising her voice but neither retreating by so much as a fraction of an inch from her own convictions.

She fantasized, while her brother regaled them with miraculous predictions for the new year, and her mother and sisters shot baffled glances at her as they organized the loveliest and most lavish banqueting table that had even been seen in that home. She fantasized about leaving the kitchen as if heading for the restroom, instead only to head her for bedroom, with a quick stop to plant a kiss on her father's cheek as he sat intently reading the newspaper. She fantasized about getting down her large travel bag, the one she'd used to go to the seaside summer camp the previous year, when she'd first met Manfred. She fantasized about filling it with a few select items: a couple of changes of undergarments, a dress, her various objects of toiletry. Putting on her overcoat and hat. Waiting for the hall to be empty and then leaving the apartment in utter silence.

The concierge, that kindhearted gossip, would have asked her: Signori', where are you going at this time of night, on the evening of the last day of the year? Look out, be careful, people throw old junk out the windows, you know.

And Enrica herself, at age twenty-five, felt old. Perhaps her mother ought to have tossed her out the window: a daughter who stubbornly insisted on remaining an old maid, turning her back on the best of opportunities, the most eligible catch.

But she wouldn't run away, nor would anyone throw her out any windows. Reality and fantasy aren't the same thing, so she'd have to meet Manfred and act perfectly natural, as if she hadn't turned down his proposal just two months ago, as if she hadn't turned her back on him and withdrawn to the kitchen to stare at the window across the way.

Instinctively, almost without realizing it, she looked up. No light, aside from the glow that arrived from the next room over, the somewhat impersonal drawing room where Rosa, the housekeeper, now dead, had served her an espresso.

That meeting seemed like an eternity ago, and yet it had happened only recently. It had given him a chance to talk with her. She had told him clearly that she was at a crossroads, that he would need to take a step in her direction, if he really desired her. In response she had received silence. Nothing but silence.

She'd dressed soberly, without any frills or fripperies, and her mother had shot her a glare of reproof. She'd have liked to see Enrica dressed in something more coquettish, something that expressed delight at the officer's return visit; but Maria knew there was only so far she could push her daughter. It was sufficient to know that her daughter would be there and would behave politely. Time would take care of the rest; little by little, everything would be squared away.

Someone knocked at the door.

Her mother looked at the pendulum clock on the wall: punctuality was typical of Germans. She shot an imperious toss of the head in Enrica's direction, directing her to go and open the door. It was up to her. It was Enrica who had behaved rudely two months ago, and now she had to make up for it.

With death in her heart, the young woman went to answer the door.

As soon as she heard the news, Nelide asked herself only one question, the same question she asked constantly in the face of any new problem, small or large. What would Zi' Rosa do? Usually, the answer came to her quickly, because she knew her aunt to perfection, being as she was herself a faithful replica of her aunt.

This time, though, she was assailed by doubts. Someone has shot the commissario, the officer had told her. He's at the hospital, the officer had told her. We don't know anything else, the officer had told her. The doctor is operating on him now, the officer had told her. They sent me to inform you, the officer had told her. With your permission, I'll go now, the officer had told her. Whereupon he had left.

Nelide wasn't built to lose heart or depair. Fear, anguish, and anxiety were emotions unknown to her. Life was something you faced up to, and that was that. It made no sense to weep and wail, it served no purpose to despair; what you did was roll up your sleeves and fight.

The young master was wounded and her place was at his side.

She had to watch over him and make sure that no one made a mistake in his care, that no one took advantage of the opportunity to rob him, that any wishes or needs he might have would be satisfied. She needed to stand by his bed, wide awake and alert, as she'd done during her aunt's brief illness. That's what Rosa would have done, and now it's what Nelide should do.

But where was that hospital? What streets would take her there? And once there, would they even let a young woman from Cilento in, a young woman who didn't know how to express herself well in proper Italian, and would therefore struggle to explain what she was doing there? She needed someone capable of stating things clearly. Someone who cared as much about the young master as she did.

Nelide's eyes had gone decisively to the window across the way.

Enrica shut her mouth. Her heart was pounding in her chest. All around her, the world had dissolved in an instant. The fog had descended again: she saw nothing, she understood nothing.

Hurrying up as the second member of the family to extend cordial greetings of the house to Manfred, Maria was left with her smile frozen on her features when she found herself face to face with that remarkably homely young woman, with her determined eyes, narrow mouth, and decisive jaw covered in dark fuzz, wearing an overcoat that reached all the way down to her stump-like ankles and a cloche hat jammed firmly down over a thick and furry unibrow.

This stranger returned her glance impassively. She'd said what she needed to and now she waited.

Enrica turned to her mother, tears streaming down her cheeks, a trembling hand covering her mouth. She collected herself, stepped around Maria, and ran into the living room to find her father.

Bianca was sitting on the sofa in the large living room in Palazzo Marangolo, but this time she wasn't listening to music. This time she was crying.

The duke stared at her, worried.

"Bianca, darling, be reasonable: it wasn't advisable for you to dally in a hospital waiting room on New Year's Eve. Dressed like this, in the midst of people from every walk of life, you'd have . . . And after all, what right did you have to be there? It's one thing to defy the gossips and the backbiters, but this would have been going too far. You're still a married woman, you have a name to worry about. It's one thing to be accompanied to the theater or a reception, it's quite another to rush to the bedside of a man who's been shot outside of a theater."

The contessa stared at her friend with puffy eyes.

"Carlo, don't you understand? That young woman was just a few yards away when she pulled out her pistol and . . . He hadn't even noticed it: if I hadn't screamed and he hadn't turned, that would have been the end of him. And then that blood, all that blood, the chaos, the people, the brigadier lifting him up in his arms . . . And if it had gone . . . Oh, my God, Carlo . . ."

The duke reassured her: "He isn't dead, he's being operated on. I sent my chauffeur to find out the latest. The doctor is a friend of his: something of a hothead, but apparently very good at his job. So he's in good hands. In any case, for you this was an unseemly situation. That's why I ordered that you be brought here. I couldn't imagine you out on the streets on a day like this."

He turned his gaze to the balcony. All around the dark seawater, the city seemed to be at war: smoke, explosions, flowers of light that challenged the stars and the chilly wind. Through the locked windows came the muffled noises of the celebration.

Bianca, trying to stifle her sobs, said: "Just seeing him there,

Carlo . . . on the pavement . . . I was petrified. They taught me how to behave on all occasions, and yet . . . What am I to do, Carlo? What am I to do now that I know . . . that I know . . . "

In the dim light, the duke smiled at her with tenderness and melancholy.

"Rest, Bianca, rest. Tomorrow morning, when the sun rises, all will become clear. And then we'll decide what would be best. I'll help you. The new year is always better than the old one. And by now it's almost midnight."

Enrica burst into the hospital at a dead run, her hair a mess, red in the face, her eyeglasses befogged with weeping.

Heading out of the apartment building's front entrance downstairs, followed by her father and by Nelide, she had crossed paths with Manfred carrying a large bouquet of flowers; the German's dazzling smile had died on his lips the minute he'd glimpsed the young woman's overwrought expression. She hadn't even slowed down to say hello to him.

Now she stood in front of a closed door behind which lay written the destiny that awaited her. Now it was clear to everyone that in her life there was no room for love, joy, or sorrow uncoupled from the future of the man who lay suffering behind that glass. Now there was nothing more to say or do, other than to turn the handle and find out what was to become of her.

Nelide and the Cavalier Giulio Colombo looked each other in the eye. In their respective inner worlds, which couldn't have possibly been any further apart, the same, identical conviction had taken root: it was up to Enrica to open that door.

And Enrica opened it, plunging into the room without hesitation, without stopping to catch her breath, with a heart that had stopped beating for the moment.

Inside stood Brigadier Maione, ashen-faced, cap in hand, his uniform jacket smeared with clotted blood, his features hardened with concern. Dr. Modo, pale with exhaustion, his white hair plastered to his forehead with sweat, stood beside him; he was drying his hands in a large linen handkerchief, his stained lab coat open over his waistcoat.

In the middle, lying on a gurney, pale and in pain, was Ricciardi. His eyes, glazed with sedatives, focused on Enrica's face, and a weak smile appeared on his lips.

Modo was the first to speak.

"The bullet entered and exited his shoulder, resulting in no lesions of any organ; but that was a matter of inches. Old Ricciardi is indestructible, it would seem. Certainly, if he hadn't turned to one side at the very last second, things would have gone differently. Anyway, hell doesn't want him, for now."

Enrica stepped close. But the commissario was no longer looking at her. He was staring at the embarrassed face of the man behind her, the one with a drooping mustache and spectacles, so similar to his daughter.

He opened his mouth and coughed. And then, in a faint but firm voice, he spoke: "Cavaliere, *buonasera.* I apologize for the disagreeable circumstances, but I'd like to ask for your permission to see your daughter, Enrica. Let me assure you that I have only the most honorable intentions toward her."

Outside, beyond the shut door and the courtyard, a frenzy of jubilation exploded at the death of the old year and the birth of the new year. Which had finally arrived.

ACKNOWLEDGMENTS

Ricciardi dedicates this tenth novel to two wonderful mothers, who both passed away just as he was assembling ideas for his investigation: the mother of Antonio Formicola, who is the strategic mind behind every story, and the mother of Giulio Di Mizio, his green-eyed gaze upon death. He is grateful, to these departed mothers, for these two pillars without whom his stories would never have existed.

He's grateful to Severino Cesari, first and foremost, because it is from him, through him, and with him that these stories go, thus it has been, thus it is, and thus it always will be. And like always, he is grateful to Francesco Pinto and Aldo Putignano, his noble sires.

He is deeply grateful to Stefania Negro, skillful and unique weaver of research and custodian of the memory of his life and the existence of the other characters. He is grateful to Roberto de Giovanni, for the medicine of the living, and to Sabrina Prisco of the Osteria Canali, who prepares the foods of Cilento. He is grateful to Nicola Buono of the Fattoria del Campiglione, a historian of cuisine and a refined chef, who nourishes souls and bodies.

He is grateful to the Einaudi team, Rosella and Daniela, Chiara and Tommaso, Riccardo, and above all, Francesco Colombo; he is grateful to them for the magnificent work that they do, and because they heroically manage to put up with Paolo Repetti. And he is grateful to Paola, Manuela, Simonetta, Stefania, and Stefano who take him everywhere around the world.

He is grateful to Luisa Pistoia and Marco Vigevani, without whom none of all this would have been possible.

These are the people who invent Ricciardi, and that world. The author, on the other hand, has been imagined, invented, and constructed by another person to whom goes the loveliest rose of my heart: my sweet and delightful Paola.

NOTE

The verses on pages 23, 160, and 254 are taken from the song *Rundinella*. Lyrics by Rocco Galdieri and music by Gaetano Spagnolo (1918).

The verses on page 91 are taken from the song *E allora?* Lyrics and music by Armando Gill (1926).

The verses on page 144 are taken from the song *Body and Soul*. Lyrics by Edward Heyman, Robert Sour, and Frank Eyton and music by Johnny Green (1930).

The verses on pages 151-155 are taken from the song *Caminito*. Lyrics by Gabino Coria Peñaloza and music by Juan de Dios Filiberto (1926).

The verses on pages 165, 171, 216, 222, 244, 245, and 258 are taken from the song *Scetate*. Lyrics by Ferdinando Russo and music by Mario Pasquale Costa (1887).

The verses on page 207 are taken from G. Verdi, *Un ballo in maschera*, to a libretto by Antonio Somma, from the romanza *Re dell'abisso, affrettati*, Act I.